falling for LUCAS

The Falling Series Book #6
TRACY LORRAINE

Marianne
#love worth the risk

Tracy Lorraine

Copyright © 2017 by Tracy Lorraine
All rights reserved.
Proofread by Pinpoint Editing
Cover design by Tracy Lorraine
Formatted by Tracy Lorraine
No part of this book may be reproduced in any form or by any electronic or mechanical means including information storage and retrieval systems, without permission in writing from the author. The only exception is by a reviewer, who may quote short excerpts in a review.

This book is a work of fiction. Names, characters, places, and incidents either are products of the author's imagination or are used fictitiously. Any resemblance to actual persons, living or dead, events, or locales is entirely coincidental.

www.facebook.com/tracylorraineauthor
https://twitter.com/Tracy_L_Author
tracylorraineauthor@gmail.com
tracylorraine.com

Dedication

Lindsay, my sister from another mister.

Prologue

Lilly

I pull the door open and know instantly that something isn't right. His eyes are crazy, he's sweating and his chest is heaving up and down with his increased breaths.

I've had moments in my life where I have been scared, but I have never felt like this—like I need to be scared for my *life*.

I rack my brain for what I could have done to annoy him this much, but I can't come up with anything.

"Jake, what's wr—" I don't get to finish asking my question, because he reaches out his hand and grasps the top of my arm tightly.

"You fucking whore," he grates out in a really eerie voice.

I'm too shocked by his words to reply. Apparently, this doesn't please him though.

"YOU FUCKING WHORE," he repeats—only this time, at the top of his voice.

"I...I haven't—" my words are cut off as I get pulled harshly towards him.

"You've been sharing my pussy with other men, you fucking whore."

I think about Ewan, the guy Taylor's been seeing who walked me home after turning up in the same bar earlier tonight. Does Jake really think I brought him home?

"Ugh," I grunt as my body hits the wall with a thud.

Jake is still shouting, spitting at me with each vile word, but the only thing I can focus on is the blinding pain in my shoulder where it just collided with the brickwork of our hallway.

"Argh...Jake...stop. I haven't—"

I'm suddenly flying through the air like a rag doll. The pain of my back hitting the stairs is unbelievable, and when my head smacks down on one concrete step I swear I hear a crack before everything goes black for a few seconds. I roll down the last few stairs until I am laid out on the landing. I'm aware that I'm screaming, vaguely aware that my neighbours in the other flats on this floor could hear me and come to my rescue. The second I open my eyes and see him leering down at me, I shut my mouth. I know it's no good. I'm about to experience the full force that is a drug-filled, alcohol-fuelled, angry Jake.

"Fucking whore," he says again before he jolts towards

me.

I roll onto my side, clutching at my stomach, hoping that I can do something to ease the excruciating pain. It's all consuming. I've never felt anything like it.

I lift my hand when I feel something run down my fingers and sheer panic rushes through me when I see my hand is covered in blood. My blood.

I'm going to die here. Alone and in the hallway of my building.

I'm fading in and out, alternating between the spinning vision of the stairwell in front of me and the blackness that keeps taking over my body. I like the blackness. The pain and the memories of the last few moments disappear when that comes.

When I come to again, a ringing sound gets my attention, and after a few seconds I remember putting my phone in my back pocket before answering the door. I feel a rush of relief as I realise that I might not die here after all.

My arm feels like lead as I try to move it to grab my phone. I'm moving so slow that the ringing stops and my panic starts to set in again. What if I can't get to it?

Thankfully, the person trying to get hold of me rings again, and it gives me a renewed sense of strength. I try with everything my weakening body has to get to it.

When I eventually pull it in front of my face I'm not even a little surprised to see who it is. He will know something is wrong; he will always be there to help me.

"Lilly, what's wrong?" Dec shouts down the line when I answer.

"Ambulance," I whisper.

"What, I can't hear you." The panic in his voice is

increasing with every word.

I take a moment to find the energy to talk.

"Ambulance. My flat."

"Fuck, Lilly, what's happened? Are you okay? FUCK," he screams into the phone.

"Don't tell Mum and Dad. Need you," is the last thing I remember saying before everything goes black again.

I'm suddenly awake, sweating and panting. I push my wet hair off my face and will my heart to slow down. I pat my bed, reminding myself that I'm safe and everything is fine. My hand finds its way to rest on the scar on my stomach and I begin to sob, just like I do every time I wake up this way.

It isn't just a dream. It's a nightmare.

One

Lilly

"Roxanne's been sacked for unacceptable behaviour, so…" my boss says as she looks at all of us.

I glance to the side to see the same apprehensive look on my colleagues' faces that I'm sure I have. No one wants their name to be said next.

"Lilly, you've been here the longest, so you get to clean the King's lair. Stay behind and I'll go through everything with you."

I say goodbye to my usual work mates, Imogen and Eve, and await my fate.

I've been working mornings cleaning at the hotel since I started uni and discovered most days I don't have to go in until the afternoon. It's the perfect opportunity to earn some money so I'm not sponging off Mum and Dad. They've done enough, buying the flat Taylor and I live in. I don't want to take any more from them.

I mostly love it. I say mostly, because you wouldn't believe the state we find the rooms in some days. And some of the things people bring to a hotel and leave out for the cleaners beggars belief. That being said, it does mean we have some very entertaining mornings!

I watch everyone else leave and follow Hillary towards her office. I spend the next ten minutes listening to what I already know. Mr. Dalton, the hotel's manager, has very particular tastes and expects things not only to be done his way but also to perfection, hence so many cleaners have come and gone before me. I think the longest one has lasted since Mr. Dalton took over here is two months. I've got no hope. I'll be the first person to say that my cleaning standards aren't up to scratch for his requirements.

"Can you just read through this and sign please, Lilly?"

I look down at the paperwork Hillary has just pushed over and my chin drops. I always thought it was a rumour that any cleaner that entered the King's lair, as we've all nicknamed it, has to sign an NDA. I mean seriously, what are we likely to find? Let alone tell the world about?

I quickly scan over the paperwork and sign without much thought. I have no intention of spreading whatever gossip Mr. Dalton is worried about around the place. All I really want to do is my job, although that job has just got a million times harder.

"You could look a little more excited, Lilly. You get to work in the best room in the hotel," Hilary says, trying to focus on the positives.

"Yeah, but how long for? Denise was the best cleaner we've had for years and she was gone after two months. I don't stand a chance." Not only does Mr. Dalton have immaculate taste—I would say bordering on OCD where cleaning's concerned—he is young and drop dead gorgeous. Not my type, but still gorgeous. Add his obvious wealth to that and his reputation as a ladies' man, and some of the women around here have issues containing themselves.

Like I said, he's hot, but *so* not for me. He always looks perfect, not a single slicked back piece of hair out of place and not a speck of dust on his sharp suits. I like my men a little more rough around the edges. I want a tattooed bad boy who is actually the biggest sweetheart ever under all the ink and the scruffy, brooding image.

I let out a huge breath as I follow Hilary to the penthouse. I thought I'd found all those things in Jake, until he found drugs and alcohol.

I try to shake off my depressing thoughts as we wait for the lift to take us higher. I promised myself I was going to fight it. I'm moving on with my life, putting that waste of space behind me.

It takes over an hour for Hilary to go through everything: exactly how he prefers his towels to be folded, the order he expects the bottles on his vanity unit to be in, and the perfect little point on the toilet roll…and that's just the bathroom. Apparently, I've even got to line the remote controls up a certain way on his coffee table. It's utterly insane. By the time she leaves me to it, my head is spinning with everything I've got to remember so I still have a job this time tomorrow.

I clean everything in the bathroom twice then triple check everything is in the correct position before attempting the rest of the suite. The chances of me making it to uni this afternoon are slim to none. I'm going to be here for hours. I just hope I get used to his quirks fast so I can speed this whole process up slightly.

I've dusted the coffee table and arranged the remote controls exactly as I was shown when my phone rings. I shouldn't really have it on me, but after everything that happened with Jake, I like to have it to hand at all times. It's like my security blanket. I also shouldn't really have black jeans on either, but there we go. Typical that today of all days is the one I forgot to wash my usual black trousers. I'm just hoping the King doesn't appear while I'm still here because being out of the standard uniform is sure to push his buttons.

I pull it from my back pocket as I fall back on the sofa. The second I see it's a text from Connie, my stomach does a little flip. I immediately unlock my phone and open the message. My eyes start to well up immediately, because staring back at me is not only my smiling friend but a tiny baby wrapped in a blue blanket. Under the photo it says *Noah Fredrick Willis, 7lb 6oz, born at 06.33 on 14th February.*

I'm so happy for Connie and Fin, I really am, but as my first tear hits the phone screen I can't help feeling hollow.

I zoom in on his little face. His eyes are shut tight, he's got a cute little button nose and full lips. He's Fin's son, that's for sure.

I drop the phone into my lap and rest my head back on the sofa. I'm so jealous of Connie right now and I hate that I feel that way, but I can't help it. I'm desperate to experience what she is right now. I'd give anything to have the chance.

My phone ringing interrupts my depressing thoughts. I pull my head up and look down at the screen.

It's Molly, my unofficial sister. She knows I'm at work, so wouldn't call unless it was important.

"Hello," I say as cheerfully as possible when I put the phone to my ear.

"Lilly, what's wrong?" So that was successful, then.

"Nothing. Connie just sent me a photo of her and the baby and I got a little emotional."

"Oh my God," Molly squeals, "Connie's given birth?"

"Yeah. I thought that was why you were ringing, to tell me."

"No, I've got other news. What did she have?"

I go on to tell her all I know. "So what did you have to tell me?"

"You will not believe what Daniel's done," she exclaims.

"Go on." Knowing Molly's brother, it could be anything.

"He whisked Beth back off to Paris and proposed on the Eiffel Tower. I just got a photo of the two of them still up there with her wearing this massive rock on her finger. And when I say massive, I mean it's fucking huge, Lills."

"Wow, that's amazing," I say, trying to muster up as much happiness as I can. Because just like Connie, it's not that I'm not happy for them. I'm ecstatic that Daniel's found someone. I just feel like everyone is moving on with their lives. All this amazing stuff is happening to them but I'm stuck. I'm fighting every day to pull myself out of the pits of hell while everyone around me is enjoying everything life is throwing at them. I feel like I'm still lying in my stairwell six months ago, wondering if I'm going to survive.

I just about manage to get Molly off the phone before I completely break down. Dec, my twin brother, is the only member of my family that knows what happened last summer. Everyone I love has been through so much in the last couple of years with losing my older sister, Hannah, that I kept everything from them. Dec wasn't happy with my decision, but he stuck by me.

I'm unattractively sobbing on the sofa when I suddenly hear a throat clearing behind me. I jump up from my seat in panic and turn around to see who's walked in.

My eyes run from his spotlessly polished shoes, up his perfectly pressed trousers and over his waistcoat and crisp shirt until I reach his eyes. They are dark and staring daggers at me. His glare renders me motionless but my heart starts to race. A huge part of me wants to run, run as far away and as fast as I can from this situation. I've barely had this promotion two hours and I've already screwed it up.

I square my shoulders and stand up. I wipe the tears from my cheeks with the backs of my hands as I wait for the ear bashing I'm about to get for slacking on the job.

Only it doesn't come.

His eyes start of hard and vicious but as the seconds tick by they begin to soften as he continues to stare at me. I must be mistaken though, because there is nothing about the man stood in front of me that's soft. He's a ruthless businessman who tramples on anyone who gets in his way. I have no reason to suspect he's going to go gentle on me just because I've shed a few tears. I raise my chin slightly to him as I prepare for him to tear a strip off me.

He opens his mouth to say something but what comes out shocks the hell out of me. "Are you okay?" There is no harsh demanding tone. Instead, there's concern. Weird.

"I'm…uh…" I stutter because this is so unexpected. I thought I'd already be on my way home with my P45 in my hand by now. "I'm fine. I just received some news and I…" I don't continue, because I realise that he really doesn't care; he's just trying to be kind and I appreciate that, but I'm here to do a job. "I'll just get on with it," I say, gesturing to the room.

I pick up my phone and go to walk past him. I don't make eye contact. I'm scared he'll return to his usual self once I get back to work.

I'm frozen to the spot when he moves and clamps his hand around my wrist. I daren't look up at him because I don't know what I might find looking back at me—and also because he really doesn't need to see the fresh tears in my eyes.

"If you need to go and have some time…"

I'm so shocked by his words that my eyes snap up to his. Close up, they look bluer than I thought.

"It…it's fine, honestly." My voice quivers, showing that I'm anything but fine really.

"Well, if you're sure," he says hesitantly. I can only presume that being in the presence of an emotional woman isn't the norm for him.

He holds my eye contact and I'm powerless to look away. There are only inches between us. I'm surrounded by his scent and his kindness touches me. Then I do something so unlike me and so utterly stupid that I can't even comprehend it.

I lean forward and kiss him. I actually kiss him!

I pull back the second my lips touch his, like I've been burned. What the hell am I doing?

"I'm sorry," I mutter before rushing out of the room.

My heart's pounding and I'm sweating from running the short distance from the hotel to my flat. I rush up the stairs and through the living room before landing face down on my bed. I scream into my pillow to release my frustration and anger at myself for my appalling behaviour. I scream until the tears take over, then I sob for what feels like hours. I cry sad tears for what I had, for what has been taken from me. I cry happy tears for Daniel and Beth, then some more for Connie, Fin and little Noah. Connie and I have become close friends over the last few months while I helped with her and Fin's house renovations. Connie's best friend is my older sister, Emma, and Fin is Emma's husband's best friend. It's all a bit close and complicated, but it's safe to say I'm jealous of all of them. I know I'm only young and I've got all the time in the world, but knowing that doesn't make me feel any better. It doesn't even matter when I *do* find 'the one'; the chances of me having my own family are slim to none now, thanks the Jake.

I eventually drag my sorry backside into the bathroom for a hot shower, hoping it might wash some of my misery down the drain. It's wishful thinking though, because when I step out I don't feel any better. The muscles in my shoulders might be a little less tense, but that's about it.

I tug on a pair of jogging bottoms, then pull one of Taylor's giant hoodies over my head. All thoughts of going to uni, or even leaving the flat ever again, are completely gone. Instead, I head to the kitchen and pull out everything I need to lose myself for a few hours. I kick the coffee machine into action and get started.

When Taylor finds me hours later, it's with flour in my hair, cake batter splatted over his hoodie and a bottle of vodka and cans of Coke littering the coffee table in front of me. There are also cold mugs of coffee littering the surfaces of the living room and kitchen.

"What happened, Lil?" he asks after he's assessed the situation.

I met Taylor not long after I started uni. He's a couple of years older than me as he started late, but he's also coming towards the end of his degree. He's studying photography while I do interior design. My wonderful parents bought this flat towards the end of our first year, and we moved in together as soon as we could. We know each other inside out, so I shouldn't have been expecting him not to question me right now.

"Connie had her baby," I slur sadly, focusing on the news I've received that I can talk about. I have no intention of telling him yet about the disaster that was work this morning.

"Oh," he responds, looking half happy for Connie and half sad for me.

"A little boy. Noah," I say, holding my phone up for him to see.

"Aw, cute." Taylor puts his stuff down, then comes to sit next to me and pulls me to him. He totally engulfs my tiny frame when he bear hugs me, making me feel like a china doll. "It's going to be okay, Lil."

Along with Dec, Taylor knows everything that happened last year, as does Connie now as well. None of them agree with me keeping what happened to myself. They think it will help me come to terms with it all if I tell the rest of my family, but I can't bring myself to do it. My parents and Emma have already been through too much heartache, and my childhood best friend, Nicole, is going through her own nightmare at the moment. None of them need me to burden them with more.

"I know," I reply as I swallow down my sorrow. "Daniel also proposed to Beth on the Eiffel Tower."

"No shit. She's really got him whipped," he says with a laugh.

When he pulls back from me, he leans down to his bag and grabs something.

"Happy Valentine's Day," he says with a smile as he hands me a single rose. The gesture makes my eyes fill with tears. He's such a sweetheart.

"Thank you, Tay."

"Dave wasn't in, so…" he says with a shrug but laughs, telling me he's joking.

"I love you," I say as I wrap my arms around his neck. Taylor's like my adopted brother, there isn't anything he doesn't know about me. I'm feeling a little out of the loop where he's concerned though. He's been out a lot recently and I have no idea what he's up to. He's reluctant to share when I question him about it.

"So what have I got to eat then?" He walks off towards the kitchen that is covered in all sorts of baked goodies, including cupcakes, flapjacks and millionaire's shortbread. "Bloody hell, Lil, you were on it this afternoon," he says with a laugh as he shovels an entire cupcake into his mouth in one go. "So good," he mumbles with a full mouth.

When I get up the next morning, the kitchen is still covered in a dusting of flour and icing sugar. There are bottles and cans all over the living room and my head is spinning. I take one look at all the cake and run to the toilet to throw up.

"Too much noise," I hear mumbled from Taylor's room as I walk past after showering.

I stare daggers at his closed door. I should still be in bed sleeping the effects of the vodka off, not getting dressed to head to work, where I'm pretty I'm going to be fired and sent straight back home the second I get there.

I curse myself when I realise my work trousers are still wet in the washing machine, and pull my skinny jeans back on again. Well, if I'm going to be sacked anyway, I guess it doesn't really matter. As I do up the button, I notice how big they are on me, reminding me how much weight I've lost. I didn't really have any to lose in the first place. I've always been skinny and tall. Where most women work towards losing weight and reducing their curves, I've always wanted more. I'm practically straight up and down; it makes me feel like a little girl. Especially when I stand next to Molly and Emma—they have such amazing curvaceous figures, and I look like a six-year-old. No guy's going to look twice at me like this.

I let go of my waistband and look at myself in the mirror. My ribs are sticking out along with my hipbones, and my belly…it's totally non-existent. The only thing I see now when I look at it is the ugly scar I've been left with. A constant reminder of my what happened, of my mistake.

I shake off my thoughts and continue to get ready before heading out. It's still dark as I walk the short distance to the hotel. I could drive but I find the walk soothing, especially at this time of morning. The early spring is the best when the mornings are crisp but the sun is rising and the birds are singing. It makes everything seem that little bit better. It distracts me from the fact I could be about to go and clean a hotel room that might have used condoms scattered around the place, or some guy's stained underwear abandoned on the floor. I shudder at the thought of some of the things I've found over the last couple of years. But then, I remember my new promotion—if you can call it that. It feels more like I've slipped down the ranks having to comply to all the King's weird quirks. I'm pretty sure only the man himself could do the job. Not that it matters now, because I'm about to be sent on my merry way. I don't think I've got the energy to find a new job right now. I'm in my last few months of uni, and I really don't need the distraction. I'd hate to have to ask Mum and Dad for money, though. I want to fend for myself where possible.

I'm the first to arrive, exactly as I planned. I want to get this out of the way before the others appear and have to watch me do my walk of shame after handing my ID badge in. I couldn't bear to see the looks on Imogen and Eve's faces as I leave.

"Lilly, you're early," Hilary says as I walk into the cleaners' room that houses her desk. "Keen to get started?"

"Something like that," I mutter. I don't move to put my stuff in my locker. I just stand behind her, waiting for the inevitable.

"Did you want to ask me something?" Hilary asks when

she turns and finds me still stood there. I go to open my mouth, but nothing comes out. "Mr. Dalton was very happy with your work yesterday."

My chin drops open in shock.

"What's that face for? I knew you were the right woman for the job, Lilly. Give yourself some credit."

"I...uh...thanks," I mutter before turning towards the lockers.

My head is spinning as I head up towards the King's lair. I kissed him and he hasn't sacked me. Everyone else who's tried it on with him has been sent away instantly. Why hasn't he done that to me?

By the time I'm standing in front of his door, I'm completely confused by the whole thing. Hopefully I can just put the stupid incident behind me and move on like it never happened.

Thankfully, his suite is in silence when I enter. I don't think I could have coped with seeing him again. In fact, I would be quite happy never seeing him again.

I've only got the bedroom to do when I hear the door open. My heart lurches into my throat. But when someone shouts, it's not the voice I was expecting.

"Lilly?" I want to groan at the sound of her high-pitched voice. It's a little like nails down a blackboard. Catherine is the operations manager. She's in charge of us and likes to make sure we know it. Hilary can't stand her, and that's saying a lot because Hilary is the sweetest woman I know. Catherine is a class A bitch. She likes to throw her weight around and get involved with stuff she has no idea about. She's the one who put a time limit for cleaning each hotel room. She's never cleaned a hotel room in her life—how the hell would she know how long it takes to do it properly?

"Yes, in here," I answer quietly in the hope that she won't hear me and go back wherever she came from. "Oh," I say in surprise when I see her in the doorway. In her arms is a huge bunch of lilies. And I mean huge.

"Please refrain from having people send you flowers at work," she snaps before putting them down on the side and marching off.

"Who on earth is sending me flowers?" I question as I walk over. My first thought is Taylor. He must know I'm not feeling great today, but he's never sent flowers before. Dec, maybe?

I stand in front of them and admire the gigantic flowers for a minute before hunting down the card.

When I pull it out, I'm even more confused.

Our condolences

What the hell?

I leave the flowers where they are for now and set about finishing the King's bedroom. I change the sheets, then spend a ridiculous amount of time faffing around with the show pillows and throw to get them just right. It's frustrating as hell. I like things clean and organised, but this is just crazy. I briefly think about the state I left the flat in. Something to look forward to after uni this afternoon…

The rest of my morning goes by in a haze of confusion as I think about who the flowers could be from and what they mean.

I'm just finishing up when a thought hits me. No, surely not. They couldn't be from Jake. Although I refused to press charges against him in fear it would make it drag on, I know that Dec and Taylor 'sorted' the situation, so to speak. I would like to think he's long gone.

The small amount of doubt that they could be from him has me looking over my shoulder all afternoon. I know it's crazy, but I'm terrified of ever seeing him again. His memory is enough.

I've just about got the flat sorted by the time Taylor appears later that evening. He looks pleased to see me in a better state than yesterday. Keeping my job has perked me up a little.

"Feeling better?" he asks as he leans a hip against the worktop.

"Yes thank you."

"I'm going out tonight. Come with?"

"No, you're okay. I've got loads of work to do."

"Oh come on, Lil, you haven't been out for a drink with me in forever."

It's true, I haven't. But I just don't feel like it. I'll feel like an idiot dressed in whatever I pick out that is too big for me. Plus, I'm still hanging on to a bit of last night's hangover. "I'm sorry, I've got a deadline." This is true, but it's not for a long time.

"Fine," he says as he rushes off to his room to get ready. I feel bad not going with him. Over the past few months I feel like we've been drifting apart. Taylor's always out doing whatever—or whoever—it is he does while I've been hiding here. I've no idea what's going on with him but I have a suspicion that it involves a man.

I spend the night working, just like I said I was going to. I've just got into bed when I hear a commotion at our front door before the noise disappears into Taylor's bedroom. His room is the opposite end of the flat, but sometimes that isn't far enough away, and I get the feeling that tonight is going to be one of those nights.

Two

Lucas

I can't get the image of her grief-stricken face out of my head. It's been four fucking days and it's still there.

I couldn't fucking believe it when I came back to my room at the beginning of the week to find my newest cleaner laid out naked on my bed. Seriously, what is wrong with these women? I must have been through at least ten different cleaners since I took over this hotel just over six months ago. Why can't they just do the job they are paid to do, and not think that just because they are cleaning my room it gives them the right to think I want them? I made the mistake of getting too close to a colleague once before, and it's not happening again. Unlike her, though, thankfully cleaners are pretty easy to come by, so I can get them replaced pretty quickly.

Then *she* turned up. Even her tears didn't distract from how stunning she was with her golden hair, blue eyes and pink lips. I usually don't waste any time where the opposite sex is concerned—I just take what I want, then move on. But as I stood staring at her, a little voice in my head kept saying, *She works for you, don't do anything stupid.*

I stood watching her cry for the longest time as my head and body argued against each other. My body wanted her; my head knew it was wrong. Then the business side of me wanted to demand to know why she wasn't doing her job, or wearing the correct uniform, or why she'd been on the phone. I almost marched down to Hilary and demanded to know where she finds these women from. All I want is someone who can do a half decent job of keeping the place clean and tidy. Is it really that much to ask?

When I made myself known, I was shocked by the fear in her eyes. I've been told before that I can be intimidating, but no one's ever said they've been actually scared of me before. The second she looked at me, her eyes widened and I swear her hands started to shake.

She went to leave, but for some reason, that felt wrong. Not only had she affected me, but she was clearly very upset. I couldn't watch her leave though, and for some reason as she stepped past me my arm moved without instruction and grabbed her.

I raise my fingertips to my lips. No matter how much I

try, I can't get rid of how it felt when she kissed me. It was the most innocent of kisses, but it's affected me like no other.

I've kept away from my room every morning since. I've almost convinced myself that I dreamt it all and she doesn't exist.

I've managed without my phone all morning. I know exactly where it is—it's on the shelf above the basin where I left it in the rush to get to my meeting this morning. Deciding it must be safe, I head up to my room to get it before I leave the hotel for the afternoon.

It's silent as I pass through the living room, so I relax a little. Everything looks great as I walk through. Apparently, I have a reputation for being a pain in the arse when it comes to how I want my stuff. I think it's been blown out of proportion though, because as long as it's clean and tidy, I don't really care. I couldn't care less how the towels are folded or how the pillows on my bed are arranged. I'm a guy for fuck's sake, I don't even know why I've got to have extra pillows on my bed. I'm more than happy with the normal amount just used for sleeping on.

My head is already focused on the meeting I have this afternoon with the builders to discuss the renovation for this place. I bought it just over six months ago. I had planned to start work on it right away, but it was clear from the first day that the major problems with it were the systems in place to run it. I brought in Catherine, and together we've basically started from scratch. Thanks to her, this hotel is now running like a well-oiled machine, so it's time for it to have a new look.

All thoughts of golden blonde hair evaporate as I focus on

what I need to talk to the builder about, but that's all shattered when I step foot in my bathroom.

She's bent over the bath with her arse stuck right up in the air.

The desire to walk up behind her is huge. Instead, I grab on to the sides of the doorframe to keep me where I am. My movement must catch her attention, because she instantly flicks her head around to look at me before standing up.

"Good afternoon," I say as I try to keep my eyes on her face and not let them roam.

"Af…Afternoon, Sir." Her response makes me smile.

"Please don't call me that. It makes me sound ancient." It's obvious I'm older than her, but I don't need her making me sound like I'm heading for retirement.

"Okay…sorry Mr. D…Dalton," she stutters out nervously. I can't help the rush of excitement that goes through me as I think about her reactions around me.

"It's Lucas."

"Okay, well…I'd better get on." Just as she finishes her sentence, the sound of her stomach rumbling fills the bathroom. She flushes pink and turns away from me.

"Have you had lunch?"

"No," she mumbles as she starts scrubbing the tiles harshly.

"I'll get you something sent up." She drops the sponge and spins my way. The shocked look on her face makes me smile.

"I'm fine, thank you." As if to prove she's lying, her belly does it again.

"Have you even had breakfast?"

She shrugs one shoulder up as she whispers that she had a

banana on the way to work this morning.

"That was hours ago. I'm getting you lunch, no arguments."

Her mouth drops open as if she's going to say something, but she decides against it. She must realise she won't win if she starts something.

"Thank you," she whispers, looking slightly embarrassed. "That's really kind of you."

"Any preference?"

She just shakes her head in response. Now the shock has worn off, I can see some of the sadness she had the other day seep into her features.

"Did you get the flowers?"

"They were from you?" she asks, completely startled.

"Yeah."

"Why? I'm sorry, I mean, thank you, they were gorgeous. But why did you give them to me?"

"You said you'd had some bad news, I presumed…" I trail off when the look on her face tells me I've missed something. "No one died?"

"No," she says with a laugh. That laugh does funny things to my insides. "One of my friends had a baby."

"Oh…but you looked so sad," I say as I take a step towards her.

"Long story. They were happy tears."

"You're lying," I state, because it's true.

"I'm not. I'm really happy for them."

"I'm sure you are, but they weren't happy tears."

My body continues forward until I'm stood right in front of her. Her breath catches at my closeness. Her scent mixes with the cleaning products she's been using and it makes me mouth water. I reach over her shoulder and grab my phone, which is exactly where I left it. The screen tells me I need to shift my arse if I'm going to get to this meeting on time.

"Have dinner with me tonight?" The words are out of my mouth before my brain realises it's happened. Fuck, I shouldn't have said that. She works for me. It goes against everything I've told myself I shouldn't do. Maybe she'll say no. It's wishful thinking, since I've never been turned down before, but it's worth a shot.

"Thanks for the offer, but I'm okay, thank you." I'm still close enough to her that as she speaks her breath tickles my neck, and fuck if it doesn't bring my body to life. I haven't had sex in…a long time for me. I've been too busy sorting this place out. This is fucking torture.

I step back once her words register.

"No?" I ask, in case I heard that wrong.

She bites down on her bottom lip and I almost groan. Shit, I want to be the one doing that.

"I'm sorry, Lucas. I don't think that's a good idea."

"Right…okay. Well, I'll see you around then." I quickly turn around and leave her standing there as I head for my car. I sit in the driver's seat for a few minutes, processing what just happened.

No one's ever said no before.

She might as well have just kicked me in the bollocks.

Lilly

The look on his face when I said no stayed with me for a long time after he'd gone. He really wasn't expecting that. He's good looking, yeah, and loaded, but who does he think he is? Brad bloody Pitt? The idea that a woman couldn't possibly say no to him makes him even less of my type than before. I don't want a guy who thinks that much of himself.

I shake the thought from my head as I continue eating the lunch Lucas sent up as promised—a huge cheese and tomato baguette with chips and a side salad. I can't deny that I wasn't starving, so this is gratefully received and will get me through uni this afternoon.

I don't see or hear from Lucas again for a week. To begin with, I start to think he's avoiding me after I refused to go out with him, but when I learn he's been away at his other hotels I want to slap myself around the face for even considering that he might have cared about it that much. I'm sure the sting of my rejection lasted all of ten seconds. He'll have found some other woman to stroke his ego, I'm sure.

Weirdly though, it seems he's still thinking about me, and I'm not sure how I feel about that, because every day I've been at work I've found something left for me. The first day, there was a tray on the coffee table. It had a card with my name on it, a plate of chocolate biscuits and a pot of tea. I wanted to be defiant and refuse his gift, but the chocolate called to me, so after arguing with myself for a whole five minutes I sat down and enjoyed my morning snack.

Day two was a Danish pastry and a freshly squeezed glass of orange juice. Day three was fruit scones and another pot of tea. And finally, on day four, which was Sunday morning, an entire plate of a full English breakfast was delivered to the door. I almost sent it away. This whole thing was getting ridiculous, but second the smell of bacon hit my nose I knew I couldn't do that, so I took the tray from the sheepish looking guy stood at the door and wolfed the lot down. I barely came up for air it was so good.

I hate to admit it, but I missed my little treats on my days off. It wasn't the same, having to make my own breakfast.

Although I knew when he was due back—the gossip around the staff in this place is just like being in a school playground—I could tell from the moment I stepped foot in reception the next day. It was like everyone I'd seen was on edge. I hadn't realised the atmosphere around the place had relaxed over the past week, but seeing the difference today makes it obvious.

"He's back," Imogen whispers in my ear as we gather for our morning briefing.

"I know, everyone's running around like they've got rockets shoved up their backsides," I say with a laugh as Hilary comes in, looking a little flustered.

Everyone gets given their schedule and a pep talk before they all disappear.

"Lilly, hang on a minute." Hillary lets the others grab their stuff and leave before she says anything. "Sorry I haven't touched base with you the last few days. I've been busy training up new staff. How's it going up there? I've heard great things."

"Yeah it's…uh…good, I guess. Great things from who?" I ask, a little baffled.

"Mr. Dalton, obviously. He says you're doing a great job. Apparently, the place was perfect when he arrived back last night."

I can't help a surge of pride rush through me that the man who has such high expectations thinks I'm doing a good job. And then another thought hits me. Is he just saying this to sweeten me up for a date, just like he must be doing with the food deliveries? A bolt of anger hits me the second I think about it. How dare he? Just because he's not bossing me around, then sacking me like all the others, it doesn't mean I have to accept his dinner invitation.

I say goodbye to Hillary and storm towards his room, thoroughly ticked off. I do my usual routine around the suite, but it doesn't take as long as usual as he hasn't been here all week, so I continue a job I'd started but not finished recently—the high up stuff that hardly ever gets touched.

I'm quite happily balanced on the arm of the chair dusting the very top shelf in the living area when the slamming of the door makes me jump. I spin around in fright but manage to lose my footing at the same time. I close my eyes and brace myself for the pain of hitting the floor, but it doesn't come.

Instead, I find my face squashed against a rock-solid chest that just so happens to be covered in one of his usual expensive suits.

"What are you doing, balancing on there? We have health and safety procedures for a reason, Lilly," he chastises bluntly. Now this is more like the Mr. Dalton I was expecting since I started cleaning his suite: rude, abrupt and arrogant. I knew his true colours could only be covered for so long.

Thankfully, he puts me back down on my feet. I step away from him because his smell is messing with my brain's ability to function.

"S...sorry, Mr. Dalton," I say like a naughty child.

"It's Lucas," he snaps.

"Sorry," I repeat.

"What the hell were you doing?"

"Dusting."

"Well, get a ladder next time. The paperwork I'd have to do if you'd hurt yourself is a bitch of a job," he says sternly, but his lip twitches up at the side, so I'm not sure how serious he's being.

"Okay, well…thank you for…saving me?" I say, but it sounds like a question.

I just bend down to pick up my duster when he speaks again. Only this time, his voice is deeper and huskier—dare it say it? Sexier.

When I look back up at him, his blue eyes have darkened and he has a smirk on his face. "You should probably thank me properly."

"Should I?"

"Yes," he states and he takes a step towards me. "Thank me by agreeing to dinner with me tonight."

"I don't think that's a good idea, Mr…Lucas," I say, correcting myself.

"I don't care if it's a fucking good idea or not, Lilly." I cringe at his harsh words. "I want to take you to dinner."

"No, Lucas," I say, mustering up some strength from somewhere. Being this close to him and under his gaze makes it hard to think, let alone stand up for myself. "I think I'm finished for the day," I say in a panic, because I need to get away from him as soon as possible. I have a feeling that he's going to do whatever he can to get his own way here.

"Fine, but you will agree eventually." Thankfully, he steps aside and lets me leave. It's not until the door closes behind me that I let out the breath I was holding. I lean back against the wall and shut my eyes. I try to relax, but he's got to me more than I want to admit. Eventually, I push off the wall and get as far away from him as I can.

"Lilly, you've got a visitor."

I quickly wrap a towel around my body before pulling the door open to see who it is. I'm presuming it's either Molly or Emma, so I don't think twice about covering up more. I realise this is a huge mistake when I turn the corner to the living room.

Stood in the middle of the room, with Taylor gawping at him, is Lucas. What the hell is he doing here?

Taylor doesn't notice I've walked in because he's too busy drooling. Lucas is just his type, perfectly put together and once again wearing a suit. Taylor will be gutted he bats for the wrong team. Lucas spots me the second I enter, though. His eyes hold mine for a second before they slowly take in my towel-clad body. Damn it.

"Lilly," he says, after clearing his throat. "We're going to dinner."

Lucas' words distract Taylor, who turns to me with a massive grin on his face. Oh, here we go.

"No, we're not. I'm fairly sure I turned down your offer of dinner earlier."

"Lilly," Taylor starts. He grabs my arm and turns us so we are slightly away from Lucas. "You cannot say no to that. He's fucking gorgeous."

"Meh, he's alright. But I'm not going out with him."

"Yes you are. One, he's gorgeous," he starts using his fingers to count his points. I inwardly groan as to how many reason he's going to find that I should go. "Two, you haven't been out in…well…forever. Three, he looks like he's got money. Have you seen that suit? You're guaranteed to have an amazing meal. Four, you need to enjoy yourself, maybe get laid—you work too hard. Five, did I mention he's gorgeous? Six—"

"Yeah, alright, I get your point," I snap, interrupting him. "He's my boss, Tay. I have no intention of dating him."

"*He's* your boss?" he asks, turning to look directly at Lucas, who is still stood in the middle of the room with an amused expression on his face. I can only presume he's heard every word, because Taylor isn't exactly being quiet.

"Yes, he's my boss. I'm not going out with him."

"Can you get me a job with you? I could do with seeing that daily."

"Taylor, can you be serious for a minute? It's a bad idea. Plus, he's not my type."

"Oh, perfect isn't your type?"

Taylor and I stare at each other for a solid minute having a silent conversation. When it becomes clear I'm not going to win, I look away. "Oh, for goodness' sake."

"She'll be ready in thirty minutes. Make yourself at home."

I get dragged none to gently to my room, then shoved down on the bed while Taylor starts raiding my wardrobe.

"There's no point looking. I haven't got anything to wear—not that will fit, anyway."

"Yes, you have. Where is that little black dress?"

"No no no, I'm not wearing that."

"Yes, you are," he states. "You'll look hot."

After draping the dreaded dress over the edge of my bed, Taylor turns and starts rummaging through my underwear drawer.

"I knew I bought you these for a reason."

When I look up, I see he's got the tiny bit of fabric he

bought me for Christmas hanging off his index finger. He decided I was too young to be spending my days in cotton knickers. I disagreed.

"I'm not wearing that." I can't imagine anything worse.

He gives me a look that tells me I'm going to do exactly as he says. Great.

Twenty minutes later, I'm stood in front of my full-length mirror. I might be looking at myself, but all I can see is Hannah, my older sister. She died in a car crash two years ago. She was such a huge part of our family, and it left everyone crushed, especially Emma, her twin, who was in the car with her at the time.

Things haven't been the same since she died, but what I really struggle with is how much I look like her. Not only does it affect me when I look in the mirror, but I know everyone else sees her when they look at me. Emma is the only one who has admitted she's found it hard to deal with, and apologised for distancing herself from me after the accident. Dec, my twin, is a typical guy and would never admit his feelings, but I know him almost better than I know myself, and I've seen how he looks at me sometimes. Mum and Dad would never admit it, but deep down I know they feel it. I can only imagine what it must be like to lose a child, your first born, let alone having a younger child that looks just like them.

Although it's hurt, I've tried to give them all some space while they've attempted to get their lives back on track. I hate that I'm not as close to them all as I used to be, growing up. I know I've always got Dec on my side. He may be hundreds of miles away in Exeter, but we're so close that most days it feels like he's right beside me. Plus, I've got

Taylor, Imogen and Eve here in Cheltenham with me. They are amazing, and I don't know what I'd do without them.

"You look incredible, Lil," Taylor says as he comes to stand behind me.

I run my eyes over my body. I'm not sure *incredible* is quite the right word, but I look good, better than I have in a long time. My dress, although a little looser than it should be, is hugging my body. It has tiny spaghetti straps, an open back and a short hemline. My very minimal chest is just about covered with two triangles of the black fabric. I never show this much skin. I only bought the damn dress for someone's twenty-first at uni last year; she demanded a dress code for her Vegas-style night.

I tug at the fabric, trying to cover up some side boob, but my hand gets slapped away by Taylor. "Stop fussing. You look perfect. Now get out there and knock his fucking socks off before I attempt to turn him."

"Fine," I mutter as I give myself one last look over in the mirror. I grab my blazer and my bag before heading for the living to find my boss—I mean date—while attempting to ignore the feeling of the scrap of fabric I'm meant to be referring to as underwear as I walk.

Three

Lucas

She's been inside my head all fucking day. By the time six o'clock rolls around, I decide that enough is enough. So what if she said no again when I asked her out earlier? I need to see her. I need to find out why, with only a few minutes of interaction, she has wiggled her way inside my head.

I'm hopeful that if I spend some time with her I'll realise I've built her up to be something she's not in my mind, and I'll be able to put her to one side and get on with my life.

I'm Lucas Dalton, successful businessman. I run eight hotels, five restaurants and employ hundreds of people. I need to be focused. I shouldn't allow someone to take up my thoughts—especially a certain golden-haired goddess called Lilly.

I convince myself I'm doing the right thing as I go through my employee records to find her information. I only wanted her address, but curiosity gets the better of me and I ended up looking at everything. I make a mental note of her birthday after writing down her address and shutting the computer back down.

I go about my usual routine as I get ready. It almost comes naturally now to look this way, like my colleagues and employees expect me to look. It doesn't mean I like it, though. I stick my fingertips into my tub of wax and smooth my naturally shaggy hair back off my face. I repeat the action a couple of times until it's perfect and looks the part. I pull on my grey suit and finish it off with a sky-blue tie, the colour of Lilly's eyes. I give myself a mental slap around the face for that thought.

Before I know it, I'm stood at the entrance to her building and ringing the buzzer. She lives in one of the traditional Regency style buildings that make up the town. The front door is huge, along with each of the windows facing out over the park on the other side of the road. It isn't the kind of building I was expecting a Cheltenham University student to be living in. It doesn't exactly say student accommodation.

The second I hear a male voice answer the intercom, I'm on edge. Fuck, of course she's got a boyfriend. I didn't even give it a thought. My selfish brain decided it wanted her, and that was that.

"Hello?"

"I'm looking for Lilly."

"Well, you're looking in the right place. I'll buzz you up." Halfway through the sentence, I know I haven't got anything to worry about. I'm pretty sure the guy on the other end is gay. What I don't expect to see though, when the door to Lilly's flat opens, is a giant of a guy. Whoever her roommate is, he's seriously stacked.

"Hey, I'm Lucas. I'm looking for Lilly. I'm taking her out for dinner tonight." I expect him to say something back, but he just stares. "Uh…hello," I prompt.

"Shit, yeah, come in. She's in the shower."

I expect him to go and get her or something, but he just calls out and then stands and stares. I'm not really sure what the hell's going on or what I'm meant to do in this situation. Thankfully, only seconds later I hear footsteps heading our way, and then Lilly appears. Wearing only a towel, thank you God.

I run my eyes down from her wet hair, over her slender neck and shoulders. I watch as the pulls the towel tighter around her before dropping my gaze to her long legs. Fuck, they're incredible.

The roommate is still staring at me while Lilly stands there looking very uncomfortable. I decide it's time to break the silence.

"Lilly, we're going to dinner."

I sit myself down and ping out a few emails while I wait—no point wasting time. If I have my way, I'll be way too distracted to do any work for the foreseeable future. I'd much prefer Lilly to keep my mind—and body—busy.

The feel of her pressed up against me earlier pops back into my mind. How her body felt up against mine, how light she was. I could throw her around and get her exactly where I want her without much effort at all. The thought alone has me reaching down to rearrange myself.

Eventually, I hear a commotion down the hall and when I look up she's stood at the entrance to the room, looking very unsure of herself. The sight of her takes my breath away. She is perfect.

"Wow, you look stunning, Lilly." I see a small smile twitch her lips at my compliment, although I can still see she's questioning this whole thing.

"Have fun you two," the roommate says, walking up behind her.

"Oh, I'll make sure of that," I say with a wink.

The roommate's face lights up, before responding with, "Good, she needs someone to show her a good time."

"Taylor," Lilly gasps before smacking his shoulder. "Come on, let's go," she adds and begins walking towards the front door. And who am I to argue? I follow her out, staring at her arse the whole way.

The second the lift door closes, the atmosphere changes. Well, I think it does, but that probably has something to do with wanting to back her up against the wall. I glance over at her and her face doesn't tell me she feels the same.

"Why are you doing this?" she asks, looking totally confused—like the idea of me wanting to take her out is that unbelievable.

"I just want to spend an evening with you, Lilly. Is that so much to ask?"

"But you're my boss. You sack everyone who so much as sneezes at the wrong time, yet here I am. I don't understand."

I can't help but laugh at her assessment. "I only sack people who can't do their job properly, Lilly. You do your job perfectly well, and I'm intrigued by you."

"Was that a compliment?"

"No, just a fact. A compliment would be me telling you your hair looks so good I want to run my fingers through it. Or that you smell divine. Or that you look incredible in that dress and I can't help but imagine what you look like without it." I watch as a flush of red spreads from her cheeks and down her neck.

"Okay, that's enough."

"It's all true, Lilly," I state.

I come to a stop next to the passenger side of my car and open the door for her. When I stand back up, she's running her eyes over it before moving to me and running them up my body. "Like what you see?"

"This is crazy, Lucas. I'm your cleaner, and you're…" She doesn't explain, just gestures towards my car.

"Just get in."

As I walk around to the driver's side, I can't help being unsure of whether I'm pleased or not that people fall for this act. But then, I guess I've played the part for so long now it's almost normal. The suits, the money, the flashy cars. Lilly might have the impression I'm something impressive, but under all this, I'm far from the person she thinks I am. I know she's thinking that she's not good enough for all this, but if she only knew the truth: that she is the one that is way too good for me.

She's silent as we drive further into town towards the restaurant I booked earlier. I wish I knew what was going on inside her head.

"Where are we going?" she asks when I bring the car to a stop.

"A restaurant just down here."

Lilly stares at me for a beat before letting out a breath and allowing me to help her out of my car.

"Reservation for two under Dalton."

"Sir, Madam, if you would like to follow me to your table."

I glance back at Lilly as we follow the hostess. Her eyebrows are drawn together as she looks around at the lavish decoration. I can only presume this isn't her normal night out.

I don't get to check she's okay until we are introduced to our waiter, have our drinks order taken and have been talked through the specials. I make the decision for her and order the nine-course taster menu and a bottle of wine. Lilly looks so overwhelmed that I just go ahead. I'd never say it to her, but she needs a little meat on her bones, so the nine courses should help towards that. Don't get me wrong, she has a stunning figure, but she is a little too thin.

"Are you okay?" I ask once we're alone. I reach my hand across the table to hers, but the second I touch her, she pulls her hand away as if I burned her.

"I'm just not used to this," she replies.

We get interrupted again when the wine is delivered. I shoo the waiter away before he gets the chance to pour it for us. I have no desire to have him hovering around our table. I've already seen the look he's given Lilly; the farther away he is the better.

"I wanted to spoil you for the night."

"Thank you, but why?"

"Because you deserve it." I don't get to say anymore, which is probably a good thing, because her phone rings.

"I'm so sorry," she says, clearly embarrassed by the noise blaring from her handbag. She rummages around, then pulls it out and looks at the screen. She looks torn as she tries to decide what to do.

"Go ahead," I prompt, and after a couple more seconds she answers it and puts it to her ear.

I hear a male voice as soon we the call connects on the other end, and I can't deny that it puts me on edge. I don't want her talking to another guy while she's out with me. Fuck it, I don't want her talking to another guy full stop.

"Stop, listen," she says, trying to get a word in edgeways with whoever it is on the other end. "I'm on a...date?" she whispers, sounding unsure of what to call this, as she turns away from me slightly. I hear his muffled voice before she states, "Well, I didn't know he was a psycho until he turned into one." There's some more talking on the other end before she tells him it's fine and that she'll call him tomorrow.

I watch as she slowly puts the phone away before turning back to me.

"I'm—"

"It's fine," I interrupt, because I have no intention of allowing whoever it was on the phone to ruin our evening. As much as I want to ask about the psycho she mentioned, I won't.

When the first course gets delivered, I begin to think Lilly isn't going to eat anything. She just sits and stares at it.

"What's wrong?"

"Nothing, it looks delicious. Too good to eat. I'm sorry,

Lucas. This is just...not me. I don't dress up like this or go to fancy restaurants. I feel totally out of place."

I instantly feel bad about my choice. I wanted to show her a good night, treat her, but my effort has fallen completely flat and instead made her uncomfortable.

"We can leave," I offer, putting my knife and fork down.

"No, no, no. I'm sorry," she says again. "I'll be okay, it's just a shock I guess."

"Well for the record, Lilly, you look exactly like you belong here. You're the most beautiful woman here." I'm relieved to see a small smile twitch her lips as her cheeks flush red at my compliment.

"Thank you, Lucas."

Once she's had another glass of wine, Lilly loosens up a little. I see her shoulders relax and the conversation starts to flow a little better, although the focus is mostly work. That's not a bad thing, but I already spend my life there—it would be nice to have a little reprieve. On the other hand, though, it's better than her asking about my past.

"Let me take that," I say to the waiter when he returns with her jacket after I've paid the bill. Lilly tried to argue and wanted to pay half. That was not fucking happening. I already feel bad enough for making her uncomfortable with my choice of restaurant tonight.

"Thank you," she says, turning back towards me once she has her jacket on. I can tell the wine we've consumed tonight has had an effect on her. Her eyes are bright and her cheeks pink. "Tonight was incredible." Fuck knows why, but I feel like puffing my chest out with pride at her words. All I did was bring her to a fancy restaurant, yet she's looking at me like I'm something special. That is so not the case, and once she discovers how true it is, she'll be running a mile.

As soon as we step out of the restaurant, Lilly wraps her arms around herself in an attempt to keep warm.

"Here," I say as I shrug my jacket from my shoulders and drape it over hers.

"You'll be cold," she says in a pathetic attempt to refuse the offer, but I can see she's so cold that she doesn't mean it.

"It's fine," I say, trying to sound convincing because it's anything but fine. It's fucking freezing.

We set off back towards Lilly's flat. I glance to the side to see her resting her head back as she stares out the window. I can't help but reach my hand over and place it on her thigh. Her head snaps to mine. I expect her to look angry and push me away, but she surprises me. She just smiles and places her hand on mine.

"Thank you for tonight," she says again. "I shouldn't have enjoyed it is much as I have."

"What makes you say that?"

"You're my boss, Lucas. We shouldn't be doing this."

"I could sack you, would that help?"

Lilly lets out a little laugh and it feels like it hits me right in the chest. I don't waste time thinking about what that might mean. "No, Luc, I need the money."

"I could still pay you…just not for cleaning," I say with a smirk on my face, because I can feel her looking at me.

"Lucas!"

"That's a shame. I think we would enjoy it." I give her thigh a little squeeze and I don't miss the feeling of her muscles tightening. Fuck, I want my hand on more than her thigh.

"Well…thanks again, I guess," Lilly says sheepishly at her

front door. I walked her up here on the off chance that I might get invited in, but it's not looking that way.

"You're welcome, Lilly." I reach up and hold her jaw in my hand while rubbing her cheek with my thumb. "It's been a pleasure."

She stands still for a few seconds, but to my relief she starts to lean towards me. If it's the result of the wine or my actions I have no idea, but I'm grateful anyway.

Our lips are about to touch when there is an almighty crash from inside. Lilly jumps a mile and looks scared witless. My instincts take over and I grab her and pull her behind me before walking into her flat. When I get inside, I see a woman dressed in a man's t-shirt, stood around shards of glass.

Just as Lilly steps inside, Taylor comes running around the corner, dressed in only a pair of boxers.

"Shit, sorry," he says to no one in particular as he rushes over to help the woman tidy up.

"Are you okay?" I ask Lilly, because when I look back, she still looks a little scared.

"Yes, it just made me jump."

"Come here," I say as I pull her to me and wrap my arms around her. I wasn't ready for our moment to be over, but I'm expecting to be kicked out any minute.

She stays put while Taylor and the random woman sort out the kitchen and then disappear.

"Do you want a coffee?" Lilly asks when she pulls back.

I really want something stronger, but I have a feeling I'm going to be driving soon so I regretfully agree to a coffee.

Lilly joins me on the sofa with two steaming mugs a few minutes later.

"Wow that's impressive," I say as I take in the barista style cappuccino she hands me.

"My mum runs a coffee shop in Oxford. I've spent my entire life making coffee," she explains.

I take a sip. "It's gorgeous."

"Good to know. I can't stand the taste of the stuff. I love the smell though, it reminds me of home. Sometime I just make some for that reason."

I look over at her mug and see if full of tea, not coffee.

"How do you grow up making coffee and not like it?"

"No idea. You'd have thought it would have grown on me by now, wouldn't you?"

Taylor and the woman reappear after a couple of minutes of silence. The woman is now wearing a barely-there dress; it makes Lilly's look huge in comparison. We both watch as Taylor backs her up against the door and shoves his tongue down her throat before watching her disappear. I continue to stare at Taylor for a few seconds as I try to figure him out. I thought he was gay.

"Sorry, I'll leave you guys to it. Pretend I'm not even here," he says with a wink before leaving again. "Have fun!"

The silence spreads out for another few minutes. Lilly is intently staring down into her mug, trying anything not to look at me, I think.

I place my mug on the coffee table before reaching over and taking Lilly's out of her hands and putting it with mine. She looks up at me through her lashes, and the move has my dick twitching. Fuck, she's so beautiful.

I grab her arm and pull her over until she's pressed up against me. I run my eyes over her soft facial features, down her neck and across her exposed cleavage. My mouth waters for a taste of her.

I raise my hand up to her cheek so we are almost in the same position as earlier. "Where were we?" I whisper before leaning in. I keep my eyes open until the last minute, watching her reaction. As soon as my head moves, her eyes close and her lips part. She's been good at playing her cards close to her chest this evening, but it's clear by her reaction that she wants this as much as I do.

Lilly

My heart starts racing the second he pulls me to him. I was gutted when we got distracted earlier. I know I keep saying that we shouldn't be doing this, that he's my boss, but I don't really mean it. As the night's gone on, or maybe as the wine has gone down, I've been looking past all the reasons I'd told myself why I didn't like him. But being up against his hard body on my sofa, all I care about is having his lips on me. All thoughts of him being my boss are gone, along with my reasoning about him not being my type. It's been so long since anyone showed any interest in me that now I'm desperate for more, no matter what the consequences may be.

As soon as his lips touch mine, it's like I lose all control, which is very unlike me. I've never been forward when it comes to this sort of stuff—I've always been happy to sit back and let the guy take over. My hands come up to the side of his head and my fingers tease the short hair before running over his shoulders and down his chest. Without instruction from my brain, my fingers find their way to his tie before starting work on his buttons, all the while our tongues dancing together in the most amazing kiss I've ever experienced. And to think I thought the feeling of his hand on my thigh in the car brought me to life…this is something else.

I sit up and throw one leg over his thighs so I'm sat on his lap. I look down on him and I can't believe the difference. His perfect hair is now perfectly messy, his blue eyes dark and hungry, and his chest…well, there aren't words for how perfectly defined every muscle is, and the scar that runs a couple of inches across his left pec sets the whole thing off.

Lucas sits with an amused look on his face as I stare shamelessly at him. Where's the sophisticated businessman gone? This man between my thighs is a bad boy. Excitement bubbles up in me at the thought.

"Bedroom," he states before lifting me as if I weigh nothing. I wrap my legs around his waist as he carries me in the direction I point.

As soon as the door is kicked shut, I am dropped on the bed none to gently before I feel the fabric of my dress being pulled up my thighs. The sudden realisation of what he's about to see makes me panic. I bring my hands down to his to make him stop.

"What's wrong?" he asks, looking up through his dark lashes at me. The sight makes my breath catch. He lifts one of his hands and runs it through his hair, pushing the inky black locks away from his forehead.

"I've…uh…got a scar." His eyebrows draw together in confusion. "It's ugly and no one's ever seen it like this." I gesture between us in the hope he understands what I mean.

"Scars are beautiful, Lilly. They show who you are, your strength, they tell your story. But more than anything, they show that you are a survivor, no matter how you got it."

I feel myself tear up at his words. I so badly want to believe that my scar is all of those things, but all I see when I look at it is everything I lost.

Lucas can obviously see that I'm close to stopping this, because he stands up and drops his trousers. The first thing I see is the huge—and I mean huge—bulge in his boxers. I'm not sure whether I should be scared or excited by that, but soon my eyes drop to another scar that runs almost the length of his thigh. My breath catches for a very different reason, because it looks pretty nasty. That definitely wasn't done in surgery.

"You've seen mine. Now it's your turn."

Lucas drops to his knees after kicking his shoes, socks and trousers off, then slowly runs his hands from my ankles up to my thighs. He stops for a second when he grabs the fabric again, but this time I don't stop him. I sit up when he has it over my arse and lift my arms so he can pull the dress off. He throws it over his shoulder, but his eyes don't move from mine.

After a few more seconds, I have to break my connection with him. It's too strong, too confusing, so I shut my eyes and allow him to look at me. I hear his intake of breath when he sees it. My eyes fly open and I go to sit but I'm stopped with hands on my shoulders.

"You're beautiful, Lilly," he whispers before I feel his lips kiss across my scar. He doesn't stop at the bottom though, he keeps going until he is kissing my mound through the thin fabric of my knickers. He nudges my knees apart with his shoulders before I feel him run his tongue over me. I shudder at the unfamiliar sensation. It's been so long, I'd forgotten how it felt. I soon feel the fabric brushing my thighs as he pulls them off, and then his hot mouth is on me. Taylor's words from when I was getting dressed briefly bubble up to the surface, about me not doing any maintenance down there, but the feel of Lucas' tongue against my clit forces them away.

Lucas slides two fingers inside me, and it's all I need after months of nothing. I fall head first into the most intense orgasm I think I've experienced. I'm aware of noise around me, but it's not until I come back to earth that I realise it was me shouting. Wow, that was good.

I feel the mattress dip either side of me, forcing my eyes to open. When I do, I'm looking up into the smug face of Lucas Dalton.

"Good?" he asks, his smirk only growing with the question.

"Hmm, it was okay."

Clearly that wasn't what he wanted to hear, because his hands come under my armpits and he practically throws me up towards the headboard before settling himself between my thighs.

"Condom?" he asks before doing anything else. I just shake my head at him and he smiles down at me. "Second time lucky then," he says before thrusting into me.

I cry out at the alien sensation that takes over my entire body. Thankfully, he takes it slow for a bit, allowing me to adjust to his size and giving my body time to remember what to do.

Tracy Lorraine

Four

Lilly

I wake with a start. Something's not right. When I open my eyes, I know immediately what it is.

Lucas is propped up with his back against the headboard and he's looking down at me with an amused expression. I blink a couple of times, thinking I'm seeing things, but then the memories of last night slam into me.

Oh holy cow, I slept with my boss and he's still in my bed. Naked. Crap.

"Good morning, beautiful."

"Oh my God," I whisper before diving under the covers. I can't believe I've done this. I should never be allowed to drink wine ever again. I'm naked, in bed, with my boss. I mean, could I screw this whole situation up any more? I was just meant to be cleaning his room, and now look. I was more than happy when I thought he was a smooth-talking businessman, but now I've seen that's only one side of him. Last night, he was anything but. I'm in trouble. Serious trouble.

"Lilly?"

I feel the duvet being tugged and hold tighter as I try to come up with a plan.

"Lilly, for fuck's sake, come out."

I let go of the duvet at his demand and sit up. I keep it clutched to my chest and focus on my chest of drawers at the other side of the room. I'm scared to look at him. I'm scared for a couple of reasons. One, because all that bad boy in the bedroom that I'm remembering might have just been a good dream, and two, if I see him naked when I'm sober, I'm not sure I'll ever be able to look at him the same again. Every time I do, his suits will melt away and I'll be seeing his tanned skin.

When I pluck up the courage to say something, it's definitely the wrong thing. "Shouldn't you be at work or something?"

"I've cleared my schedule. I thought we could spend the morning together, get breakfast or something." The hurt in his voice surprises me.

"I've got to go to work, Lucas" I snap a little harshly.

"Ring in sick. I'm sure your boss won't mind."

"I can't. I can't just blow off work to hang out with you. I need that job, the money. Just because I made the stupid decision to go out with you—and sleep with you—last night, doesn't mean I don't have to do my job."

Lucas is silent for a minute and I almost apologise because it did come out a little harshly. I won't allow him to give me special treatment though, just because I slept with him.

"Fine," he states. "I was only suggesting it for this morning. I've got more important things to be doing anyway." With that, he flings the duvet back and gets out of bed. His sudden movement makes me look his way and I wish I hadn't, because he's perfect.

We both stare at each other for a few seconds, me admiring his perfection and he, I guess, waiting for me to change my mind. It's right there on the edge of my tongue, but it's wrong. I won't do it.

When he breaks eye contact with me, I feel like bursting into tears. I don't want to admit to myself how much I would like to spend the morning with him. Instead, I focus on what I should be doing, on what is right. That is, until he turns and I get a full view of the tattoo I only caught glimpses of last night. His entire back is cover with a stunning black and grey phoenix. The artwork is incredible. My breath catches when I see it, and his body pauses when he hears my reaction. He soon rights himself though, and starts pulling on his suit.

Then he's gone without so much as a goodbye. Did I just play that all wrong?

"Oh my God," I groan when I get out of bed. I can't believe how much everything hurts. My muscles pull and ache as I grab my dressing gown from the back of my door and pull it around me. I've always been pretty agile with all the yoga, but I never went back to classes after I was given the all clear. I couldn't bear to go out in public in my usual crop top and leggings, so I've stuck with doing the odd bit in the flat every now and then. I hadn't realised how out of practice I am.

I hobble my way to the bathroom for a hot shower. I lean back against the bathroom door and breathe a sigh of relief that I made it without bumping into Taylor on the way. No doubt he'll have a million and one questions for me. His bedroom might be the other end of the flat, but I know for a fact that noise travels pretty well in this place, so there will be no denying what went on last night.

"Lilly, get your skinny arse out here now!" Taylor shouts through the door as soon as I turn the shower off. He bangs on it a crazy number of times—just in case I didn't hear, I guess.

"Really?" I mutter under my breath. I was hoping to escape the flat without an inquisition. I should really know better.

I pull the door open to find Taylor stood there with his hands on his hips, looking impatient.

"I want all the details."

"Don't you have uni?"

"Don't change the subject."

I get dragged to the sofa and questioned about the first part of the evening. Where he took me, what we ate and drank, what I found out about him, how much he spent. The questions get much harder to answer when he moves on to what happened here. I don't know why he bothers asking, because it's clear he heard everything. He's had enough experience to picture what we were up to.

"I've never heard you come before," Taylor says, making me turn beetroot red. I've never really been one to share the details of my love life. I've preferred to keep it inside the bedroom, hence he's never heard anything before. I wish I could say the same for him. "It was seriously hot, Lil. I'd only just got laid but I was in my room knocking one out after the other listening to you guys."

"Ew, really, Tay? I don't need to know this," I say, getting up to get ready for work. I've already annoyed Lucas this morning; I'd better not be late as well.

Unfortunately, Taylor follows me and continues to question me about every intimate detail of my night, as well as demanding to know why I sent him away this morning if he was good enough to make me scream. Taylor looks about as confused as Lucas did first thing this morning when I explain my reasons. Apparently, he thinks I should have blown off work as well. I don't mention that one of the reasons I refused was because, in a round about way, Lucas would basically be paying me to spend time with me, and that didn't sit well with me. I knew Taylor would tell me I'm being stupid, and I probably am, but that doesn't stop me feeling that way.

I eventually get out of the flat only thirty minutes later than usual. Thankfully, my rust bucket of a car starts first time and I'm rushing through reception to dump my stuff in my locker in no time.

I burst through Lucas' hotel room door with my cleaning supplies in hand. I instantly look around for him and I can't help feeling disappointed that he isn't here. What was I expecting though, after this morning?

I let out a huge sigh and crack on, trying to put all memories of last night and this morning behind me. Obsessing over them will not help me in the slightest.

It's a shame my little pep talk doesn't help, because I'm totally lost to the feeling of his lips on my body when a throat clearing behind me makes me jump. I drop the bathroom cleaner and sponge I had in my hands in fright. I spin around and gasp at the sight. My heart starts racing and my temperature instantly increases.

Lucas is stood in the doorway wearing a black hoodie with the hood up over his head, and a pair of grey jogging bottoms. The hood comes down to his eyebrows and the shadow it causes makes his eyes look even angrier.

I swallow down a lump that's formed in my throat. He looks dangerous, like he could seriously hurt someone. Weirdly, I have no fear. I know he won't hurt me. This shocks me, because after everything I've been through, I'd have thought this would set me on edge.

"I need to use the shower," he states coldly.

"Uh…right…yeah."

I gather up my stuff and get out. I can't stop myself from turning back to look at him as I walk away, and of course he catches me. And just to torture me further, he pulls his hoodie off, exposing that stunning tattoo to me. Frustratingly, he doesn't shut the bathroom door, so as I go about dusting the bedroom, all I can picture is the water running over his hard muscles.

I need to get a grip.

It's only a few minutes before he appears with a towel wrapped around his waist and water droplets running down his chest.

"Lucas, can we talk a minute?"

"No, I'm busy. Just do your job, Lilly. It's what I pay you for."

His vicious words cut me. They actually hurt.

"I thought you took the morning off," I say with as much strength as I can muster, because I don't want him to see that he's affecting me.

The look I receive has me cowering away. Now that's the Mr. Dalton I knew of before I started working up here: a ruthless and powerful arsehole. As much as it hurts that he's reverted to that when he's never been anything but kind to me, it actually grounds me a little. This is what I was expecting; this is how it should be.

Lucas

After I spend the night with a woman, I usually spend the following days—fuck, even weeks sometimes—trying to get rid of them. So why is that Lilly kicking me out this morning hurt? I would like to think it was only my ego, but unfortunately, it's more than that.

I knew she'd be here when I got back from my run. If I'm honest, I wanted her to be. A part of me hoped she might have changed her mind. The second I saw her though, I was pissed off again. My relaxing run was long forgotten. I saw how she was with me last night—how sweet, how responsive, how forward she was. I was not expecting this today. I shake my head at my thoughts, because how she is acting right now is all I've ever wanted. Why is it that I've found her, yet I want the exact opposite of what I have before? I want more time.

After cancelling my meetings this morning, I haven't really got anything to do, but a quick call to my designer gets me a meeting with her to see how everything is progressing with the refit. I know Dad wants to be involved as much as he can with this, so I arrange for the meeting to be at their house.

"Good morning, Luc," my mum greets when I walk into their kitchen.

"Morning," I mutter before giving her a kiss on the cheek.

"Son, how's it going?" Dad calls out as he walks towards me.

"It's good," I say, but I don't put much enthusiasm behind the statement, which earns me a concerned look from my mum. I can't hide anything from her. Coming here was probably a mistake.

The designer is the same middle-aged woman Dad has worked with for years. Her designs are good, don't get me wrong, but they're so safe. I'm trying to make our hotels something a little different to the competition—*safe* isn't going to do that. Dad loves it though; he sees all the standard fittings, the same decoration in each room, the same bedding, and thinks it's all great. I'm sure I could convince him otherwise, and most days I do, but I just haven't got it in me this time. So I sign off on the designs and put an end to the meeting.

Dad almost immediately disappears to his greenhouse, leaving me alone with Mum. Fuck knows what he's doing in there in February.

"What's going on, Luc? You look stressed. Is everything okay at the hotels?"

"Yeah, everything's fine. Occupancy rates are higher than ever. I'm actually on the look-out for a new one. I know we've only had Cheltenham a few months, but I really want to push on. Now I've got the right staff and systems in place, it's practically running itself. There's no real need for me to be there."

"You work too hard. Why don't you have some time off? Go travelling or something, blow off some steam for a while."

I hate that when my mum mentions blowing off steam, the only image that pops up in my head is one of Lilly in bed last night. Fuck's sake.

"Lucas?" she prompts. "You're worrying me."

"It's nothing, Mum. I'm fine."

"Oh my goodness," she gasps. "It's a woman, isn't it?"

"No, Mum," I lie. She sees it though, because I can't meet her gaze.

"Oh, at last! Do you have any idea how long I've been waiting for this?"

"Yes, I have an idea," I mutter, thinking of all the times it's been brought up. How she wants me to find someone to settle down with, get married, have babies. I've even seen pictures of possible hats before now.

"Oh, tell me all about her. I bet she's beautiful, and smart. Oh, I just can't wait to meet her."

I just about manage to hold in my groan at her excitement. "Mum…" I start, not really sure where I'm going with this. "Yes, okay, maybe I met someone, but I've already fucked it up, so calm down. I've told you before that none of that stuff is going to be happening, and you know why."

"Oh Lucas, you can fix it. Whatever it is you've done. If she means enough to you that she's affected you, then she's worth it. And watch your language, young man."

I can't help but smile at her. How she's not used to my foul mouth by now, God only knows.

I apologise as I always do, and make my excuses about being busy.

I don't go back to the hotel until I know Lilly's gone. I think it's best for both of us if we stay out of each other's way. I'm too drawn to her, and she seems too intent on running in the opposite direction.

Five

Lilly

It's been eight weeks since my night with Lucas, and I haven't seen him since he walked out of his hotel room that morning. Some days I think it's probably for the best, but others, I'm less convinced. I barely know him, so how I miss him is beyond me.

He's making it hard to forget him though. Not only am I in his private space multiple times a week, but he's kept up the food deliveries. I'm grateful because I never have time for breakfast, but I'm confused by it all. He won't let me forget him and I'm starting to hate him a little for it. He can swan off wherever it is he disappears to and hide from me, yet I'm stuck here cleaning his damn toilet and making his bed. And as if that isn't bad enough, he's showing me he's thinking of me. Well, that's how I see it, anyway. If he didn't care and had forgotten about me, he would have stopped, surely?

I managed to convince Dec when I spoke to him that the date was a disaster, and it must have worked because thankfully, he hasn't mentioned it again. He was so excited I'd put myself back out there that I felt bad for missing out the finer details of the evening, but I'm pretty sure he didn't really want to know that I had a one night stand with my boss. He might be happy oversharing his many conquests with me, but I'm not comfortable doing the same.

Connie has been on at me to visit her and Noah since she got home from the hospital. Up until now, I've managed to make every excuse under the sun. I'm desperate to see them both, but I don't know how it's going to affect me. I'm hoping I'm strong enough to be happy for her and be able to look at him with the love I should, but I'm still worried. My excuses of working and uni have run dry, so I pull my boots on and head towards the village they live in. Connie is well aware I'm putting it off, although she never comes out and says it. She knows everything, and I know she understands, but she is right: I need to put all that behind me and move on. I can't let it hold me back.

The house looks gorgeous as I pull up. Towards the end of last year, Emma asked me if I'd help out with Fin's house. It was the perfect distraction I needed at the time, and the perfect project I needed for my final uni year. I couldn't have been more grateful. The house was a mess, but after a few months of hard work, it's almost as good as new. All the features are back to how they would have been when it was first built, the floors stripped back to reveal the stunning wood hiding under years of dirt, and the walls fresh and bright.

Connie is already in the doorway with her little bundle of joy in her arms as I get out of the car.

"Lilly, it's so good to see you. Come here," she says, holding out her free arm so she can wrap it around my shoulders.

I don't get a chance to get a look at Noah, because Connie spins around and heads for the house, leaving me no choice but to follow her.

When I get in the living room, I see she has lunch all ready for us. It was only an hour ago that a bacon sandwich appeared in Lucas' room, but the sight and smell of Connie's homemade soup and fresh bread makes my stomach growl.

I take a seat on the sofa as Connie places Noah in his bouncer. I get the impression she's making every effort she can not to force him on me. I know as a new mother it must be killing her not to shove him under my nose so I can tell her how cute he is. I'm beyond grateful for her thoughtfulness.

"You look really good, Lilly. You've put some weight on," Connie comments as she hands me over a tray. "Why have you just gone bright red?"

"Oh, have I?" I ask, trying to pass it off as nothing. The fact I've put some of my weight back on makes this whole thing with Lucas worth it, I think. My jeans are no longer hanging off me and I look less ill. "No reason."

Connie gives me a curious look before demanding I spill it. I give her some of the truth.

"So he just randomly sends you food for no reason?"

"Yeah, pretty much."

"Your boss, who you say is an epic dickhead—"

"I've never said that," I interrupt.

"Okay, so you're too polite to use those exact words, but that's what you meant." I can't exactly argue with that, so I let her continue. "So, as I was saying, your dickhead boss has suddenly started sending you food while you're cleaning his room. I call bullshit, Lilly. It sounds like he wants more than his room cleaning, if you know what I mean," she says with a wink.

Why do I have to have such pale skin? I can't hide even the smallest of blushes.

"OH MY GOD," Connie squeals. "You *have* cleaned more than his room, haven't you?"

I drop my head in my hands and groan. I'm starting to think her shoving Noah in my arms would have been less painful than this.

"Lilly, come on, I need details. The last you told me about this guy was that he was a slick Rick with a fancy suit and a bad attitude. How did you end up falling into bed with him?"

I lay it all out for her. It actually feels good telling someone the whole story. Taylor only knows bits and pieces, and I haven't told Nicole anything—she has too much of her own stuff to deal with without me landing my drama on her. She sits and listens to the whole sorry story and bites her tongue until I've finished.

"Oh my God, he sounds hot, Lilly—fancy pants businessman by day, bad boy in the sack by night. On a more serious note though, I can't believe you had a one-night stand with your boss. That is so unlike you."

"I know. I still don't know what came over me, other than the wine."

"Or Lucas," she interjects with a laugh that makes me blush again. "Sorry! So, anyway…what are you going to do?"

"No idea. I've thought about handing my notice in, just getting away, but I need the money and I really haven't got the time to be worrying about starting something new. Plus, I'm almost at the end of my course and I'll be looking for a design job soon enough. I just need to stick it out for a few months. With a bit of luck, he'll stay in the shadows and I won't have to worry about him."

"But you will, because you're cleaning his room and picking his fucking dirty underwear up off the floor." I don't mention that he's too much of a neat freak for that to ever be one of my jobs.

Our conversation gets interrupted when Noah starts fussing in his chair.

"He needs a feed. Do you want to hold him while I go make a bottle?" Connie asks tentatively.

"I…uh," I stutter, looking between her and the baby. 'Yeah, sure," I say when I realise I need to get a grip. I can't let what happened rule my life. I want to enjoy my friend's baby. I won't let him take that from me as well.

"Okay?" she asks once Noah is settled in the crook of my arm.

"Yeah, I'm good. He's a proper cutie, Con."

A huge proud smile breaks across her face. "He is, just like his daddy. I'll only be a few minutes."

"Take your time. We're good." And I really mean it.

From as early I can remember, all I've wanted is kids of

my own. I was obsessed with my dolls when I was a child. Although I always knew I wanted a career first, kids were always next on my list. When I was a teenager, it soon became clear that things weren't as they were meant to be down there. I still held on to my hope that one day, when the time was right, it would still happen for me—even though my chances were low. I always hopped I'd be a younger mum and when I met Jake I thought maybe I'd get the chance. I had a wonderful boyfriend, uni was going well, and I had amazing friends and family. He was incredible, too good to be true almost, until his life was turned upside down and he found alcohol and drugs. It made him crazy.

I'd always sworn never to have anything to do with drugs. I should have ended it with him the day I found him with white powder on his nose but I rationalised he was going through a rough time and that it would get better. He promised it would. Well, it definitely didn't, and he ended up taking away that small chance I had of ever having my own children.

Noah distracts me from my memories when he makes a cute gargling sound. I stare down at his cute face and little button nose. I was worried how I would feel, holding an almost newborn baby again. I had a complete meltdown the first few times I held Lois. Thankfully, Dec could see what was going on and rescued me. I was so relieved he was there, because I wouldn't have been able to explain my freak out to everyone else without telling the truth, and I really didn't want to do that.

This time it's different, though. More time has passed and I've slowly been dealing with it all. When I look down at Noah now, all I feel is happiness for Connie and Fin; my anger and pain is barely noticeable. To say I'm relieved would be an understatement. I hated the idea of having to stay away because I couldn't handle it.

Connie looks a little teary eyed when she comes back in and sees that Noah is still cuddled in my arms.

"You'll make a great mum one day, Lils. Just because you might not be able to carry your own, doesn't mean you won't get the chance."

"I know," I say, looking back down at his little face. And I do. I've realised in the past eight months that even though I won't carry my own children, I won't allow it to stop me from having what I've always wanted. I've been brought up to believe that everything happens for a reason, so maybe I was never meant to carry my own—maybe I was always meant to adopt. When the time is right, there might be a child or two out there who need a good home and a loving family, and I will welcome them with loving arms as if they are my own. I can't imagine anything more rewarding than giving someone the life they deserve.

"Shall I take him or do you want to feed him?" Connie says, dragging me from my inner musings.

"Can I do it?" I say to my utter shock. I've never fed a baby before, so this will be an experience.

By the time I need to leave Connie's, she has to practically rip Noah from me. I knew I'd love him, but having him sleeping in my arms contently made me realise how quickly I'd fallen for the little guy. I give him a gentle kiss on the forehead before handing him back to his mummy and saying goodbye.

I head straight to my parents' house for our monthly

Sunday dinner that my mum still insists on, although more often than not only half of us are in attendance these days. When I arrive, I see it's only Emma, her husband Ruben and me today.

"Oh my goodness, Lilly, you are looking really well," Mum says as I enter the kitchen to join everyone.

"She's right, you look really good," Emma agrees. It's the third time I've heard similar things today, and I'm starting to realise how bad I must have looked. I know I lost a lot of weight, but I didn't realise everyone had noticed so much. It makes me wonder how much they believed about the lie I spun about having the flu. Dec swore to me that he didn't tell anyone, and I believe him. I know he wouldn't break my trust, but seeing their reactions to how I'm looking now really makes me wonder.

As always, lunch is amazing and the conversation is easy as we all chat about our lives and what we've been up to. Emma tells us about her latest book and Mum fills us in on stories of Lois. Molly and Ryan have taken her away on her first holiday and are currently up in the Lake District.

I'm in a really good mood by the time I get home. I have the place to myself so change into my pyjamas and get some uni work done.

When I curl up in bed my thoughts, as they often do, turn to Lucas. I hate that he still fills up my headspace, but I can't shift him. He's made some kind of impact on me and I wish it would stop.

Everything seems normal when I walk into Lucas' room. Well, that is until I turn the corner to the en suite.

"Oh my God, Lucas," I say in a panic as I run towards

his lifeless figure on the tiled floor.

I didn't expect him to be dead, but I'm seriously relieved when I see no blood. I couch down next to him and place my hand on his shoulder. His skin is burning to touch and he's covered in sweat, yet he's shaking.

"Lucas," I say gently, but there's no response. I try again, with a shake to his shoulder this time.

It does the trick and he starts groaning. His eyes open to slits as he looks at me. "Go away," he says croakily before shutting his eyes again.

"Don't be so damn stubborn. Come on, we're getting you into bed." God knows how long he's been lying on the tiled floor.

"No," he groans but I can't just leave him here.

When I stand up, I notice the state of the toilet and decide for myself what's wrong with him. I quickly flush it before attempting to pull him up from the floor.

He refuses to help and lies there like a dead weight for ages. He must realise that I'm being serious about getting him off the cold floor because eventually he helps by pushing himself up.

I help him towards his bed the best I can. He's way too heavy for me to take the weight; if he didn't put some effort in then he wouldn't be going anywhere.

He drops down on to the bed and lies back, throwing his arms over his eyes and letting out a huge breath.

"Can I get you anything?" I ask quietly.

"No, just leave." No sooner have the words left his mouth does he start retching. I run out to where I dropped my stuff and grab my cleaning supply bucket. I get back just in time. He snatches it from me before sticking his head in it.

I stand there for a few seconds, unsure of what to do, until I decide to sit down next to him. I place my hand on his back and slowly rub up and down, admiring his artwork. What he hides underneath his suit is all bad boy.

"That's why I was in the bathroom," he complains when he's finished.

"Just lie back. I'll sort this out."

Thankfully he does as he's told, and by the time I come back with a clean bucket he's fast asleep. He's lying like he was earlier, on his back with his arm thrown over. I run my eyes down his chest and abs before taking in his cotton pyjama trousers that are hanging low and giving me a great shot of his V lines.

I shake my head and give myself a good talking to. He's sick, and here I am checking out his body!

I put the bowl on the floor next to him before grabbing him a glass of water and placing it on his bed side table for when he wakes up. I then set about cleaning the bathroom. I've no idea if it's a bug or something he ate, but I get the bleach out just in case.

He's still out cold when I'm finished, so I pull his bedroom door to and make myself busy in the living area.

It's almost an hour later when I hear his phone ringing.

I grab it from the coffee table and answer it before really thinking. I just wanted to stop it ringing in case it woke him.

"H…hello. Lucas?" a soft female voice asks.

"Uh…no…it's his…cleaner."

"Oh um…Is he there?"

"He is, but he's in bed."

"That's what I feared. Both him and my husband had the seafood platter last night and Joe's been up all night. I just thought I'd check on Lucas."

"It looks like he's been up all night, too."

We exchange a few more words before she says her goodbye and I hang up.

When I glance at the clock and see the time, I realise Lucas probably has meetings and stuff planned that someone is going to have to do something about.

I pick his phone back up and call one person I really don't want to speak to.

"Good morning, Lucas," she sings when she picks up.

"Catherine, it's Lilly."

"Who?"

"Lucas' cleaner," I answer, hating the way it sounds. It doesn't feel like the right description, although it's the truth.

"Can I help?" she snarls.

"Lucas is ill in bed. I thought I should let you know so you can cancel anything he had planned."

"I'm sure he's capable of telling me that himself," she snaps. I'm taken back by her attitude. "I'll be up to see him as soon as I get in. I suggest you go home, Poppy."

"It's Lilly," I correct. I don't know why I bother, though; it's obvious she did it on purpose.

I bite back any response that would be unprofessional—she is kind of my boss, after all—and choose to thank her and say goodbye politely. Okay, so I say it way too politely and sweetly in the hope it annoys her.

Lucas

I roll over and instantly regret it. My stomach turns over and I begin the heave again. I lean over the bed and am surprised to see a bucket waiting for me. I'm thankful it's there, however it got there. I reach out and grab it before throwing up for the thousandth time since leaving the restaurant last night. I knew the seafood platter was a bad idea, but the scallops in that place are award winning and I couldn't resist.

I rest myself back against the headboard when a banging on my hotel room door starts. I go to swing my legs off the bed when I hear movement in the living area. Suddenly, images of her blonde hair filter into my brain, memories to her finding me on the bathroom floor, making me get up and then passing me a bucket when I was sick again.

Staying away from her these last few weeks has been a challenge, to say the least. Knowing that every morning she's here making sure everything is clean and in its place has been torture. If I'm honest with myself, I was too scared to show my face. I've haven't allowed myself to care about anyone for a very long time. I hate letting people close to me—especially new people. There are very few in my life that I trust—five, to be exact—and I'm more than happy with that number. I don't need a little blonde haired beauty upsetting my well-structured life.

"I already told you he's in bed ill," I hear her say when I eventually make it to the doorway.

"And I told you to go home," a very familiar voice snaps back.

"Oh, here we go," I groan to myself as I make my way towards them.

"I'm not—" Lilly starts, but I interrupt whatever she was going to say.

"Enough," I state when I have them in my sights. "I

won't be in today, Catherine. Please cancel everything in my diary. Actually, cancel tomorrow as well, while you're at it," The longer I stay upright, the more I realise that I'm not going to be fit for a few days. "Then you can leave."

Both of them look at me with shocked eyes. Okay, so maybe that came out a little harshly.

"You need someone to look after you," Catherine says so sweetly it sets my teeth on edge. Why I ever went there, God only knows.

"I'm good, thank you. Now, you've got work to do," I say, dismissing her.

I stand and watch as she stares at me for a few seconds longer before turning her hard stare on Lilly.

"Grab your stuff then," she snarls.

Lilly turns to do as she's told, but I'm soon behind her with my hands on her shoulders. "Goodbye, Catherine. Only contact me if it's urgent." With that said, I reach around Lilly and swing the door shut.

Six

Lilly

"She's right, I should go if you're feeling better. I just thought you might have needed something, but now you're up..." I ramble while removing myself from his grasp.

"I'm only feeling better if you stay."

"What?" I ask, thinking I must have heard him wrong.

"I'm sure I'll feel much worse if you leave, so I think you should stay."

"You're blackmailing me into staying with you."

He makes a non-committal noise as a response and just stares at me. I can see from here that he's really struggling, so I decide not to fight.

"Fine, get back to bed."

After some disagreement, he finally caves, and once he's brushed his teeth he goes back to bed. I wait until he is settled before asking if he needs anything. He says he doesn't, but I head out to the living area and place an order for some toast anyway.

When it arrives, Lucas takes one bite before rushing back to the bathroom. Maybe it wasn't such a good idea, after all. Listening to him heaving into the toilet seriously put me off eating as well, so I have it cleared away and on a tray out in the corridor to be picked up by the time he reappears.

I think he manages about ten minutes before he is asleep again. I can only imagine how irritating being ill must be for a guy like Lucas. I don't get the impression from him that he spends many days lazing around in bed—he's too busy trying to take over the world, or whatever it is he spends his days rushing around doing.

I get a huge sense of déjà vu when his phone starts ringing again. I jump up from the sofa where I was sat quietly doing some uni work after he passed out. Again, I don't look at the screen; I just swipe it and put it to my ear.

"Hello?"

"Oh my, is it you?" another female voice says.

"Uh…I guess that depends on who you think it is."

"Are you the girl that's got my Luc tied up in knots?" Something happens inside me when the lady on the other end says those words. I can't quite describe it. A bubble of excitement? Dread? Hope? I have no idea.

"I'm just his cleaner," I say, and I feel just as much like a nobody as I did when I was talking to Catherine earlier. I enjoy my job most days, and I have total respect for people who do this day in and day out, but it's not my calling in life. I want more than this, and I've worked damn hard to hopefully have that.

"Hmmm, what's your name, my dear?"

"Lilly."

"That's pretty. Is my son there?" It's not until she says it that I realise who's on the other end. Mrs. Dalton. The woman is a bit of a legend with all the female staff around here. She must be in her sixties, but she is the most elegant woman I've ever seen. The way she holds herself is like nothing I've ever seen before. Weirdly, it's not pretentious though. She also has this soft and gentleness to her—much like my mum has, I guess. Mrs. Dalton is just a richer, more sophisticated version. I bet she hasn't ground a coffee bean in her life.

"He is, Mrs. Dalton, but he's sick. From what I gather, he went out last night and got food poisoning."

"Oh my goodness. Let me whip up some of my famous chicken soup and I'll be right over."

"Oh, that's so lovely of you, but I should warn you that he just tried some toast and it didn't stay down. I wouldn't want you to waste your time."

"Nonsense. My chicken soup fixes everything."

"Well, okay then."

"You'll still be there; I'll bring extra. Thank you for taking care of him, dear. Now I know it's not my place, but I just need to say something." Everything inside me wants to groan out loud at her statement. She is reading far too much into this situation. "Lucas doesn't let people in. He has a handful of trusted people and that is it. He also doesn't let his walls down easily. What I'm trying to say is that he'll push you away at every possibility, but it's only because he's scared. If you care for him like I know he does you, then you need to give him time—and whatever you do, cling on tight, because it will be a bumpy ride. I can guarantee it will be an amazing one as well though, because my boy is a one of a kind. And if you do show him that he can trust you and let you in, you'll never regret it."

My mouth drops open to say something, but no words come out.

"Oh, I'm sorry, my dear. I didn't mean to scare you. I just thought it best I say those things now before it could be too late. I'll see you soon. I hope you're hungry."

The phone beeps in my hand, telling me she's hung up. I drop back on to the sofa and let her words roll around my head.

If you care for him like I know he does you.
Cling on tight.
Bumpy ride.
You'll never regret it.

My head is so all over the place that I gather up my stuff, leave a note next to Lucas and run as fast as I can. I need to get away before Mrs. Dalton appears and potentially starts filling my head with more thoughts I don't need or want.

I go down to the cleaners' office. Thankfully, there is no one around. After finding an empty room, I head back up in the lift with the key in my hand.

I spread my stuff out across the double bed and try to carry on where I left off. The only problem is that all I do is stare at the blank sketchpad page in front of me. None of the wallpaper samples, paint colours or fabric swatches draw my attention. My sole focus is still on everything that happened upstairs.

I don't really understand how I got here. I was more than happy just cleaning rooms with either Eve or Imogen, and now? Here I am. I've slept with the boss, and I have his mother telling me not to let him push me away. I'm pretty sure I've been the one doing the pushing, though. Lucas was the one who went after the date, turned up even after I said no, and has since tried to spend more time with me. Granted, I haven't seen him for two months until this morning, but I think that might have been because of his bruised ego.

I've discovered over the past year that when I need quiet time to work, finding an empty hotel room is perfect. No one knows where I am—they can't interrupt me like Taylor would at home, or other students would at uni. I can hide away and gets loads done. It also helps that the rooms I'm currently designing are these exact hotel rooms. Using this hotel for one of my final projects has worked perfectly. I have access to most places, plus it's in desperate need of an overhaul, so I can imagine my designs actually being put to use.

I get two hours of solid work in before my phone starts ringing. I ignore it and let it ring off the first time, hoping it's someone ringing about my non-existent PPI claim, but no sooner has it stopped than it starts again. I reluctantly reach down and pull it from my bag. The second I see it's an unrecognised number, I know exactly who it is. I guess I shouldn't be surprised to have a call this quickly.

"Hello?" I answer, like I don't know who it is.

"Where are you?" Lucas demands. I almost didn't put my phone number on the note I left, but in the end, the idea of him being up there and needing something made me do it.

"I'm working, Lucas. Do you need anything?"

"Yes, I need something. You didn't answer my question. Where are you?"

I hesitate, because I shouldn't really be occupying an empty hotel room for my own peace and quiet, but in the end I cave. "Room 319."

"You're cleaning. I thought you only did my room," he says, sounding confused.

"I do. I'm…uh…using it to do uni work. I know I shouldn't, but—"

"It's fine."

"What is it you needed, Lucas?" I know I might sound a little harsh, but he's ruined my peace by demanding to know where I am like he owns me.

There's no response—he's already hung up.

"Argh, you irritating man," I moan to no one but myself.

I sit back against the headboard and look at what I managed to achieve. I'm pleased with the designs I've come up with—they are a little edgy and unique. Definitely not the chain hotel look like the room I'm currently sitting in. I know Lucas is organising a refurbishment of this place, and I'm really intrigued to see what they do with it.

Bang, bang, bang.

I let my head fall back against the wall behind me with a thud. Why didn't I think he'd just turn up?

I pull the door open and find a very rough looking Lucas staring back at me. The man in the doorway is almost unrecognisable from my perfectly put together boss. His hair is a mess and falling across his face. He's got stubble on his chin and he's wearing a white V neck t-shirt and grey jogging bottoms. If I saw him in the hotel, I don't think I'd realise it was Lucas. He looks incredibly hot even though he's got dark rings around his eyes. Those and his pale skin the only signs he's ill. I feel my temperature increase and between my legs starts to throb as memories of our night together run through my mind. I shake the thoughts from my head and banish them. They are not helping this situation.

"I would have come up if you'd asked."

"No, you wouldn't." He's right. I may not have done.

"So did you actually need something?" I ask, stepping to the side as he pushes his way in.

"Yes. You."

My lips snap shut with surprise.

"What are you doing in here, anyway?" he asks as he walks towards the bed. "Wow."

I watch as he crouches down so he can get a better look at my designs. He's silent as he studies each room laid out in front of him.

"I'm sorry, I'll make sure the room is put back perfectly. I just like the peace and quiet," I say, going over and starting to tidy everything up.

"Lilly, these are incredible. You've basically done the whole hotel."

I feel my face flush at his compliment. I mutter a thank you before continuing to tidy up.

"Do you fancy a job as my designer instead of my cleaner?"

"Don't be stupid, Lucas. I'll meet you upstairs when I'm sorted," I say in the hope he'll leave me to it for a bit. He's taken me by surprise, turning up looking all sexy bad boy. I need a moment to compose myself and remind myself he's my boss. Unfortunately, he doesn't leave. Instead, he helps me get everything together before insisting on carrying it all back upstairs.

The second I step foot in his room, I realise what was missing this morning. There was no music. Every single time I've been here, whether Lucas has been here or not, there has been music playing. Usually it's easy going kind of stuff that is easy to work along to. This afternoon is different, because the sounds of Tinie Tempah filter through the entire suite.

I look over my shoulder at Lucas but he ignores the question in my eyes and just walks past me before putting my stuff down next to the sofa. I can't help but watch his backside as he bends down.

When he looks up, he catches me staring at him. A smirk tugs at the corners of his lips.

"See something you like?" he asks, reminding me of the night he took me out.

As he stands looking smug and waiting for my reply, I spot a flask, a loaf of bread and bowls on a tray on the coffee table behind him.

"Ah, your mum's famous chicken soup," I state before heading in that direction.

When I look over my shoulder, I see him looking at me with his mouth open. "How do you know about that?" he asks but then immediately answers his own question. "You spoke to her this morning, didn't you? I wondered how she knew I was ill. I just presumed the gossip got back about my cancelled meetings."

"I'm sorry. Your phone rang and to stop it waking you up, I answered it. I'm sorry," I repeat, because I have no idea if he's going to be annoyed with my actions.

"It's fine, Lilly. I bet she was thrilled that a female answered my phone," he comments with a laugh.

"You'd already told her about me."

"Not really. She's tenacious, my mother. Once she gets something in her head she won't stop."

The fact he's not denying telling his mum about me is a shock. Maybe she's right—maybe there is more here than the one night stand I thought it would be and that Lucas does actually want to spend more time with me. I thought maybe it was all a bit of a joke or something. I mean, not every hotel owner wants anything to do with his cleaning staff.

Once I gather my thoughts, my mouth runs away with me. "And what did you tell her exactly?"

"Well nothing, actually. I went over the day after we went out for dinner and… she can see everything, that bloody woman."

"What do you mean?"

"Would you like some soup?" Lucas asks, completely ignoring my question.

The soup is delicious—I even have seconds. Lucas, on the other hand, has a couple of spoons full, then puts the bowl down. When I glance up at him, he looks a little green. After a bit of an argument, he eventually concedes and takes himself back to bed. He looks exhausted.

Just like before, he was almost asleep before his head hit

the pillow. I pull his bedroom door shut before finishing off the cleaning I escaped from earlier. Once everything is looking as it should, I peek my head around his door to see if he's still asleep. I'm surprised to see a bright blue pair of eyes looking back at me.

"Hey."

"Hey, yourself."

"I was just coming to say that I'm heading off. I've finished cleaning, so…"

"Don't go." My eyes snap back up to his. "Please," he says, in an almost begging tone. He sounds so sad and looks a little pathetic with his green glow that I haven't really got a choice but to agree.

I slip inside the room, pulling the door closed behind me. I stand at the side of his bed and he lifts the covers for me to join him. I'm feeling a little unsure of myself now. I may have just agreed to stay, but what happens next? It's only just getting dark outside, so going to bed seems a little crazy, and I can guarantee nothing untoward is happening in said bed. And that's not only because he's ill. I can't go there again, even if my memories alone are enough to get me revved up for it.

"Lucas, I don't think-"

"Just get in. I'll behave, I promise." There's a twinkle in his eye as he says this that makes me question his sincerity.

I stare at him for a few seconds as I try to tell myself to leave. But I can't.

I slip my shoes off and slide in next to him.

Lucas

I don't put much thought into the fact I don't want her to leave. It was bad enough that I woke up earlier with only a note to say she'd left to greet me. I'm keeping her here this time.

I don't waste any time moving her so her back is tucked to my front. It's not what I really want to do, but it's all I'm allowing for a number of reasons. Mostly because I promised I'd be good. Smelling like vomit is also pretty high on my list.

I don't remember falling asleep, but it must have happened pretty quickly. I can't recall the last time I was ill, but I don't think I've ever felt this drained before.

It's a fight to pull myself from my sleep, but I can hear my phone ringing. I push the haziness away, drag my eyelids open and swing my legs from the bed.

I eventually find my phone down the side of the sofa. It's unlike me to leave it lying around; it's usually no farther than a foot away from me at all times. I blame Lilly—she's messing with my head.

When I look down, I see it's the manager of our hotel in Yorkshire. "Dalton," I bark into the phone. I don't mean to be rude, but it's three o'clock in the fucking morning.

"I'm sorry, Sir," her timid voice says on the other line. "But there's been a fire."

Shit. "How bad?"

"Bad. I think you'd better get up here."

"On my way," I say, already walking back towards the bedroom to find clothes.

I'm dressed and out the door in ten minutes. I feel better than I did yesterday, but not much. I push thoughts of my dodgy stomach down as I race towards the underground garage. I floor the accelerator of my Jaguar and head out into the night.

Thoughts of the mess I might find when I eventually arrive are forgotten as the image of Lilly's blonde sleep-messed hair filters into my mind. I tried to slip out without waking her but just as I was about to leave I heard a sleepy voice whisper my name.

"I'm sorry, beautiful. I've got to go—there's been a fire and I'm needed." My words made her sit up.

"Where? Is everyone okay?"

"I don't know any details yet. I'll ring you when I can. Go back to sleep." I gently pushed her back down to the pillow before pressing my lips to her forehead. I wanted to pick her up and take her with me, but I knew I couldn't. I wasn't going for a jolly; I was going to assess the damage to our most lucrative hotel and hopefully not have to organise rebuilding it from the ground upwards.

After a few seconds, I pulled away and walked straight out. If I'd have looked back and seen her, it would have stopped me going. That realisation hits me hard. Since the day I started in our family business, I have always put work first. I wanted to show my parents they hadn't made a mistake in giving me a chance. I wanted to prove to them that I could be a better person, someone they could be proud to call their son. Not the walking disaster that I had been. I've never lost focus, but there I was, questioning whether I should take her with me or say fuck it and let someone else handle it.

"FUCK," I shout when I turn up the driveway to the hotel and see smoke bellowing from the top. All thoughts of Lilly are immediately banished as I look at everything me, my dad and his dad built smoulder in the heat from the flames.

The place is a mess. It's going to need a lot of work before it's fit to have guests staying in again. Every square inch of the place is going to need redoing. I just pray that the structure of the building is safe and we won't need to do any major building work.

The day is long and stressful—not one I will ever look back fondly on, that's for sure. Once I have as much sorted as I can with the fire brigade, police and members of staff that are still hanging about to help, I book myself into a local hotel to get some rest, ready to start all over again tomorrow. Hopefully, I'll be able to properly assess the damage better and make some kind of plan.

My arse barely touches the sheet covering the bed when my phone starts ringing.

"Mum," I state as I put it to my ear. I'm too exhausted to be bothered with pleasantries.

"Your dad wanted me to let you know that he's just left. He'll be with you in a few hours. How are you feeling?"

"Better than yesterday," I answer. It's the only slightly positive thing I can think to say.

"That's good. How about the hotel? Is it salvageable?"

"I haven't got any details yet. They're still investigating the fire, but the fact the sprinkler system didn't go off isn't helpful. The police are concerned it might have been done on purpose."

"Oh, really? Why would someone do a thing like that?"

"No idea, Mum. I'm sorry, but I need to go," I say as I feel my body start to give in.

"Of course, you get some sleep before your dad gets there. I love you, son."

"Thanks, bye," I respond with a lump in my throat. No matter how many years go by, it never gets easier hearing those words.

I'm just drifting off to sleep when my phone starts up again. I can't ignore it—the control freak in me refuses in case it's important.

I sit up and grab it off the bedside table. When I see who it is, I'm suddenly much more awake.

"Lilly," I greet with a much lighter tone than I've used all day.

"How is everything?"

"Fucking disaster. The place is a total mess. It's going to take a lot of work to get it functioning again and fuck knows how much time. Thankfully, there wasn't anything more serious than some mild smoke inhalation and a few scratches and scrapes. The thought of something more serious happening doesn't bear thinking about."

"I know. So how long are you going to be up there, do you think?"

"Honestly, no idea. My dad is on his way up to help out. I'll be back as soon as I can."

"Really?" The way she asks the question makes my heart beat that little bit faster. I don't think anyone has ever really cared that much about when I was coming home before—other than my parents.

"Do you miss me already?" I say with a laugh, but I'm seriously curious about the answer.

"I'm just worried about you; you were ill and everything." Her evasive answer makes me smile.

"I'll take that as a yes then, shall I?" Just before she responds, I drop the tone of my voice and say, "And just so you know, sleeping here won't be the same without you."

I hear loud and clear the huge rush of air that escapes her. It's good to know that I can affect her from this far away. She's the master at hiding her true feelings and running away, but I feel like I might be breaking down her barriers. The only thing I worry about with that is I think she might just be doing the same to me.

Seven

Lilly

"Are you free this week?" Nicole asks the second I put my phone to my ear. She doesn't wait for me to respond; she just keeps talking, knowing the answer doesn't really matter. "The carers have organised for me to have a week of respite and got a room for Mum in the local hospice at the last minute. Apparently, I look like I need it. Anyway, I've got to be back for the weekend, but if you're free I'll get in the car right now."

"OH MY GOD," I shout into the phone. "YES, YES,

YES, get your butt down here now."

After a bit more overly excited chatter about her imminent arrival we hang up. I fly around the flat like a mad woman, getting it cleaned for our guest as well as making up spare sheets for the sofa bed.

I obsessively check the clock every ten minutes, hoping the four hours have miraculously gone by. It's been too long since we've seen each other, and life has been really tough for Nicole recently. I need to give her a huge hug.

Nicole and I met at playschool. She was a tiny little thing with bright red hair and freckles. We hit it off instantly over our love of My Little Pony, and were inseparable from then on—until she moved up north with her mum to look after her grandparents. I now realise it was for financial reasons as well. Nicole's mum brought her up on her own after her dad died. She was living in Oxford and working three jobs to try to support them. She was desperate not to uproot Nicole, but in the end her parents' deteriorating health meant they had to make the move. I was gutted to lose my best friend, but we've stayed in touch and apart from the distance we are still as close as we ever were.

Lucas is still in Yorkshire with no idea as to when he'll be back. I'd be lying to myself if I said I didn't miss him. Something changed for me the night I slept in his bed when he was ill. I can't put my finger on what it was, but suddenly I didn't have the urge to run anymore. Which is weird, because after what his mum told me I think I should be running faster.

He texted me earlier in the day with a brief update, but it seems they are still no further forward in working out what happened.

Thinking it will pass some time, I pick up the phone and call him.

"Hey, beautiful," Lucas says in his sexy, deep voice. It sends goosebumps rushing over my skin.

"Hey, is this a bad time?"

"I've always got time for you." Swoon! "So, what's up?"

"Nothing. My best friend is heading down for a few days. She lives in County Durham and can't get away much at the moment. I'm just waiting for her to arrive."

"So you're telling me you're bored and need distracting?"

"Uh," I think about how he knows me so well. "Something like that," I admit.

"I'm joking, Lilly. Call me whenever—whatever you need."

"Thank you. I wanted to let you know that I've booked last minute holiday as Nic's coming, so your room might not get cleaned."

"You didn't need to book holiday. I don't have a problem with you not going in while I'm not there. I hate that you have to clean my room at all."

"Lucas, it's my job, and just because you and I are…whatever, doesn't mean I want special treatment. That's not why I'm—" Thankfully, he interrupts me.

"You're looking too much into it."

"Am I? Because the way everyone else will see it is that I let you in my bed and now I can turn up to work when I feel like it. That doesn't sit right with me, Luc."

"I've told you before, just quit. Focus on your last couple of weeks at uni."

"NO," I shout, a little too forcefully. "I need my job, Luc. I have things to pay for. I'm not like you with thousands sat in your bank account."

"I'll make sure you have money, don't worry."

"Oh great, so now everyone's going to assume you're paying me for sex!" This isn't the first time we've had this discussion. I thought he understood—clearly not.

"Lilly, that's not how it is."

"No, because we've only had sex once. I've got to go. Goodbye." I jab my finger against the phone screen to end the call in a huff. How dare he? Just because he's some rich fancy pants businessman he thinks he can tell me what to do. I don't think so.

By the time the buzzer goes off, I've already had half a bottle of wine while ignoring my ringing phone. My mood instantly lightens when I think about who is at the other side.

I pull the door back and launch myself at Nic, we hold each other for the longest time on the doorstep.

Eventually I let her go, grab her bag and together we walk into the flat. Nic kicks off her shoes as I pour her a glass.

"Wow, you've already had a good go at that by the looks of it," she comments when she sees the half empty wine bottle.

"Don't worry, I'll tell you all about it." And as if on cue, my phone starts ringing.

"Who's Lucas?"

"The reason I'm already tipsy."

I go on to tell Nic everything. I can see she's a little annoyed that this is the first time hearing it, but she understands when I explain that I didn't want to put any more on her plate. I think she feels guilty that I felt the need to hide what's going on in my life.

Her mum was diagnosed with breast cancer a few years

ago. She had all the treatment and got the all clear. Nic was convinced that was it, that she'd beaten it, but towards the end of last year her mum was getting headaches. One scan later and Nic had the news she was terrified of. Not only had her dad died when her mum was pregnant, she had lost both grandparents in the last couple of years, and now she was going to lose her mum as well.

Nic's incredible. The strength she has amazes me. She's given everything up to care for her mum. She dropped out of college the first time round and never ended up perusing a career in music like she always wanted. This time, she's given up her job, her life, everything to be her sole carer. She has some help from carers that come in daily, but every other minute of the day it's just her. It kills me to be so far away and unable to help. Not that Nic would accept it, mind you. She is stubborn to her core.

"Give him a break, Lil. His hotel just burnt down and he's had food poisoning; he's probably not thinking correctly," Nic says once I've told her everything. I think she's giving him too much credit. He knows exactly what he's doing.

"I'm not so sure," I mutter.

"Anyway, enough about that. I can't believe you had a one-night stand with him. That's so unlike you. Mind you, it's about time. How long ago was it you broke up with Jake?"

"Eight months."

"Exactly. Time to get back in the game."

"That's rich. When was the last time you showed any interest in a guy?"

"I haven't got time, you know that."

"I do, but that's only been recently. What about before that?"

"I don't know. No one interested me, I guess."

Nic and I have an incredible couple of days. Having booked holiday from work, my mornings were free, and while I went into uni in the afternoon, Nic went shopping before meeting for me dinner and more drinks. I don't think I've ever drank so much, but I was grateful that Nic was relaxing and enjoying herself, so the hangovers were worth it.

I skive off uni on Friday so we can spend our last together. I book us both in for a hair appointment, followed by eyebrows and spray tans. Nic's usually gorgeous red is looking seriously drab, and the tan should help her look a little less exhausted.

"Thank you for the last few days, Lils. I really needed it."

"You're welcome. I just wish you didn't have to go so soon."

"I know, but one day soon I'll be able to do as I please," she replies sadly.

Listening to her talk about it on the phone is hard enough, but having her here in person and listening to what her life is currently like is heart breaking. Although she's had a good rest, I can see that being so far away has been playing on her mind. She's well aware that the phone could ring at any minute.

"We're going on holiday," I state to try to cheer the conversation up slightly. "Where do you want to go?"

"Somewhere hot, with a beach, a bar and a load of hot guys," she says with a laugh and a genuine smile on her face.

"Done. We'll get it booked as soon as we can."

Our excited chatter about sun, sand and hot men is soon distracted by my ringing phone.

"It's Dec," I say, going to grab it. Fair play to Nic, because she manages to contain the groan I know she's desperate to let out. It's no secret that Nic and Dec do not get along—they never have, and I'm pretty sure never will.

"Hey, what are you doing ringing on a Friday evening? Shouldn't you be out on the pull?" I say, teasing my brother. It's unlike him that he's not already on the hunt for tonight's partner.

"Ugh, you sound just like Mum," he complains. "I've had a busy day. I thought I'd be a good brother and call you before going out, as we haven't really spoken much this week." My twin brother can be sweet when he wants to. "So, what've you been up to?"

"Nic's here," I reply excitedly. The noise he makes in response takes me right back to being a kid and listening to the two of them bickering. "We've spent the week chilling out and drinking mostly. She's heading back tonight though."

"Okay, well I'll leave you to it and we'll catch up over the weekend then, yeah?"

"Yeah okay. I haven't got any plans so call me whenever."

"Okay, bye."

"Bye."

As I hang the phone up, Taylor walks in all dressed to the nines and smelling incredible. He hasn't been around much again this week, and it looks like tonight isn't any exception. His bed-hopping is getting a little over the top now.

"Going somewhere nice?" Nic asks.

"Heading to a gay bar in town. Hoping it's my lucky night," he says, wiggling his eyebrows.

"Isn't every night your lucky night?"

"Now, now, Lilly. Just because your boss hasn't banged you into next week again, doesn't mean you can take your frustration out on me," Taylor replies with a laugh, making Nic smirk and me throw a cushion at him.

"Whatever," I mutter.

Before I know it, Nic's getting ready to leave. We're just grabbing her bags, ready to head towards her car, when there's a knock at the front door. It's unusual not to be buzzed first; people in this building are pretty good a not just letting randomers in, which I'm thankful for.

When I look through the peephole though, I'm not surprised. I'm sure he could sweet talk just about anyone to get what he wants.

Besides a couple of short texts, we haven't spoken since the other night's argument. His text was a pathetic sort of apology, but I figured that was probably more than he was used to. I can't imagine he apologies for much.

"Hey," I say when I pull the door back. He immediately steps forward, his hand slides around the back of my neck, and he pulls my lips to his. It's an innocent kiss, but it still gets my blood pumping. Having Nic here helped me forget how much I was missing him, but having him here, his scent in my nose, brings all my feelings back.

"You must be Lucas. I've heard quite a bit about you," Nic helpfully says and distracts us from each other.

"Is that right?" Lucas says with a smirk. "I'm sure it's all been good."

"Something like that," Nic mutters, making Lucas laugh.

"I guess I deserved that."

"I'm glad I stayed a little later than planned now so I got to meet who has Lilly all tied up."

"Nic, please stop," I beg when I see Lucas' eyes light up and a smile start to tug at his lips. He does not need to know any of this.

"No, please, continue. What else has she said about me?" His eyes are sparkling with amusement, whereas I'm dying inside.

"Nothing I could share," Nic says with a wink. "Right, I need to get going."

"Thank you for coming. It's been so good to see you."

"You too."

Lucas stands and watches as we say our goodbyes. Neither of us makes any promise of when we'll see each other again. I think it's easier for Nic that way. Her life is so up in the air and I'm scared to say *I'll see you soon* because we both know what that means for her.

By the time we walk away, we both have black mascara stains down our cheeks.

"Hey, come here," Lucas says, stepping towards me and wrapping me in his arms.

"I'm sorry, I've just not seen her for so long and I've no idea when I'll see her again, other than that I'm pretty sure whenever it is, it'll be for a sad reason." Lucas gives me a look that prompts me to explain Nic's situation.

Once I've finished, he wipes the tears from my cheeks with his thumbs and kisses my forehead. He's so gentle with me and I can only imagine gentle is the last thing he wants to be—especially if the urgency of the kiss he gave me when he arrived was anything to go by. It may have been gentle, but there was a promise behind it. A promise that made my knees weak with anticipation.

"Go and get packed. I'm taking you away for the weekend."

"What?"

"You heard—now go pack. And make sure you bring that black dress you wore out last time. I really liked that," he says, dropping his hooded eyes to run the length of me.

Butterflies erupt in my stomach when they come back up to mine.

"O…okay," I stutter before rushing towards my bedroom.

I pull out a small case and start throwing things into it. I don't need to turn around to know that Lucas is stood in the doorway watching me. I can feel his presence.

"Are you going to tell me where we're going?" I ask when he grabs my case from the bed and starts to move towards the front door. I quickly slide my feet into my Converse and rush after him.

"I'll explain when we're in the car. Come on, it's already late enough and I've got plans for you."

I don't respond; I just lock the flat door and follow him into the lift. The atmosphere is thick as we descend in the enclosed space. I so badly want him to kiss me properly but I'm aware that if he does the only place we'd probably end up tonight is back upstairs and in my bed.

"So you said you'd explain," I remind him when he pulls out of the car park.

"You're my guest for a charity auction I'm going to at the end of the month so we're going to London so we can get you a dress."

My mouth falls open as his words register in my brain. "What if I don't want to go?" I ask, trying to be irritated by his demanding attitude. Unfortunately, my body is thrilled that he wants to spend more time with me.

"It's a charity for underprivileged kids. You can't say no."

"That's a low blow, Lucas. How could you use kids like that?"

"Because I was one of them."

His words shock me into silence. I look over at him and his eyes are a little wider than usual. I don't think he meant to say that out loud.

"Have you been to the London Dalton before?" he asks suddenly, obviously trying to change the subject.

"No, I've only ever been in the Cheltenham one."

"This might be a shock then. It was the first one I took on when my dad allowed me to work for him. I had a lot to prove. He never said it but I know he was waiting for me to fail, to fall back into my old ways. He was worried about me being back in London but I told him to trust me and I think he's glad he did now."

"Did you live in London then?"

"I'm not sure you could describe it as living. I *existed* in London. It wasn't a good time in my life and it's not something I like to talk about."

"Okay," I whisper as I think about the secrets I have. It looks like we both have skeletons hiding in our closets. "How's it going in Yorkshire?"

Lucas spends the rest of the journey talking about his burnt down hotel. I get the idea that he really needed to get it all off his chest so I sit and listen and make the right noises in the right places.

"Mr, Dalton, such a pleasure to have you with us," the concierge says as we enter his swanky London hotel. He was right when he said I would be shocked. It is very different to Cheltenham. The hotel sits inside a very similar old building but inside has been modernised within an inch of its life. Everywhere is blue and silver to match the Dalton brand but it's much more like the design work I've been doing than the hotel chain look I was expecting. I now understand why Lucas was so taken with my ideas. It looks like we have similar design tastes.

As predicted, we head straight up to the top of the hotel to the penthouse suite. The colossal size of it makes Lucas' suite in Cheltenham look tiny.

"Lilly, are you nearly ready? Our reservation is in five minutes," I hear Lucas shout through the bathroom door. Practically as soon as we entered the room he told me to get dressed as he'd organised a table downstairs for dinner. I wanted to take in the stunning room but all I've really seen so far is the bathroom. It's a nice bathroom—I'm not complaining, but I don't get that excited by them. Plus, I haven't seen Lucas all week. I was hoping for a bit of time together before having to go out in public.

I turn my straighteners off and run my fingers gently through the curls I've just created. Even I can see that I look better in this dress than last time. Instead of hanging around me, it is now hugging my body. Let's face, it my figure is too athletic to ever really be described a curvy, but I'm definitely seeing more curves than a couple of months ago. The woman looking back at me in the mirror now has a sparkle in her eye and a smile on her face. It's a very different look to what I had been beginning to get used to.

"Okay, I'm ready. Let's go," I say as I pull back the bathroom door and find Lucas sat on the corner of the bed in his standard suit and tie combo. The more I see him dressed like that, the more I'm beginning to like it. Not as much as when he takes it off, mind you, but the sophisticated look is growing on me somewhat.

Lucas stands and I'm expecting him to step in the direction of the door. What I'm not expecting is for him to step towards me but then not stop until my back hits the wall.

My mouth drops open to ask what he's doing but I don't get the chance for any words to come out because he's on my lips. Both his hands come up to my head and I feel his fingers thread through my hair.

I forget about dinner. I forget about everything he said at the beginning of the week. Hell, I pretty much forget my own name. Holy cow, this man can kiss. I remember it being good, but I was pretty drunk the last time. I don't remember it being *quite* this good.

His hands slide down my neck and over my shoulders before skimming down my sides. His thumbs brush over my nipples as his hands descend down my body. The sensation causes a shudder to run through me. He must feel me shake under his hands but it doesn't make him stop kissing me.

The kiss goes on forever as his hands explore my body. My heart races and tries to beat its way out of my chest.

My hands follow suit and I reach out to grab on to him. I slide them inside his jacket and run them up his stomach and chest until I reach his shoulders. I gently shove the fabric so it starts to fall down his arms. The movement stops Lucas in his tracks and he pulls back. His breath is coming out in quick pants as he looks at me with dark and hungry eyes, like he wants to devour me.

"Fuck dinner. I'm having you," he states before shrugging his jacket off so it falls on the floor. His tie follows and then he's back on me. His hands go to the back of my thighs and run up until the fabric of my dress is bunched around my hips.

I suck in a breath when I hear the lace of my knickers rip under his touch.

"Not sorry," he mutters against my jaw as he moves his way down to my neck.

He sucks hard on my skin as his fingers find their way between my legs. He gives my thighs a nudge and I widen my stance to give him access. The second his fingertips connect with my sensitive skin, I cry out. He circles my clit a few times before going lower and sliding a finger inside me. My legs quiver and I struggle to keep myself upright as he increases the tempo and adds another finger.

My head falls back against the wall as I feel the pressure building. I feel the straps of my dress being pulled down my shoulders and then Lucas' hot breath across my breasts. It teases my nipples and makes them form tighter buds.

"Oh God," I whisper-groan.

I feel his tongue flick my nipple once more and I'm gone. I fall into the most intense pleasure as heat surges through my body and lights flash behind my eyes. Lucas continues whatever it is he's doing inside me and eventually the waves start to lessen as I come back to reality.

I lower my head and look at him though hazy, lust-filled

eyes. He's stood back up to full height. His hair is a mess, his eyes darker than ever, and his lips parted. The mess my red lipstick has caused makes me smile. I reach my hand out and run the pad of my thumb over his stained lips. It doesn't get to do its job though, because as soon as it hits his lips Lucas sucks it into his mouth.

He keeps his eyes on me. They hold a promise that has me feeling the tail end of my orgasm slightly more intensely.

I barely blink and I'm on the move. Lucas lifts me so my legs wrap around his waist and he squeezes my arse cheeks as he walks us over to the bed. I can feel his hardness against me and I almost feel like begging, knowing it's so close.

He drops me down but doesn't make a move to stand back up. He kisses my lips again before descending my body. He nips at my neck and collarbone before paying attention to my breasts. I've always worried they're too small but Lucas doesn't seem to have any issue with the size. When he starts tugging them into his mouth my back arches off the bed. Just that alone is enough to start building orgasm number two. He moves down again and places kisses across my ribs before jumping over the fabric of my dress that is still around my waist and starting on my hipbones. I worry that he hasn't moved it because it's covering my ugly scar but the second I feel his tongue heading south I lose all train of thought.

By the time I'm on the brink of coming again, Lucas has positioned me so that only my shoulders are touching the mattress. My entire bottom half is up in the air and at his mercy as he laps at me with his tongue.

It's just as I'm about to come that I feel something new. He pulls his finger from inside me and runs it lower before pressing gently. I'm just about to question him but suddenly fireworks ignite and I'm hit with one unbelievable orgasm. It puts the last one to shame.

Lucas continues gently until my body relaxes under his touch and he lowers me back down to the bed. He sits back on his heels and looks at me. He's still practically fully dressed while I'm lying here with everything on display.

I prop myself up on my elbows and look back at him.

"Strip," I demand. I'm a little shocked by my words. That isn't really me.

I watch as he slowly undoes each button. The slow pace is torture but I know it's going to be worth it. I already know what's under those posh boy clothes.

His shirt gets shrugged off once he pulls out his expensive looking cuff links and it gets dropped to the floor by his feet. He toes off his shoes and then removes his trousers, boxers and socks all at the same time.

He stands back up and waits. Our eyes lock for a few seconds before I tear mine away in favour of looking at him. He stays still and allows me time to get my fill. His only movement comes after a few seconds when he moves his hand and fists his cock. It's the most erotic thing I've ever seen. I feel my already swollen core flood with more moisture the longer I watch him.

"Fuck this."

Then he's on me and everything goes a bit wild. There are hands and mouths everywhere. He bites down on my neck as I run my nails down his back. I grip on to his hair as he sucks on my nipple. The franticness stops the second I feel him at my entrance though. He moves forward slightly and looks at me—I presume for my approval. I nod slightly and it must be what he wants because he slides all the way in slowly.

I watch as the muscles in his neck pull tight. He throws his head back and lets out a huge breath.

After a few seconds he starts moving, and he falls down on top of me. I grab on to his arse to try to get us closer—if that's even possible.

"I don't deserve you." I hear him whisper into my neck and it reminds me of the things he was saying about his past in the car earlier. I'm desperate to know his secrets, although I'm aware that will mean spilling mine.

My third orgasm of the night is no less powerful than the previous two, and only seconds after I scream his name do I feel him twitch and groan as he comes inside me.

The next thing I know, the sun is shining through the windows and Lucas is looking down at me with a smile on his face.

"Ready to hit the shops?"

Eight

Lucas

This week's been hell. The fire at the hotel has been a fucking disaster. I have no idea when we're going to be able to start refurbishing it, let alone when we might be able to think about reopening. The police are still looking into the fact it could be an inside job because of where it started and that the sprinkler system didn't work. I've had multiple staff and guests in hospital. Thankfully nothing serious but it's still not great. I've had meeting after meeting but things are going absolutely nowhere. And then, just to top all that off, I had that fight with Lilly and then haven't been able to get in contact with her. I knew she had a friend down, but would it have been so much effort to text me back? I know I was out of line, trying to take control of her life. She's independent and wants to make her own decisions. That's one of the things I love about her. I've met so many women who are just after an easy ride and my money. It's refreshing to spend time with someone who doesn't care about all that.

The thought of going to the annual charity auction I attend with my parents was filling me with the usual lack of excitement. Don't get me wrong, I totally support it, but it's not my kind of evening. I spend every day of the week dressed up in a suit trying to be something I'm not. I don't want to spend my Saturday night like it as well. The little time I do get away from work is precious. If it wasn't for my mother insisting I be there, I'd just give my usual donations and be done with it, but I can't say no to her—I've never been able to. Then, it struck me that I could take Lilly, and my feelings about the night changed.

"Lucas, I can't afford a dress from here," Lilly complains as I pull her into Harrods.

"Who says you're buying it?"

"Lucas," she warns and I know I'm about to get the speech again so I cut her off.

"I know you don't want me spending my money on you, but you wouldn't be going to this event if it wasn't for me, and you are the only reason I'm looking forward to it. So please, just this once, let me spend my money. Trust me, it'll be for my own benefit more than yours."

She looks up and me and opens her mouth to argue but

must see something on my face that changes her mind, because she falls back into step next to me.

"It's a formal event, so you want something gown-like, I guess," I say as we start walking through the ladies' section. I look around to see if anything catches my eye but I'm seriously in over my head here. I've done a lot in my life but never once have I been ladies' clothes shopping. I'm pretty sure it's not something I'll be rushing to do again any time soon, either.

I trail behind Lilly as she looks around but she doesn't stop or show interest in anything. This is going to be harder than I thought.

"Don't you like anything?" I ask when we come back around to where we started.

"They are all stunning, Lucas. But did you see the prices? I know I agreed to this but it's crazy."

"Lilly, enough about the price. I will pay whatever, I want you to look and feel amazing. It's the first time ever I'm going to have a date, and I know I sound like a dickhead but I want you to be the best dressed woman there. I want everyone to look at you on my arm and think, wow that's what he's been waiting for."

I see her chin drop open at my words and I swear her eyes water a little. Okay, so maybe that was a little much. But it's the truth. I'm sure everyone at those fancy events thinks I'm gay because they are always filled with beautiful women, none of whom ever take my interest.

"Fine," she mutters and begins walking off again.

This time I watch as she strokes some of the dresses as we walk past. She even pulls a few out slightly to look at the backs. But again, she doesn't make any choice.

"Come on," I say as I grab her hand. I saw the sign for a personal shopper on the other side of the floor. We're going there.

"I'm sorry, Sir, we're booked at the moment." Lilly goes to walk away but I stand my ground. There's always a way to get what you want.

Twenty minutes later and I'm sat on the plush sofa with a glass of champagne while a petite woman brings in dress after dress for Lilly to try on. Maybe this shopping thing isn't so bad after all. I even manage to bang out a few emails while I'm sat here.

"I'm so sorry, Lucas. Wearing these sorts of dresses is unusual for me. I have no idea what I want or what suits me," she says after the fifth dress gets escorted away.

"We've got all day," I reply, but hope we aren't just going to be doing this.

Another two dresses get refused before the woman returns with a black dress draped over her arm.

"Isn't that a little plain?" I ask as she gets closer. There are no ruffles, flowers or diamonds as far as I can see, which is unlike everything else that has been whisked passed me so far.

"No, Sir. Sometimes, simple is the best." And then she's gone again behind the door where Lilly is stood. Probably only in her underwear. The thought has my dick twitching. Last night wasn't enough. After weeks of being away from her, my body is now craving her like a drug. My fingers dig into the velvet fabric of the sofa in an attempt to stay where I am and not join Lilly in that little room behind the door. I've never had sex in a shop before.

My mind flashes back to last night when Lilly walked out

of our hotel en suite in the same little black dress that she wore the night I took her to dinner. It had the exact same effect one me as it did that first night.

It was even more incredible than the first time. I didn't think that was possible. Her body is unbelievable; it's like it was designed for me in every way and I can't get enough.

"Holy shit," I exclaim when she appears in front of me. She's standing looking very unsure of herself in the black dress. It's perfect, just like woman said it would be. It hugs her in all the right places and the V at the front shows off the swell of her breasts perfectly.

"Is it okay?" she asks nervously.

"It's fucking amazing. You look…wow. Incredible." A small smile starts to tug at the corners of her lips at my compliment.

"We'll take it," I say to the assistant as she comes to stand behind Lilly. I'm not thrilled by the smug *I told you so* look on her face as she glances at me.

"Okay, Sir. Are you going to need accessories? Shoes, jewellery a bag?"

"Yes, everything please."

The time it takes for her to pick everything out and come back is torturous as Lilly perches herself on the sofa next to me. It gives me a look at the back, which has a long line of diamond buttons running from the base of her neck to the top of her arse. The desire to undo each one and reveal what is beneath is seriously high. I almost give into temptation when the assistant reappears with a pile of boxes in her hands.

I watch as Lilly tries on shoes and picks the bag she wants. Thankfully, it's a much faster process than finding the dress. Before long, the assistant disappears with the dress draped over her arm again and Lilly's chosen accessories, saying she'll get everything boxed up ready for payment. The second she's out of sight, I make my move.

I open the changing room door quietly and step up to Lilly. A little shriek comes from her but it's silenced when I put my hand over her mouth. I look over her shoulder and into the full-length mirror in front of us. Perfect.

Lilly is exactly as I was hoping—just in her underwear.

"You're going to have to be silent," I whisper in her ear before undoing my fly and pulling out my already hard cock. "This is what you do to me, Lilly. Now, can you be quiet?"

She bites down on her bottom lip and nods once. It's all the approval I need. I bend her forward at the waist and pull her knickers to the side before lining up.

"Put your hands on the mirror. This is going to be fast."

The glow of Lilly's cheeks when we leave the changing room leaves nothing to the imagination about what just went on in that little room. She was quiet for the most part, but not quiet enough for the couple of middle aged women also in the personal shopper changing rooms not to know what was going on.

"I can't believe we just did that," Lilly says in shock as we leave the shop with her purchases in tow. "I'm sure we could have been arrested or something for doing that."

"It's fine. I'm sure the other women loved it."

"Lucas," she squeals with a slap to my shoulder. "What are we doing tonight?"

"I thought we could have the dinner we missed last night. Do you want to get a new dress for the occasion? I may even allow you to buy it," I say, but it pains me to do so. I've never had anyone but myself to spend my money on before but I'm finding that I quite like doing so.

"Can I choose what we do tonight?" she asks, taking me by surprise.

"Don't you want to go for a meal?"

"I have something better in mind," she says with a cheeky smile.

Lilly

I take us straight back to our hotel room so we can drop the stuff off. I am in love with the dress; it's stunning, but the price is obscene for something I may only wear once in my life.

I can't believe I allowed Lucas to do what he did in the changing room. My face still feels hot with embarrassment. But the second I saw him in the mirror behind me, I knew there was no way I'd say no. He had that dark look in his eyes again. The one that basically means I'll do whatever he says. It was quick, but it was by no means any less enjoyable that the other times we've been together.

It's late afternoon when we walk back out through the entrance to the hotel. I glance over at Lucas. I can see that he's trying to be himself but for some reason he won't allow himself to fully let go. I guess it's because we are staying in one of his hotels and he feels like he needs to keep up his boss persona.

He's wearing a pair of dark jeans and a jumper. It's a little more casual than his suit, but not a lot.

"What's the plan then, beautiful?"

I wanted to do things my way. I wasn't up for fancy restaurants and even fancier food.

"Come on," I say as I wave down a taxi and jump in.

"Please can you take us to Hyde Park? But we need to stop at a supermarket on the way," I instruct the driver.

The taxi lurches forward and I can feel Lucas' eyes on me.

"Lucas," I say, not really knowing how to put into words what I want to say without offending him. "I know that the whole suit thing is a lie; that isn't who you are. I can see that now. The designer labels, expensive restaurants…I think you're almost as uncomfortable with that as I am. So we're going to do things my way."

Lucas doesn't agree with me, but he doesn't argue either. We both know I'm right, and I will get him to open up eventually.

"Here?" I ask as I look back at Lucas who is loaded down with all the bags. I know he's trying to be a gentleman, but I have no problems helping.

"Sure." He still looks a little unsure about this, but I couldn't think of a better way to spend a sunny spring evening.

I pull out the picnic blanket that I luckily found in the BBQ isle of the supermarket and lay it out in the sun. I sit myself down and start rummaging through the bags for everything else I bought.

In only a few minutes, I have our picnic laid out in front of us. Lucas, however, is still stood with his hands in his pockets, looking down at me with complete confusion written all over his face.

"You swerved a posh meal in a restaurant for a picnic in Hyde Park?" he asks, like it's the most insane thing he's ever heard.

"Yeah. Is that not okay?" I ask, now a little concerned that I've done the wrong thing.

"No, I think it's perfect," he says as a wide smile creeps across his face.

My heart jumps into my throat, seeing his happiness. He's serious so much of the time that it's a real pleasure to see that smile.

He lowers himself down next to me but makes no attempt to reach for the food. We haven't eaten since breakfast so he must be starving, I know I am. Instead, his hand wraps around my neck and he pulls me to him. He kisses me gently to start with bit it soon begins to turn into something that shouldn't happen in a public place.

"Calm down," I say with a laugh when I pull back from him. "We're in a public park. We could *definitely* get arrested for doing that kind of stuff here," I say.

He huffs in disappointment as he looks down at his lap. I can see his issue; there's not really any hiding that he's hard but the look on his face makes me laugh.

"I'm sure you can wait a few hours. Come on, let's eat."

We've almost polished everything off when Lucas' phone rings. He stretches out his legs so he can pull it from his pocket. I'm expecting him to silence it like he has most of the calls he's gotten today, but instead, he looks at me as if for permission to answer it.

"Of course, go ahead," I say, feeling a little weird that he felt like he had to ask.

"I wouldn't usually but it's Joe," he responds before

answering.

The name rings a bell but it only takes a second of listening to Lucas' friendly banter into the phone to remember that it's his friend who also ended up with food poisoning last weekend. Wow, was that only a week ago?

"I'm in London with Lilly," he says, like Joe knows all about who I am. It piques my interest so I eavesdrop with a little more enthusiasm than I did when they were talking about work stuff. "Soon," he says after Joe clearly asks a question. "Fine, yes. Okay, Friday night. Yes. Tell her she's a demanding pain in the arse," he finishes with a laugh. "Okay, yeah. Bye."

"What was that about?"

"They want to meet you. We're going out on Friday night—is that okay?"

"As long as it's not to the same place you went last time," I say with amusement because I can see the worry etched in Lucas' face. "Why do you look so worried?"

"It's…" he starts, but pauses as he finds the right words. "I have very few people in my life, Lilly…"

"And you introducing me to them and allowing me into your circle is hard for you?" I ask, finishing his sentence for him.

"Yeah, something like that. How did you know?"

"Your mum said something that day on the phone."

"Of course she bloody did. I still need to talk to her about that little stunt she pulled."

"Don't be mad at her, Luc. She's only trying to help."

"I guess," he mutters before shoving a mini pork pie in his mouth.

It's my phone's turn to start ringing then. I grab it, see

that it's Dec and immediately swipe and put the phone to my ear. Lucas will have to get used to Dec if he plans on sticking around. We kind of come as a package deal.

"Hey, how's it going?"

"Good. How're things your end?"

"Yeah, not bad." I look up as Lucas mouths the words 'not bad' at me and raises an eyebrow. "Okay, better than that. I'm actually sat in Hyde Park having a picnic as we speak."

"Sweet. Are you still with Nicole?"

"No, she went back yesterday. I'm actually with a guy."

There's a pause on the other end as the information settles in. "A guy? Like, what kind of guy?"

"A non-psycho one, I hope," I reply, thinking of the conversation we had when Lucas and I had our first date.

"Hang on, you're with the same guy, aren't you? I thought you said it didn't work out?"

"It's a long story."

"I've got time."

"I haven't. Can I ring you when I get back? I'll explain everything."

"Fine," he mutters. I'm sure he's probably pouting.

"Talk soon, okay? Love you."

"Okay, bye."

I put the phone down and smile to myself.

"Who was that?"

I look up to see a curious look on Lucas' face. I guess I should have told him about Dec before.

"That was Declan. My twin brother."

"You're a twin," he says, repeating my words.

"Yep."

"I'm guessing you're close then?"

"Yes. Although he lives in Devon. He decided to go uni in Exeter. He's a big surfer. He's actually started his own business down there now. He's a bit of a wannabe Alan Sugar.

"Do you miss him?"

"Every day. We talk as much as we can but it's not the same."

"Have you considered moving down with him? I'm presuming that now he's started a business he wouldn't come back?"

"Yeah, I've considered it. I thought about seeing if there were any design jobs down there as well as here when I start applying.

"I've never been to Devon. Always thought about opening a hotel down that way at some point. We should go."

His sudden enthusiasm for me meeting his friends and us going away and meeting Dec confuses me slightly. It was just over a week ago that he was avoiding me and now he's done a complete one-eighty and is planning time away and meeting family.

"What are we doing here, Luc? I go from not seeing you for weeks on end to suddenly planning to meet each other's friends and family. I feel like I've got a bit of whiplash."

"I really like you, Lilly. More than I should. And you are so much more than I deserve. I disappeared because I wanted you and you turned me away. I thought it was the right thing to do but it turns out I was wrong. And I don't admit that often. I can't stay away from you."

"Why don't you deserve me?"

"I'm not a good person, Lilly."

"Can I be the judge of that, please?" I ask.

"I'm serious. I've done stuff that I'm not proud of. I've *lived a life* I'm not proud of."

"Will you tell me about it?"

"Maybe. I'll want something in return, though." And there it is. A secret for a secret. "When you're ready," he adds, obviously seeing the panic in my face.

I swallow down my fear of having to explain. What's the worse that can happen?

"Ask away," I whisper.

I lie back on the blanket and wait for his question. When it comes though, it's not what I was expecting.

"That first night I came to your flat, I got the impression Taylor was gay—"

"Oh, you mean from the amount of staring he was doing?" I ask with a laugh.

"Yeah, pretty much. But when we got back, there was a half-naked woman in your kitchen."

"Ultimately, yes, Taylor's gay. He openly admits that in the end he wants to settle down with a guy, but until he finds that guy he seems quite okay with sticking it to anyone who's willing."

"Okay then. I'm not judging, I was just a little confused."

"Honestly, he confuses me as well. He's great, I love him dearly, but he's changed recently. We're not as close as we once were. I think he met someone a while ago that he really fell for and I can only presume he was knocked back. I worry about what he's doing but it's not for me to point out what I think are mistakes."

"Fair point. I can say from experience that someone

telling you you're doing something wrong won't help you. You've got to come to your own realisation. It will happen eventually."

"Go on," I prompt, hoping for a little more of an insight.

"I don't want to get into the dark stuff today, Lilly. It'll ruin our time here. Tell me about your family."

"Okay. Well, my mum and dad are amazing. They live in Oxford in the house we all grew up in. They met at Mum's coffee shop and fell in love over a slice of millionaire's shortbread and a cappuccino." Lucas smiles at the story. I so badly want what they have. Their love has only got stronger as the years have gone on; it's incredible. "Emma and…" I pause, thinking about her twin. "Emma's my older sister. She's also a twin but Hannah died in car accident a couple of years ago."

"I'm so sorry," Lucas says quietly.

"Emma's now married to Ruben. It was his sister, Connie, who had a baby the day you found me in your hotel room. She's engaged to Ruben's best friend." I look at him for a second to make sure he's keeping up. "Then there's Molly and Ryan. Molly was Hannah's best friend but she's more like an adopted sister because her parents were…uh…useless. Ryan was Hannah's boyfriend but they have since got together and have a little girl called Lois."

"Wow, okay. What about the friend you saw this week?"

"We've been friends since playschool but Nicole moved away when we were teenagers. We've always stayed in contact though. Her life's so hard at the moment with her mum, but she was given some respite care last week so she was able to relax a little."

"That must be hard," Lucas says. He doesn't say

anything else and looks a little lost in thought.

"So what about your family? I mean, I've kind of met your parents, but any siblings or adopted family like I have?" His eyes snap to mine at my final comment and I feel like I might have said something wrong, although I've no idea what it could be.

"I have a brother," he states.

"Oh, does he work for the hotels as well? I don't think I've ever come across him."

"No, I haven't seen him since I was a child."

"Okay?"

"Christopher and Elaine adopted me, Lilly."

I suck in a breath. "Oh, I had no idea."

"I like it that way. I don't need anyone questioning where I came from."

"And where was that?"

"Hell."

I watch as the shutters come down. Even mentioning it must take him back to a dark place. Lucas falls onto his back and looks up to the blue sky above. He doesn't make a noise; he just stares. I watch him for a few minutes but soon realise he probably needs a reminder that he is no longer in hell, and is here with me. I lean over and gently place my lips against his. He doesn't move for the longest time but eventually I feel his lips part and his tongue run across my bottom lip.

When I pull back he's looking directly into my eyes and thankfully he doesn't look as closed off as he previously did.

"I'm sorry," he whispers.

"Nothing to be sorry for, Lucas. We've both got demons that haunt us. Maybe it'll become a little easier to bear once we share."

"Maybe," he says but it doesn't sound like he agrees. Time will tell I guess.

"Shall we head back?" I ask when I realise the sun is starting to set behind the trees that hide us from the hustle and bustle of the city behind us.

"Sure."

Silently, we gather up all our things and walk hand in hand away from our little patch of grass. I fear that Lucas is still lost in his memories and I don't want him to spend the rest of the night that way.

"We could go somewhere," I offer.

"Oh yeah, like where?"

"I don't know. Just walk around, take it all in."

"Okay."

We walk around central London for hours. We walk up Oxford Street and take in all the shoppers hopping from one store to the next. We get a coffee and sit in Leicester Square as people set up barriers for what looks like a film premier tonight. Then, we head toward Covent Garden. We watch all the different kinds of street entertainment before finding a bar to get a drink in.

As the minutes tick by, I see that Lucas is beginning return to his usual self, and I'm more than grateful.

Some of his memories must have been lingering in the background though, because when we get back to our hotel room he drops the bags he's been carrying on the floor before disappearing into the bathroom.

I listen as the water starts running. I argue with myself about what to do. Do I stay here and wait for him to reappear, or do I go and join him?

In the end, I decide to strip out of my clothes and head for the shower. My breath catches in my throat when I get there. He's stood with his head bent forward, the water cascading down his back.

The opening of the shower door catches his attention and he looks up at me, but it's not with the kind of heat in his eyes that I'm used to. I don't think he even notices that I'm naked.

I step inside and pull the door shut behind me. I stand right up against him and place my lips to his. Just like earlier, it takes a few seconds but he soon responds and within a minute he has me backed up against the tiles with my legs wrapped around his waist.

By the time he's finished, the shadows have totally lifted from his eyes and I have my Lucas back. I hate the idea of him hurting so much when he thinks about the past, but we will have to talk about it at some point.

Nine

Lilly

The week has flown by. It seems like one minute we were in London and the next I'm getting ready for dinner with Joe and Natalie. Nothing has been mentioned about Lucas' past since Saturday night, and for the short amount of time I have seen him, he has been his usual self.

He spent a few days here before disappearing back up to Yorkshire to try to deal with some stuff going on up there. He tried to make me sleep at the hotel with him but I refused. I needed to get home so I could sort stuff out for uni and generally get some sleep. I hadn't had that much over the weekend and I was suffering for it. I only had a couple more weeks left before everything needed to be handed in— it was the final push. I've worked hard for almost three years; I'm not going to let Lucas distract me now.

I managed to pin Taylor down on Thursday afternoon so we could go shopping for something for me to wear tonight. He helped me choose a light floral summer dress, seeing as the weather is still unseasonably warm.

Taylor spotted immediately that I'd put weight on and he was beyond excited for me that I now had boobs again after the amount I'd lost after Jake. He made sure the dress we chose showed off my new assets to their best.

Taylor still isn't the same bubbly person I first met. Something is weighing him down which is so unlike him. I know his parents often take their toll on him with their overbearing opinions of how he should live his life. I can't imagine that's changed, but this is different. He won't tell me though, and it's bugging the hell out of me. Especially when he insists I tell him everything about Lucas. I'm more than happy to tell all, but it irritates me a little that he won't do the same. I can only hope he will when he's ready.

I'm just doing my lipstick when the buzzer starts ringing. I quickly finish it off before giving myself a once over in the mirror.

"Wow, you look beautiful," Lucas says as soon as he sees me.

"No—lipstick," I say, putting my hand up when he leans in to kiss me.

"Seriously?"

"Yeah. I'll make up for it later." I smile to myself as the

memory of Lucas covered in my lipstick in the hotel last weekend springs into my brain.

"You'd better," he grumbles. "Have you packed for the weekend?"

"Yeah, it's on my bed if you want to grab it."

I watch him leave the room. I wasn't sure how fancy the place was going to be tonight, but I'm a little relieved to see that Lucas is only wearing trousers and a shirt. If it was really fancy, he'd have a suit on.

"Come on then," he says once he's got my weekend bag in his hands. I might have got away with not staying with him overnight at the beginning of the week, but I didn't stand a chance this weekend.

The smiles on Joe and Natalie's faces when we walk towards the table are hilarious. When we get close enough, they both totally ignore Lucas and greet me. It's like he's not even there.

"Oh my God. We're so excited to meet you, Lilly. We never thought we'd see the day. We've nagged him for years to—" Lucas interrupts Natalie's excitement by clearing his throat.

"Oh, hey, Luc. How are you doing?" Joe asks.

"Oh, so you did notice I'm here," he says with a laugh as he pulls a chair out for me.

Joe starts asking Lucas details about the fire. I begin to listen but Natalie starts asking questions. All the usual ones, I guess. What do I do? Where did we meet? All that kind of stuff. I answer everything she throws at me and I soon find that I like Natalie a lot. She's really sweet and it's obvious she cares about Lucas.

"So have you guys all known each other a long time

then?" I ask once our starters have been cleared away.

"We all went to secondary school together in Gloucester, but we weren't friends then. Nat and I were the goodie two shoes kids. Luc, on the other hand…well…wasn't," Joe answers, but then gets a little unsure of himself at the end. I guess he doesn't know how much I know about Lucas. And in all honesty, I don't know that much, but I know enough to presume he probably wasn't a goodie two shoes.

"It's okay, you can say it," Lucas says with a laugh, letting Joe know he's not going to ruin his reputation with me.

"Okay, well Luc was either in detention or skiving. It was only by accident that we stumbled across each other a few years ago when the Dalton family accountant died on them."

"Literally," Lucas adds.

"Uh…explain please."

"Dad and I were having our end of year meeting with him and he had a heart attack and died right in the middle of the meeting."

"Oh my God. What did you do?" I ask in shock.

"Well, I got online to find another accountant and the first one I rang was Joe. Although I didn't know that until we met later that week."

"I didn't mean about your accountant problem, you fool. I meant, what did you do with the dead one?"

"Well, we didn't know he was dead at the time so we rang an ambulance like most people would. What did you think we would do?"

I shrug at him because I hadn't really thought about it. I was just shocked by the situation.

We have a great night. It's nice to see Lucas laughing with friends. I usually only see him when he's in work mode, and that Lucas can't always be that fun. I know he's only doing his job but he can be a little uptight. Okay, a lot uptight.

When we get back to the hotel we get stopped by Catherine in the lobby.

"Lucas, can I borrow you for a few minutes?"

"Can't it wait, Catherine?"

"No."

Lucas turns to me, whispers that he's sorry in my ear and tells me to wait for him upstairs.

I do as I'm told, although a huge part of me wants to go with him. I don't trust Catherine as far as I could throw her. It's obvious she wants him; she might as well be wearing a sign. I do trust Lucas though, so I head upstairs, just a little irritated that she's interrupted our evening.

I go straight to the bedroom, smiling to myself when I realise Lucas must have set up his playlist ready because the music is soft and perfect for what I have in mind. I undo the strap of my dress that is knotted behind my neck and wiggle out of it. When I went shopping with Taylor I also headed for the underwear section, much to his delight and amusement.

"Oh, so the cotton ones aren't cutting it now you've got a man then?" he said very loudly as we walked over to the fancy section. I turned around and glowered at him but it was too late—I was already beetroot red.

I leave my shoes on because Lucas seems to like that and I crawl on to his bed. I prop myself up against the headboard and wait.

Lucas

"What is it, Catherine?" I bark as I follow behind her towards her office. The extra swing she puts into her hips pisses me off. If she thinks that is going to entice me, then she's got me very wrong.

"The system's crashed. It's double booked some of the rooms."

"And I'm needed because?"

"I thought you might know what to do," she says innocently.

I can't believe she interrupted my night with Lilly for this bullshit.

"Just ring IT, have them fix it."

"No one's answering."

"Well then, wait until the morning. No one will be checking in this time of night, and if they do, we have some empty rooms that are ready for the referb next week. Just use them if you have to."

"You're so smart," she says as she runs her hand down my arm. Her act doesn't fool me. I've known her too long. Catherine hasn't always been the workaholic bitch that she is now and I feel partly to blame for it. When she first started working for me she was waiting tables. I saw something in her straight away and soon started moving her up through the ranks until she was managing one of our small hotels up north. She was dedicated but she also had empathy and consideration that's now disappeared. Her life was turned upside down and she started on a downward spiral. She had months off work. When she came back she was more determined than ever and she latched on to me, I think it was because I'd kept her job for her and given her another chance. I should have said no when she tried it on with me, but I was young and horny. She's made it clear ever since that she wants another chance but I've refused. She's turned into an amazing manager but she's ruthless. I think she's so focused on not falling back into the person she was during her months away that work has taken over her entire life. It's almost like she needs control more than I do.

"Are we done?" I snap. My blood is starting to boil.

"Do you fancy a drink, Luc?"

"No, thank you. I have company."

"I saw. But don't you want a real woman? Not just the cleaner."

"Lilly isn't just a cleaner, Catherine. Now do your job and leave me to do mine." I push past her harshly and march out of her office. She might be good at her job but she is a serious pain in my arse.

I take the stairs instead of the lift to try to burn off some of my frustration before I get to Lilly. When I step through the door the first thing I hear is the music I set up earlier. I hate being in the quiet so there is always music playing in here. Something I'm surprised Lilly hasn't asked me about. Being surrounded by silence brings back too many painful memories of my childhood.

Everything is quiet other than that. The thought of her waiting for me makes my cock twitch. I haven't been with her for way too fucking long. I almost cancelled on Joe and Nat so that we could have the night alone, but I knew I'd get no end of grief for it. We've got the rest of the weekend to make up for lost time.

I step into the bedroom and immediately spot her on the bed. She's wearing white lace underwear and she still has her pink heels on. My cock throbs for her; my mouth waters for a taste. The only problem is that she's fast asleep.

I quickly strip down and climb on to the bed with her. She doesn't stir. I really want to wake her but she looks so beautiful sleeping, so I reluctantly side her shoes off her feet and lift her gently so I can pull the covers over her. I slide in beside her and pull her into me. I breathe her in; she smells like apples.

I lie there with her in my arms for the longest time. She's touched a part of me I didn't know I had, and that excites and scares me in equal measures. She's too good for me. Too beautiful, too kind, too caring for an arsehole like me but I'm too selfish to walk away from her. I know I'm going to hurt her. It's what I do. But I can't stay away. I'm addicted, which isn't a good thing.

Eventually, I pull myself away from her and head into the living room. I can't sleep. There's too much stuff going around my head. I want to say it's work like it usually is. But it's not—it's her.

In an attempt to distract myself, I open my laptop and start replying to some emails. The referb of the hotel has started and I've had a million and one questions from the builder and architect already.

I lose track of how long I'm sat staring at the screen but at some point, movement from my bedroom catches my attention. When I turn to look, I find Lilly stood in the doorway of my bedroom. She must have turned the lamp on as there is light behind her. It makes her look like an angel.

My heart thuds in my chest. Fuck, she's beautiful. Her blue eyes are bright and her full pink lips are parted with her slow breaths. Her skin is creamy white and her small but perfect tits are covered in lace along with her pussy. As pretty as they are though, I want to rip them from her body to reveal what is beneath. I run my eyes down her stomach and linger over her scar. I know she's self-conscious of it but it's a part of her and I wouldn't change it for the world. She's perfect as she is. I'm curious as fuck to know how she got it, mind you. I'm hoping one day soon she'll be brave enough to tell me. The fear of that coinciding with me talking about my past isn't far from my mind. It's going to make her walk away, I know it will, and I would like to put that off happening for a long as possible. I can only hope she will begin to like me enough to be able to deal with my past.

All thoughts of what I was doing completely vanish when she starts walking towards me. She disappears from sight and I almost turn around to see where she is when I feel her hands on my shoulders before running down my chest and onto my stomach.

"Come to bed," she whispers in my ear. Why the fuck I got up when she was in my bed I have no idea.

"Okay."

When her fingers reach the waistband of my boxers she bends them and starts running her nails back up. My cock, already hard, turns painful and strains against the fabric.

"I've got a better idea," I mutter before practically throwing the laptop on to the table and pulling her over the back of the sofa so she's sat astride my lap. "Perfect."

I go to kiss her put she pulls away and puts her hand over her face. I see her glance over at the clock before whispering, "Middle of the night breath," behind her fingers.

I don't have time for her to start faffing around with brushing her teeth so instead of going for her mouth I turn my attention elsewhere.

I pull the straps of her bra down her arms, which causes the flimsy fabric containing her tits to fall as well. I cup them both in my hands and gently squeeze. I lean forward and take one nipple in my mouth while pinching the other one. I'm rewarded by a moan of approval from Lilly as she starts grinding down on me.

"Fuck, Lilly."

I lift my hips enough so I can pull my boxers over my arse and let my cock spring free. Before I know what's going on, Lilly is off my lap and on her knees in front of me. She doesn't waste any time. She immediately reaches forward and wraps her delicate hand around me. It feels incredible but nothing compared to when she lowers her mouth on me and sucks gently.

"Fuck," I groan as my head falls back against the sofa.

She continues to suck me gently and it feels like it's going to go on forever but she suddenly stops. My eyes fly open to see what's going on but I'm greeted with the sight of her wiggling her knickers over her hips. I watch, enthralled, as they drop to the floor and she steps out of them. Her bra follows so she is stood in front of me completely bare. What is it about this woman? Nothing is enough; no amount of time is enough. I need more. I need forever, and that is a seriously scary thought. I haven't ever wanted anything as much as I do right now since I was a kid. I learnt very quickly though that wishing and praying for something you wanted was pointless so I soon gave up and tried to deal with the shit I'd been dealt.

Lilly is different. She seems to want this as well. She wants me. Fuck knows why.

The feeling of her soft skin against mine pulls me from my depressing thoughts and back to the here and now. Her thighs encase mine and her hands come up to my shoulders. I take the hint and position myself so she can sink down on me. She waits a few seconds while she looks into my eyes. There are so many things I can see reflected back at me and it knocks me for six slightly. There's anticipation and excitement but I'm sure I can also see some fear. I've no idea what she has to be scared about; I rationalise that it's probably just my own feelings making me see things.

She blinks, breaking our contact, before slowly moving down and taking me inside her. Her eyes lock onto mine again but this time all I see is pleasure. I grab on to her hips to help her move and eventually her eyes start to shut as the sensations take over. I want to tell her to open them but I'm afraid of what she'll see in mine if I do. I'm scared she'll she how much I want her, how much she already means to me after only this short amount of time. I'm not sure I want to know all that myself, let alone have her know it too.

"Was everything okay?" she asks when we're both curled up in bed again.

"It was incredible, Lilly," I reply, thinking back to our little session on the sofa.

"I didn't mean that, you fool," she says with a laugh and a playful slap to the shoulder. "I meant with Catherine."

I want to groan at the sound of her name and the fact she's even gets to be a part of this. "Yes, it was nothing."

"She wants you, you know."

"Uh huh," is the only response I give, because I am all too aware of what Catherine wants, but I have no intention of Lilly knowing the truth.

"Oh my God. You have, haven't you?" Oh, too late then!

"It was a long time ago, Lilly. And it was a huge mistake." The look she gives me in return makes me feel like the biggest arsehole on the planet. "I've made a lot of mistakes in the past, Lilly. None of which I'm proud of. What happened with Catherine is a drop in the ocean compared to most things. I know most people see me as this posh hotel owner, but be under no illusion that that is who I am. I know you've already figured out that it's just a front. Yes, I love what I do. I love the challenge. I especially love making money, because once upon a time I had nothing. But dressing up in a swanky suit every day, looking like I belong, isn't a part of it I enjoy."

"Why can't you just be yourself then? Why put on the front?" she asks innocently, like it's the simplest thing in the world.

"When my dad trusted me to do this, I was at my lowest point, Lilly. Fair play to him giving me the chance, because I'm pretty sure if the tables were turned I wouldn't have. To say I was a mess would be putting it lightly. I needed to leave all that behind me, so the day before I started I went out and bought everything I thought I needed for my new life. It worked so far as I've been incredibly successful, but it will never take away where I came from."

"It's not how you dress, Luc, that's made you successful. That's you. That comes from inside here," she says, laying her hand over my chest. And she's right, I guess. But no one wants their boss to look like a homeless tramp.

Ten

Lilly

I think my words struck some sort of cord with Lucas because after my comment about how he dresses, he held me tight and we both drifted off to sleep. Well, I did anyway. I could see the storm cloud descending in his eyes before mine shut so I wouldn't be surprised to hear that he didn't get a lot of sleep. Especially when I realise that I'm waking up alone in his bed.

When I sit up I see the bedroom door is ajar and I hear the soft sounds of music playing as always. I find one of

Lucas' shirts to put on before I make use of the bathroom. I check each room but he's nowhere to be found.

I sit myself down on the sofa and wonder what to do. Do I just pack up and leave, or is he expecting me to wait? Whatever it is, I can't do anything until I've had at least one cup of tea.

I'm just pouring the milk in when I hear the door click shut. I look around the corner to see Lucas walking in, looking a little like the morning after we first slept together. I swear my girly parts do a little dance at the sight of him.

He just unzips his hoodie before he looks up and spots me. His eyes shine with what I hope is excitement as they run down my body, which is covered in his perfect white shirt.

I do the exact same thing as I run my eyes over every inch of the sexy bad boy in front of me. He's wearing a pair of low slung jogging bottoms with the waistband of his boxers showing. His black hoodie is undone, showing off the glistening sculpted perfection underneath. He has his hood up, making him look like the bad boy you should never talk to, let alone get close to.

I watch, amazed, as he reaches up and knocks the hood off his head. He runs his hands through his hair, making it stick out in all directions.

"Enjoying yourself?" he asks with a smirk.

"Guys in suits with perfect hair aren't really my thing. This though," I say as I start walking towards him. "This is spot on." I run my hands up his chest and over his shoulders, giving his hoodie the push it needs to fall down his arms.

I squeal in surprise when I'm suddenly thrown over his shoulder.

"Lucas, what are you doing?" I shout as he walks us to the bathroom and straight to the walk-in shower. He doesn't answer, just turns its on, and we are both blasted with ice cold water.

"Lucas," I squeal again as I wriggle in his tight hold to try to get away. I have no hope though; he's too strong.

"What? Didn't you want a shower?" he asks with an amused glint in his eye.

This is the Lucas I like: the rough-looking, demanding, slightly arrogant bad boy. Who needs a guy in a suit when you can have one of these?

I'm none too gently manhandled so I'm chest to chest with him before I'm forced back against the tiled wall with a thud.

"I don't think I said you could wear my shirt," he says before I hear a rip and then buttons pinging everywhere as he tears in from my body.

"Lucas, that must have cost you a fortune."

"Don't give a fuck. I want these," he says as he pins me to the wall with his hips and brings his hands up to my tits.

I'm grateful we're in the hotel and not my flat, because the water would have gone cold a long time before we were ready to get out.

Lucas is leaning back against the vanity unit with a towel around his waist as he watches me wring out my hair and wrap it up in a towel with a bemused look on his face.

"I've always wondered how women got that to stay on their heads," he comments when I tuck the corner under by my neck.

"Something you often think about, is it?" I ask with a

laugh as I walk past him and into the bedroom to find some clothes. "Do you like living in a hotel?" I ask over my shoulder, because I don't actually expect an answer to my first question.

"Uh…I like that there are always people around."

"I never see you talking to any of them. You only talk to the staff, and when you do that you're barking orders."

"If you want something done right, Lilly, then—"

I raise my eyebrow at him and he immediately stops talking. "Really? There are other ways to go about it, Luc. Anyway," I say, changing the subject slightly. After all, who am I to criticise his skills as a hotel manager? "Why don't you live away from it all? Get some peace?"

"I have a house," he admits.

"Oh." I wasn't expecting that response. I've only ever known him to be staying in a hotel, whether it be this or another one elsewhere in the country. "Where?"

"On the outskirts of town. I hardly ever go there."

"Could we?"

"What? Go there?"

"Yeah. It would be nice to be away from here, don't you think?" I watch as he thinks about it for a few seconds before agreeing. "So what are we doing today?"

"Going to my house, by the sounds of it."

"Okay. I'm cooking you dinner then. Let's pretend to be a normal couple."

"I don't know what normal is, Lilly."

"We'll make a normal for us."

His answering smile melts my heart. Every second I spend with him I feel myself getting in deeper and deeper. I'm pretty sure it's not a good idea. God, even his mother warned me about him, but I can't stay away. I should be at home; my final deadline is Friday, and I should be working, but here I am, spending the weekend with Lucas and not really giving my final week of uni a second thought. It's not like I'm unorganised. If I'm honest with myself, I've finished, but the perfectionist in me has me continually going back to tweak something.

"What's your favourite food?" I ask on the way to a supermarket to get supplies for his house.

"Uh...I'm not sure I have one."

"What! You don't have a dish that reminds you of something? Of being a kid and your mum calling you for dinner and being excited because you know she's made you favourite?"

The second I look at his face I know exactly what I've just done.

"No, Lilly. I would have been excited if there was any kind of food."

"I'm so so—"

"Don't."

"Okay, so what do you always pick when you go to a restaurant? Any certain cuisine, or meat?"

"Sea food, I guess."

"As long as it doesn't make you sick," I say with a laugh.

"Yeah, that's preferable."

"Okay, so I'll make you a paella."

I spend the rest of the journey looking up a recipe I'd like to cook before writing a list of everything we're going to need.

"Have you got anything to actually cook with at your

place?" I ask.

"Yeah, it's fully stocked. The fridge will be full too, but probably not with what you need."

I refrain from asking why it would be stocked if he's never there. I get the sense he doesn't really want to talk about it.

Lucas grabs a basket with one hand as we enter and my hand with the other. The simple action brings a smile to my face. Nothing about our relationship has been what anyone would class as normal so far, so doing something as every day as visiting a supermarket is a little surreal.

"Come here often?" I ask with a laugh as we head towards the in-store fishmongers.

"No, I can't actually remember the last time I visited one. That's bad, isn't it?"

"It's not bad, it's the way you live. I have to say, I find it a little weird. But then, I don't live in a hotel."

"Did you just call me weird?"

"Yep." That remark earns me a slap on the arse. "Lucas, we're in public."

"So?" To prove his point, he backs me up to the bread shelves and kisses me deeply.

Lucas' house is exactly what I was expecting when we pull down the down driveway. It's totally on its own and sat in what looks like a huge piece of land. The house itself is stunning. It's Georgian, with three floors. It has classic sash windows and a pillared entrance that I would expect from a building of its era. It is stunning and in immaculate condition—probably because it's not lived in.

I jump out the car and take a better look around at the perfectly pruned bushes and flowers in the front garden while

Lucas grabs the bags from the car.

"Come on, stop gawking."

I follow him up the handful of stairs to the front door. When he opens it, he reveals the most stunning entrance hall.

"Oh my God," I gasp as I look around. Everything is in keeping with the time it was built although it's clear it's been renovated fairly recently. I follow Lucas through the entryway and down the stairs to the lower floor into a humongous kitchen. I am in love.

"Lucas, this place is amazing. How don't you want to be here all the time?"

He shrugs before saying, "I get lonely."

My heart bleeds for him when he says things like that. It's so far removed from the image of the ruthless businessman he likes to portray.

I open the fridge to put everything away and see that he was right—it's fully loaded with everything you would expect. But no one lives here. I can't put off asking any longer; it's too strange.

"Why is it like this if you're never here?"

Lucas looks over his shoulder where's he's stood getting glasses out of a cupboard. "Sylvie keeps it stocked in case I want to come here," he says with a warm smile. Whoever Sylvie is, it looks like Lucas has a soft spot for her.

"So you do come here sometimes then?"

"No, not really. This is the first time in months."

"So why bother with all that?"

He shrugs. "I've told her not to, but she continues anyway."

After Lucas has given me the grand tour, we grab some

drinks and head out to the decking area, which is bathed in the last of the sunlight.

"This place really is incredible, Luc. I don't think you'd be able to drag me away if it was mine."

"Maybe I'll be spending a bit more time here from now on then."

His response makes me smile. It also forces a question that I've been trying to keep down up to the surface. "What are we doing here, Luc? I mean, you're my boss. I'm just about to finish uni and start looking for jobs. What are your intentions?"

"Honestly," he says, looking up at me after swallowing a huge mouthful of his drink. "I've no clue. For the first time in years, I have no plan. You have no idea how huge that is, seeing as I've lived a very regimented, organised and planned life since I started at the hotels. For the first time in forever, I have no idea of what I want and where I'm going. I just know that I really like you and I really enjoy spending time with you. Both inside and outside of the bedroom," he tags on at the end.

"Well, I'm glad you can put up with me outside the bedroom as well," I say with a laugh.

"I don't know where this is going to go but I'm willing to give it a go and see if you are," he says very seriously.

I take a moment and look into his blue eyes. They will me to agree with him and not ask for any more. At this point in my life, I don't think I could offer any more. As much as I do want to think about settling down and focusing on the rest of my life as a couple, I'm on the brink of starting my career, so that needs to be my main focus.

"Sounds good to me," I say before knocking my glass

against his when he raises it.

"To us, wherever it may take us."

"To us."

Lucas

To say I was dubious about taking Lilly to my house would be an understatement. It's a place that I hardly ever go, and one I would never take another person. My parents have only been here once. The only person who is here regularly is Sylvie, and that's only because she's cleaning the place and filling up the fridge, only to throw it all away again the following week.

Sylvie originally worked for my mum and dad, but since they downsized they didn't need her as much so I made up her hours when I bought this place. Sylvie was a huge part of my teenage years. She's kind of like a much older sister. She was there to listen to me when I needed it. I was horrible to her at times as I tried to vent what I was going through but she took it all. She just seemed to understand what I needed and allowed my anger run its course. She was always there when my mum and dad were away on business to make sure I made it to school and ate properly. I think it's safe to say that when I left home, she was the one that I missed the most. I thought often about getting in touch, but I knew how disappointed she'd be in me for the life I was living, so I always stopped myself from reaching out. I don't see her a lot these days but I know she is here trying to do her little bit for me, and it makes me happy that I can make her life a little easier since her husband passed away a few years ago.

"I'm making you breakfast," I state when Lilly appears in

the living room the next morning, once again dressed in one of my shirts.

"You can cook?" she asks, looking sceptical.

"Uh…can't be that hard."

She gives me a look that is half amused, half questioning, but I slide a cup of tea towards her and ignore it.

She perches herself on the bar stool as I start rummaging in the fridge to see what I can find.

Twenty minutes later, it's clear I really can't fucking cook. The bacon is like a fucking crisp, whereas the sausages are raw. What the fuck? It can't be this hard to make a fry up. Lilly kept trying to stick her nose in so I banished her to the living room to give me some peace, but I'm now wishing she stayed and took over.

"Lucas, I can smell burn…oh," she says, looking worried as she rushes into the kitchen.

"Looks like I can't cook. Shall we go out?"

"Nonsense," I hear shouted loudly from the bottom of the stairs.

I don't have time to think about whether I want Sylvie and Lilly to meet, because it's too late.

"Oh my days! Lucas, you've got a girlfriend?" Sylvie asks the second she claps eyes on a barely-clad Lilly.

"Good morning, Sylvie," I say as I go over to kiss her cheek. She has aged quite a bit since I saw her last and it hits me hard that I haven't made time for her. Especially now she's alone. She never had any kids of her own; I think it's why she made so much time for me.

"Lucas," she snaps, but she's too gentle to ever be mean. "Introduce us."

"Sylvie, this is Lilly, my…"

"Friend," Lilly helpfully adds.

"Right, I see," Sylvie says, giving Lilly a wink. "My Jerry and I were friends like that once. Those were good times."

I can't help but smile, seeing the happiness on Sylvie's face as she thinks back to her late husband.

"Lucas, get out of the kitchen and let an expert take over. He thinks he's good at everything, this boy," she says, looking over at Lilly. "Just because he can run a hotel or two doesn't mean he can run a kitchen. Out of the way, boy," she says again as she whips a tea towel in my direction.

Thirty minutes later and the three of us are sat around the dining table, eating a properly cooked fry up.

"That is how it's done, Lucas. I hope you took notes so next time you can make the lovely Lilly here breakfast yourself."

"Yes, Ma'am," I say with a salute.

Sylvie tried to sneak away once breakfast was made, but I wasn't having any of it. She wasn't cooking for us then disappearing once the job was done.

Sylvie and Lilly lose themselves in a conversation about the house, but I lose focus on the conversation. I'm too enthralled watching Lilly interact with another person I care about. It's like she's known Sylvie for years with the way they are talking. I thought letting Lilly meet my small circle was going to be weird. I don't bring new people into my small network, ever, but she fits in so well and makes every effort to be interested in them—I presume just because they are important to me.

As I look at Lilly laughing at something Sylvie said, I feel something I don't think I've ever felt before. I feel at home, like I've found somewhere I belong. It has nothing to do with the fact that we're in my house and everything to do with being with her. I think I could be anywhere in the world and I would feel like I was home, as long as she was with me. It's the oddest feeling after a lifetime of feeling like I don't really fit in. I couldn't have asked for better parents than Christopher and Elaine, but I never really felt like it was my home too.

We spend the afternoon cuddled up on the sofa watching old black and white westerns on the TV, as the weather had changed. I can't focus on them though; I'm too close to Lilly for my brain to think about anything but her. If I'm not thinking of all the places around this house that I would like to fuck her, then I'm trying not to think about how much she has come to mean to me in such a short space of time. If I allow myself to think about it too much, I'm worried I'll do something stupid to put her right and show her the selfish bastard I really am.

"Could you take me back now?" Lilly asks after we've had dinner. A wave of disappointment floods me that this weekend is over. I think it's safe to say it's up there with last weekend in London for my best weekend ever.

"What? Why?" I ask in a bit of a panic. I'm not ready to let her go yet.

"I don't want to, Luc," she says, obviously seeing where my thoughts were headed. "It's my deadline on Friday. Once I get everything completed, I'm all yours. Well, until I find a job."

"So you're telling me I've got to take you back now, and that I'm not going to see you all week?"

"Yeah, but," she quickly adds, "I'll be free to do

whatever, go wherever after that. As long as my demanding boss allows me."

"I think he'll agree to most things, Lilly. How about I take you back first thing in the morning?"

It doesn't take her too long to agree to my plan.

We spend a while longer in front of the TV before Lilly convinces me to make use of the bathtub in the master bathroom. I had it installed because the room would have looked empty without it. I never had any intentions of using it. But being laid out in the bubbles with a soapy, wet Lilly lying on top of me makes me glad I put it in. I couldn't think of a better way to spend a Sunday evening. Actually, that's not true, because not long after that thought, I sit her on top of me and get her to ride me. Water splashes everywhere but I couldn't give a fuck. I'm in fucking heaven.

Eleven

Lilly

"I'm so excited for tonight," Imogen says when I arrive for my shift at the hotel before heading to uni to hand everything in. Imogen is doing the same course but she's a little less organised than me; she looks like she hasn't slept a wink. "I'm going to hand everything in the second I leave here, then sleep all afternoon. I didn't think there was much point by the time I finished everything at four this morning, so I just necked a few Red Bulls and here I am. I'm getting so trashed tonight."

She says all this at such a pace that I have no doubt the fact about the energy drinks is true. "Even Eve's coming, aren't you?"

"Yes, I wouldn't miss the opportunity to watch you get wasted and make a fool out of yourself. My mum is babysitting." Eve's got another year left on her course as she took a year out when she discovered she was pregnant at eighteen. She's now trying to juggle motherhood, working and uni. Hats off to her, because I don't think I could manage all that. She's determined that Elissa isn't going to stop her getting the career she dreams of.

"I'm not going," I admit. Of course I want to go with them, but I haven't really seen Lucas all week other than in passing in the mornings, and I'm desperate to spend some time with him.

"Why the fuck not? There is no excuse under the sun that's good enough. You're coming," Imogen squeals, looking completely put out.

"She's right, wait a minute," Eve says eyeing me curiously. "Oh my God, Lilly, have you got a man?" she guesses correctly. My cheeks flame red so there's no point denying it. "Oh my God! Who, when, where, what's he like?"

"It's early days," is all I say before Hillary comes in and sets us off. As soon as she's finished, I run as fast as I can. I've been holding back telling anyone other than Taylor, Connie and Nic about seeing Lucas, and we haven't had the conversation yet about letting people at work know about us. It's obvious Catherine knows something, and I'm surprised she hasn't spread it around yet—or more likely some twisted version that makes me look bad.

"Morning, beautiful," Lucas says the second I enter the living room.

"Good morning," I reply before walking over to where he's sat on the sofa with his laptop to give him a kiss.

"Hmmm, that's what I've been waiting for," he says with a smile when I pull back. "Now, I've got to go. I'm really late for a meeting." I barely get a chance to blink and he's gone. So much for asking him about tonight and the possibility of telling other people about us.

I do what I've got to do at Lucas' before lugging all the stuff to uni. I decided it was a better idea to drive this morning so I didn't waste time walking back and forth to work. Once I decided my projects were completely done I wanted to hand them over and move on. I'm looking forward to a life that doesn't include constantly obsessing over the tiny details of each of my projects. I'm happy with what I've achieved and I'm confident in my work. Now I just have to wait to see if what I think is good actually is.

The feeling of relief when I finally hand everything over is huge. It feels like a two-ton elephant has been lifted from my shoulders.

"I was planning on going home to sleep for tonight but I'm fucking buzzing. Drink?" Imogen asks and I can't refuse. I'm flying high right now and a drink sounds perfect.

We head away from uni to a local bar and order a cocktail each.

"To success, to our futures, to rocking the fucking shit out of that course and smashing it," Imogen announces loudly for the whole bar to hear.

"To us," I say with a laugh as our glasses touch.

Excitement bubbles around in my belly as we reminisce

about our three years together and everything we've been through. I also think about the weekend ahead of me. I know that Lucas has plans for tonight, so I hope he's not going to be too annoyed that I'm going out with my friends for a bit. He's got me all day tomorrow and Sunday for this charity auction thing he's taking me to. I'm excited, but I'm also a little apprehensive, because I've never been to anything like that before. Hell, I've never worn a dress like the one he bought me.

"So it's time to spill the beans, Lills. Who's the guy that almost had you leaving us tonight?"

"It's just someone I met…uh…" Thankfully, Taylor arrives right on cue and plonks himself down at our table.

"Hey, chicas. I can't believe we're done," he exclaims.

I've seen more of Taylor this week than I have done for the past year, I think. He's been in every night surrounded by his photographs, getting everything ready for the big day.

"We are. Now to start thinking about the rest of our lives." I try to say this with excitement but I can't help feeling a little uneasy about it. I always thought I'd try to join Dec down south, but now there's Lucas. It's only been a few weeks but already I feel like leaving him would be wrong.

"Come on, have another," Taylor says once our glasses are full.

"No, I drove. I'll have more later."

"I've got a bottle of pink bubbles chilling in our fridge."

A couple of hours later and we are back to get ready for tonight. I hadn't mentioned my plans to Taylor about going out with Lucas tonight because I knew I'd get grief about it.

"Uh…what's the case for?"

"I'm going to Lucas'. It's the charity auction this

weekend, remember?"

"Yeah, I remember. Do not tell me you're not coming out with us tonight."

"I'm coming for a bit. I thought I'd ask him to pick me up when he's done."

"Lilly," he warns. "I know you've fallen for him hard but you can't flake out on us, on the last three years, for him."

"I know. I'm coming for a bit. I'm sorry if that's not enough, but I want to celebrate with him, too." Taylor pouts at me and I can tell he's not happy about it, but it's what's going to happen. I love my friends but I also want some much-needed time with Lucas.

"Whatever," Taylor mutters. "I've got other news."

"Oh yes," I say excitedly, hoping that whatever it is will explain his recent attitude to life.

"I got a job!"

"OH MY GOD! Taylor, that's amazing. Congratulations," I say, jumping up to give him a hug. "I didn't even know you'd started applying."

"I hadn't really. I saw this one and it was like my dream job, so I went for it. I didn't think I'd hear anything back, let alone get an interview."

"Oh my God," I squeal again in excitement for him.

"But I got a call and I went for the interview. I didn't get the job I applied for because I've got no experience, which is what I expected, but they said they were so impressed with my stuff that they wanted to offer me an assistant job that will give me the experience I need to go up the ladder in a year or two. It probably means I'm going to be spending my time getting other people coffee and doughnuts, but it's a start. It's such an opportunity, Lills. They do the most amazing shoots with incredible models. All the top mags have their photos in."

"I'm so excited for you, Tay. Where is it and when do you start?" I ask, but the sudden realisation that our life as we know it is about to change dramatically makes my stomach flip.

"London." And that one word makes my heart drop into the pits of my feet and I instantly feel bad because this is by far the most exciting this that has ever happened to him. I need to stop being so selfish and be happy for him like I should be. "I start in two weeks," he says, slightly less excitedly.

"Two weeks! That's so soon. Where are you going to live?"

"I'm staying with a friend."

"A friend?" I ask, because I wasn't aware of a friend in London.

"Yeah."

"Male or female?"

"Male."

"Someone you've slept with?"

"No, unfortunately, but I've tried—am trying—hard."

"I see," I say, wondering if this is the one who has Taylor a bit all over the place. "And you think living with him and trying to bed him is a good idea?"

"We'll find out soon enough."

"Well, I guess it's time for those bubbles, then," I announce as I head towards the fridge. It's obvious Taylor has no intention of elaborating on the guy he's going to be living with, so I guess I'll have to continue to bide my time. I have every intention of visiting after he moves, so I'll have to meet him at some point.

I've tried ringing Lucas to tell him about our slight change of plans for tonight, but he hasn't answered, so in the end I send him a text with where we're going to be so he can pick me up when he's done.

"Did I mention that you look really good, chica?" Taylor says once we're settled into the back of a taxi heading towards the bar where we're meeting everyone.

"Yeah, you have, but please feel free to tell me again," I say with a laugh.

"Lucas is good for you. I may not be impressed about you leaving with him tonight instead of staying with us, but I can see what effect he's had on you. And I don't just mean your body. It's so good to see you happy again, Lilly. I would have been worried leaving if you were like before, but now I know you're going to be okay."

"Thanks, Tay."

"So, tell me more about Lucas. How is he in the sack? Still insane?" I feel like I blush from head to toe at the question. "That good?" Taylor says with a smile when he sees the colour of my face.

Him questioning me about sex reminds me that I wanted to ask him something. I'm not sure the back of a taxi is the right place to have the conversation, though.

"What? Spit it out, Lills."

"Ugh. I…uh…Lucas…" I stutter trying to work out what it is I want to say. "When we were…"

"At it, shagging, fucking, banging—"

"Yes alright, any of the above. He put his finger…" When I glance up, Taylor is biting down on his bottom lip, trying to contain a smile. "What?"

"If you're about to ask what I think you're about to ask, then I'm excited because I've been waiting for this conversation since we met," he says with a laugh. "Go on. Where did he put it?"

"Where it hasn't been before," is all I can come up with that doesn't include a massive amount of TMI in the back of this poor guy's taxi.

"You mean up your arse," Taylor helpfully announces.

I chance a glance up, and exactly as predicted, the taxi driver is looking back at me in his rear-view mirror with a glint in his eye.

"Ugh, Taylor," I say as I slink down in the chair.

"What, it's true isn't it?"

"Yes," I whisper.

"So how did it feel?"

I look back up before answering to see that the driver is now concentrating on a roundabout, so hopefully ignoring us.

"Incredible, I've never felt anything like it," I say very quietly.

"OMG, right?"

"He hasn't said anything but I'm presuming he probably wants to…you know. So I just wanted to ask you about it seeing as…"

"I like that kind of thing," Taylor finishes my sentence with a laugh.

"Yeah, something like that."

"Do it, Lills. What's the worst that could happen?"

"I guess. But doesn't it hurt?"

"Yeah, at first, but then it's out of his world. Like what you've experienced but even more."

I blush at the thought. "Okay."

"Seriously, if I can give you one bit of advice in this life, it's always do anal." Taylor says this so seriously my mouth falls open. Then, when I hear an "Amen," come from the front of the taxi, I can't help but fall about laughing at the ridiculousness of this. I think the half a bottle of bubbles helped with the giggles, mind you.

Lucas

I've been stuck in fucking meetings all afternoon then the second I get out I'm collared by Catherine. Thankfully, she was slightly more composed than last time, but I could really do without her eye fucking me as she stood and talked at me about recruiting a new chef.

"For fuck's sake, Lilly, answer," I moan as I stand at the entrance to her building, ringing the buzzer.

I'm pissed off. I don't need to be stood here waiting. I've waited all week while she's been here doing her thing and I've been going to bed alone. Well, time's up. She's handed everything in; she is now mine for the weekend and I wanted it to start hours ago.

The reservations for the restaurant were for thirty minutes ago. I had to get my assistant to move them, but it's now looking like we're going to miss those too if she doesn't answer the fucking door.

I jam my finger on to the button again and hold for a good minute, but still, there is no response.

I pull my phone out of my pocket to find eight missed calls and one text—all from Lilly. I guess I should have looked at that earlier.

Lilly: *Going out with uni mates. Please pick me up from Perry's when you're finished.*

For fuck's sake. I don't need this. What I need is to be inside Lilly, forgetting about my long-arse day.

The town centre is fucking manic with students. Clearly, it wasn't only Lilly who finished today. It's like the whole fucking university is out celebrating.

I eventually find somewhere to park the car before heading towards where she said she would be.

The place is packed and spilling out on to the street when I get there. I can't see Lilly so I head inside.

It's got to be a full five minutes before I see her golden hair catching the light with a crowd of people by the bar.

As I start heading towards her, a woman I recognise clocks me before turning to Lilly and whispering in her ear. Lilly instantly looks up and finds me. I can tell from just the look on her face that she's drunk. It pisses me off. This was not how we were meant to spend tonight.

When the person in front of me moves, I pause for a second to take her in. She looks incredible. Her hair is curled, her eyes are wide and her cheeks are flushed with the alcohol. Her lips are bright red and they call to me. As I run my eyes down her body, I take in her flimsy, barely-there silver top and tight skinny jeans. I suddenly have the urge to take every fucker out who might have so much as looked at her.

A slow but sexy smile appears on Lilly's face as I make my way to her. I feel some of my irritation wash away the closer I get, but when some guy comes up behind her and puts his hand on her waist, I see red. Thankfully, over the last few years I've managed to find a way to control it. So instead of laying the handsy fucker out, I reach for Lilly and pull her so we are chest to chest. She sways a little as she stands there, showing me just how drunk she really is.

The girl I recognise is stood looking at us with her chin practically resting on the ground.

"It's the King?" she asks, looking between Lilly and me. Lilly bites down on her bottom lip but she doesn't take her eyes away from mine as she nods in agreement. "Well, I didn't see that coming. No wonder you still have your job," she mutters.

"Let's go," I state and begin marching out of the bar with her hand in mine. I don't stop or even look back. I have no intention of sharing her with all those people. My well-planned night is already ruined.

"What the hell was that?" Lilly fumes when we reach the car.

"What?" I ask. I know what the problem is, although I have no intention of explaining myself.

"You can't just turn up out of nowhere and drag me away from my friends."

"You told me to come and get you," I remind her.

"Yes, but that wasn't exactly what I meant. I would have liked to at least have said goodbye. Plus, a little warning would have been nice. I hadn't told Imogen about us; she's my friend, but that won't stop us being the hot topic of conversation in the hotel by morning."

She works for me—that's why she was so familiar. "I couldn't give two fucks about what people are talking about, Lilly. Let them talk."

"Ha that's rich," she says, narrowing her eyes at me. "I didn't think you liked gossip. Seeing as you spend your life trying to hide who you really are in case anyone learns about whatever it is you're hiding."

Her words are like a kick in the balls, because I can't really deny that they aren't true.

"Get in the fucking car," I snap, staring at her. With her shoes on, we're almost the same height. I take a step towards her but she doesn't back down, instead continues to stare at me.

"For fuck's sake, Lilly. You drive me crazy." I move forward the last inch until my lips are on hers. I force my hand into her hair and my fingers hold tight to keep her in place. My tongue opens her lips to find hers. She fights for a good thirty seconds but she's as desperate for this as I am. I lift her leg up around my waist and grind myself into her. She moans into my kiss and it only makes me harder and more desperate for her.

"Get in," I repeat when I pull back from her. My voice is deep and gravelly even to my own ears.

This time she does as she's told and in seconds I'm shutting the door behind her. I walk around the front of the car and rearrange myself as I go. I don't miss that she watches every second of it.

I waste no time in having the car on the move. I need to get her somewhere quiet—and soon, before I combust. With lust or anger though, I'm not sure; they're both simmering away on the surface ready to break free.

"I'm hungry," Lilly complains, distracting me from my thoughts. "Can you stop and get me a burger?"

"What?"

"Oh come on, posh boy. Just swing by McDonald's; it's not that far out of our way."

I glance over at her to see she's being serious. Brilliant.

I change lanes and head towards the retail park that has a drive thru.

I pull up in front of a huge speaker as someone asks what I would like. I look over at Lilly, because I have no fucking clue.

"Um…I'll have a quarter pounder with cheese meal with a strawberry milkshake and a Flake McFlurry. Oh, and six McNuggets." I look at her for a few seconds like she just spoke to me in a different language. I turn to try to relay her order when she adds, "Don't forget the BBQ sauce." Fuck me, this is new.

"Can we have a…McPounder cheese meal—" I get interrupted by laughter next to me, which pisses me off.

"Let me do it," she says as she leans over towards the speaker. The only thing that makes this whole experience bearable is that she palms my dick through my trousers while placing her order. When she's done, she sits back in her seat and puts her seatbelt back on. "What?" she asks innocently. "You need to drive to the next window to pay."

I do as I'm told and put the car back in gear. When we get to the window, there's a young girl stood there with a headset on, waiting for us. It's impossible to miss the amused smirk on her face.

"Please excuse him. He's too posh for a place like this. I mean, just look at the car!" Lilly announces before I even get a chance to pull my wallet out to pay. She thrusts her hand across me at the woman, who is now laughing, and takes the note from her hand.

I sit there stunned as Lilly takes her change and sits back like nothing happened.

"Next window," she instructs.

"Was that necessary?" I ask.

"Well, it's true. Have you ever been to a McDonald's before, or a drive thru?"

"No."

"Exactly—too posh for fast food. I can't believe you didn't even go when you were in London."

"I'm not too posh for fast food. I would have been extremely grateful for it when I was a child; I'd have been grateful for any food I could get my hands on. And when I lived in London, it was no different. What we ate was usually free from a skip." I don't realise the words fall from my mouth until I see the look on her face.

"I'm so sorry," she immediately says. "I was just having a laugh." The mortified look on her face makes me feel a little better about her banter. I do know that she was only messing about. I'm also aware that if I had manned up before now and told her the truth, she wouldn't put her foot in it like she just did.

I swallow down my unease of even considering having that conversation when a huge brown bag gets thrust in my face.

"Thank you," Lilly says politely as she takes the bag and then the tray of drinks. She must see me look at it questioningly. "I figured you'd never had one when you tried ordering, so I ordered double. I thought we could experience you having your first McDonald's together. Only clause is we have to eat it in the car."

"You want to eat that in my car? This car?" I ask, horrified by the thought.

"Yes."

"Do you have any idea how much this car cost?"

"No clue, posh boy. Now take us somewhere nice—it's getting cold."

Even though she's brought up memories I'd rather keep locked away, a drunk Lilly is kind of funny. She cares less about what she says and it's nice to know she's not holding anything back, saying what she really thinks.

I pull up into a deserted car park that looks out over the countryside. It's usually full of ramblers and dog walkers but this time of night there's no one to be seen.

Lilly immediately rips open the brown bag and starts handing stuff over to me. I can't lie, I'm fucking starving. I haven't eaten since this morning, knowing we had reservations, but that all went to shit pretty quickly. So instead of a nice restaurant with award-winning food, I find myself sat in my car eating fast food. I hate to admit it, but I actually enjoy it. Although, that may have more to do with the company than the actual food.

Twelve

Lilly

I'm ashamed to say that one kiss from Lucas made me almost forget about his pig-headed behaviour in Perry's. I know I asked him to come and get me, but that wasn't code for *embarrass me in front of all my friends and drag me from the bar at the first chance you get*.

If the kiss wasn't enough to make me forget, then our trip to McDonald's definitely was. The fact he'd never ordered one before was shocking enough, but hearing the little bit of his past he let slip broke my heart. I couldn't help visions of a skinny little boy with dark long hair and blue eyes entering my head. It's not very often that Lucas allows me to see any of his vulnerability but the fact that he does sometimes gives me hope that he is letting me in, when he keeps almost everyone else at arm's length.

By the time we're heading towards his house, I'm feeling much more sober with a full stomach. That'll teach me for drinking most of the day on a pretty empty stomach.

"Taylor's moving to London. He's got an assistant job at some swanky photography company," I announce after a few minutes of silence.

"That's good." His reply is a little short, making me glance over to see what the issue is. His lips are pressed into a thin line and he's gripping the steering wheel a little too harshly.

"What's wrong?"

"Nothing. Sorry, it's just been a long day, and as nice as eating a burger in my car was, I had other things planned." I suddenly feel guilty for ruining what he'd organised.

"I'm sorry. I couldn't get hold of you so I didn't really think twice about going for a drink."

"Stop, it's not your fault. This is my shit. I've been waiting to spend time with you all week. It's been driving me a little nuts."

"Me too," I admit. I reach over and put my hand high up on his thigh. "Put your foot down a bit," I whisper as my palm reaches up higher.

The car lunges forward as Lucas does as I suggested and presses the pedal down. I'm both impressed and scared witless by the power his flashy Jaguar has. It seems like Lucas is on a mission, with the speed he takes the last few corners.

We come to a grinding halt on the gravel driveway outside his house and he's out of the car before I have time to reach for my seat belt.

I'm just reaching down to grab the rubbish when my door flies open and I'm pulled from the seat. I expect to be dragged along behind him so am shocked when I suddenly feel myself lifted off the ground and thrown over his shoulder.

"Lucas," I squeal, "is this necessary?"

His response is only a grunt as he shuts the car door and starts marching towards the house.

The second we're inside I'm put back on my feet. I go to step away, presuming we're heading for the bedroom, but a tug on my arm ensures I stop before being pinned back against the wall.

His lips go to mine as his hands find their way under my top. The second he discovers I'm braless underneath he groans as he pinches my nipples.

After a few seconds, his hands are on the move again and he's undoing my jeans, shoving them and my knickers down my thighs.

"Turn around and put your hands on the table," he instructs, nodding towards the side table in his hallway.

I do as he says but I'm obviously not how he wants me, because he grabs my hips and pulls them back. I just about manage to stay on my feet.

"Don't move," he demands, and then I feel his fingers on me. He tests my readiness, and when he finds what he wants he pulls his hand back and lines his cock up.

I don't get a chance to brace myself before he slams into me. He grabs on to my hips to help steady me but he doesn't slow down.

He folds himself over my back once he's finished and pants in my ear. The feeling of that, along with him still twitching inside me, begins my climb towards round two. I don't mention it though, because I'm going to need a few minutes—or an hour—after that.

"I'm sorry," he whispers softly in my ear. "That was too rough. It's just, this week, today, tonight. I just needed you," he admits, and it makes my breath catch. I can't imagine Lucas admits to needing anyone very often, if ever.

"Come on, let's go to bed," he says after he's pulled out and helped me sort out my clothes on shaky legs.

"So did everything go okay handing your work in?" Lucas asks once we're in bed. It's one of my favourite places to be—possibly my absolute favourite—lying curled up into Lucas' side.

"Yeah, no problem. Now I just wait for the verdict and start looking for jobs."

"Tell me about Taylor's job. It sounds like a big deal."

We chat about work and uni and life in general for the longest time. It makes me imagine doing this with him in ten, twenty years' time. It's what I imagine my mum and dad do after work—just enjoy each other's company and talk about their days.

Eventually, I start yawning. The stress of the last few days and the alcohol from earlier have started taking their toll.

"Not yet, you don't," Lucas warns as he rolls on top of me. "I need to do this properly this time," he whispers as he lowers his lips to mine.

His actions are so far from what I experienced downstairs. Earlier, he took exactly what he needed. I wasn't

Falling For Lucas

going to stop him, mind you, but right now…this is about us. He takes his time, kissing and caressing every part of my body until I'm on fire. When he enters me, it's so slow and gentle I think I'm going to combust with the need he's aroused within me.

He continues moving slowly while he kisses me. Lucas hasn't really ever explicitly said how he feels about me, not that I have about him either, but this feels like he's telling me. It's just with his body instead of his words, and I get totally lost in it.

It feels like it takes forever, but I start feeling my release approaching. My efforts to get Lucas to increase the pace have been ignored for his leisurely speed.

"Oh my God," I groan as I feel it getting closer. It's unlike me to be vocal, but the words just fall from me. "Yes, Lucas, let me feel you. Let me feel you making lov—" My words are halted and all movement ceases as I feel his hand press down against my mouth in panic.

"Don't," he warns, before pulling out of me and marching out of the room.

"Uh…" I say aloud, trying to work out what the hell just happened. I think back over the last few seconds and what could have causes his freak out. Then the words that I said come back to me. "Damn it," I mutter as I swing my legs off the bed, grab his shirt to cover myself up with and head in the direction he disappeared.

When I eventually find him, he's sat outside on the decking, naked with a glass of what I presume is whiskey, and to my surprise, a cigarette in his hand. He's looking out over the garden but I can tell by the hard lines of his face that he's lost somewhere in his memories. I chastise myself for what I almost said. It's not like he ever warned me, but from the few things he's shared about his past I can understand why he might have a problem.

"Lucas," I say softly from the doorway. I know he's heard me because he flinches slightly at my voice, but that's the only reaction I get. "I'm sorry, I didn't think. Please come back to bed."

"Just go, Lilly," he says sadly.

I want to argue. I want to tell him so many things. That I didn't mean it, that it was spur of the moment, that he'd swept me away. And yes, all those things were true, but the real reason I said it was because it was true. He was making love to me, he was telling me how he felt, and I was doing the same. Except I can just about accept what my feelings for him are, as scary as it might be. I know I'm falling in love with him. I hadn't even considered how that might affect him. I think again about how if he had opened up to me before now then I wouldn't need to feel like I'm walking on eggshells. I would know the triggers that send him back there.

I have no idea if he means to just leave him alone or to leave the house but I make the decision to go back to bed and leave him to it.

I toss and turn for hours hoping he'll return, but he doesn't, and when I wake up in the morning the space next to me is still cold and empty.

I search the house for Lucas but come up empty. What am I meant to do now? I'm stuck here without a car and with only the clothes I was wearing last night and the insanely expensive Dolce & Gabbana dress I should have been wearing tonight. I get the feeling that won't be happening now. I'm a little disappointed that I'm not going to get to wear it, but I'm more annoyed at the epic waste of money. I know Lucas has enough, but that's not the point.

I go back to the kitchen and put the kettle on as I think about what to do for the best.

I sit looking out over the garden with a pot of tea for the longest time, lost in my thoughts. The sound of the doorbell ringing scares the life out of me. When I glance over at the clock I'm surprised to see that it's well past lunchtime. My heart drops when I walk through the empty house. Where is he? I tried ringing his mobile but went straight to voicemail.

I look though the peephole when I get to the front door. I have no idea if I should be answering it or not, but seeing a young woman on the other side, I decide to go for it.

"Good afternoon, are you Lilly?" she asks with a smile.

"Uh…yeah, why?"

"I'm here to do your hair and make up for your event tonight. Mr. Dalton booked me.

"I…uh…don't think that's necessary anymore," I say, stepping back into the house so I can close the door.

"I only spoke to him an hour ago to confirm the booking," she says. "He told me to have you ready by five."

I stand and stare at her. How is it she can talk to him but my calls go to voicemail?

"Are you okay?" she asks, looking a little concerned.

"Yeah," I say, but it doesn't sound convincing. I open the door and gesture for her to enter.

"I'm Julia," she says from behind me as I walk her though the house towards the bedroom.

"Are you okay here? I just need to make a phone call."

"Of course. Can I just see the dress? I want to make sure

we do the right thing with your hair."

Thankfully, when I open Lucas' wardrobe there is a familiar dress bag hanging from the rail. I drag it out before unzipping it and hanging on the back of the door.

"Wow, it's stunning," Julia says when I step back. I can't disagree with her because it is.

"I'll just be a minute."

"No rush," she says as I walk thought the door.

I find my phone where I left it on the table. I unlock it before redialling the most recently called number.

I'm a little shocked when it starts ringing this time. That soon changes to anger when I hear a familiar irritating female voice on the other end.

"Is Lucas there?" I snap after hearing her flustered sounding voice.

"No, I'm sorry, Poppy. He's just in the shower; we've had quite a day," she says.

I may not know Lucas all that well, but I'm pretty damn sure I know him well enough to know he wouldn't go there again like she is implying.

"Right, well…please get him to ring me when you're not too busy," I say as sweetly as possible in a pathetic attempt to sound unaffected by her. I'm not sure how effective it is though. I hang up and throw my phone back down on the table before letting out a breath and heading back upstairs. I should really tell Julia to leave and call myself a taxi. I know that's the right thing to do, but for some reason when I get upstairs and she tells me to sit in front of the mirror I do exactly as I'm told. It's just easier, and I'm too exhausted to argue.

A couple of hours later, I'm stood in front of the full-length mirror in Lucas' bedroom, staring at a pretty prefect looking version of myself wrapped in the gorgeous gown.

I want to be excited about tonight. I want to be looking forward to my first swanky event in a designer dress but all I feel is dread. Is Lucas even going to turn up? And if he does, what mood is he likely to be in.

"I need a drink," I announce after thanking Julia for her work, because my hair and make-up are flawless.

When I get to the kitchen I grab a glass and pull a chilled bottle of wine from the fridge. I offer Julia a glass but she declines and leaves me to it after wishing me a good night. I didn't really talk much while she was working, which I realise is unusual, but I didn't have the energy to fake excitement for tonight.

I stand and look out over the garden as I drink the wine in my hand. It goes down a little too quickly, seeing as I've eaten nothing all day.

I swallow down the final drop and turn around to put the glass down. A figure stood in the doorway makes me jump and I drop the glass on the tiled floor.

"Lucas," I say, as I bring my hand over my racing heart. "You scared me half to death."

"I'm sorry. Let me get that," he says, walking over and bending down to pick up the larger pieces of glass—or, more likely, crystal—that I just smashed everywhere.

"I'm sorry, I'll buy you a replacement," I say nervously, because I still have no clue as to where his head is at.

"Don't be stupid," is all he says in response as he cleans up the mess. I stand there watching him, feeling totally out of place. Maybe I should have gone home after all.

Once he's done, he leaves the room without anther word.

When he reappears, his suit has been replaced with a tux. He looks incredible, and if it weren't for the dark shadows in his eyes, you wouldn't know anything was wrong. I can see them though, and I know he's hurting after last night.

"Luc, I—"

"Not now, Lilly. We'll talk, but after the auction, okay?"

"Okay," I mutter in agreement.

When he stretches his arm out towards me, I place my hand in his and let him lead me from the house.

Lucas

I hate that word. The only thing it means to me is that someone is using me. That was all the woman that gave birth to me did. She didn't *love* me, she just used it against me.

"Lucas, baby, if you love me then you'll go and get my medication."

"You love me don't you, Lucas? I promise I'll make you nice big breakfast in the morning to make up for dinner tonight."

I accepted every word that came from her mouth when I was little. What child wouldn't? It's ingrained in you to trust your mother, that she only has your best interests at heart. Well, not for me. The woman who gave birth to me only ever thought about herself. Herself and her drug addiction.

My parents learnt very quickly that telling me they loved me had a bad effect on me. From the day they figured that out, they've always made sure they've shown me how important I am to them. They are the kind of parents kids should have. I know it must have killed them both over the years not to tell me how they feel. Especially my mum; she wears her heart on her sleeve and wants everyone to know. She will tell me now occasionally, but I've kind of got used to her voice saying it so it doesn't quite have the same effect as it did when Lilly said it.

I spent a lot of years disappointing them. I wasn't aware of it at the time but I know now that I was probably trying to push them away, to prove to myself they didn't want me like they said they did. But they stuck by me, no matter what I threw at them. They've been there to pick up the pieces and to get my life back on track.

I've never told them how much they mean to me. I'm often aware I probably should, but I really hope they know.

When I eventually make it home later that day I find Lilly, dressed and ready to go in the kitchen, looking out over the garden. I stand in the doorway watching her. From the back alone, she looks stunning. The dress hugs her curves like a second skin. I run my eyes down the diamond buttons that run down the length of her spine before taking in her slim waist, curved hips and long legs. Her hair has all been pinned up and it shows off her creamy, perfect neck. I fight back the urge to walk up behind her and sink my teeth into that perfect skin, to mark her for the night so every fucker at the event will know she's mine. I don't think she'd welcome that after what I've probably put her through in the last few hours. So instead, I continue to stand and watch her, until she turns around and I scare the shit out of her. The sight of her from the front takes my breath away as well. She is beautiful and far too good for me, I think for the millionth time since meeting her. She has a few bits of curled blonde hair framing her face, and her makeup is so natural I can hardly tell she's wearing any—the only thing that's noticeable is her red lips. And fuck me, how badly do I want to see those wrapped around my cock?

It's obvious she wants to talk. I knew she would, but I put her off until at least after this event. I'd like to try to get through it unscathed. Everyone there thinks I'm the ruthless businessman I portray. I'd like to keep it that way.

Our arrival is everything I wanted it to be. I wanted to shock people by bringing a date. What I didn't anticipate was the looks she'd get from all the other men here. Yes, I know I wanted them to be jealous, but I didn't want them looking at her like they're stripping her naked with their eyes.

"Ow, Luc, stop holding so tight," she complains as she tries to pull her hand from mine.

"I'm sorry," I whisper. "It's just that every man in this place wants what's mine."

"I thought that was what you wanted."

"I didn't think it through properly," I admit.

"Are you jealous?" she asks with amusement.

"I should be the only one that gets to look at you like that." I don't answer honestly because the truth freaks me out.

"I'll take that as a yes."

"Lucas, Lilly, it's so good to see you," my mother sings when she spots us. She completely ignores me though, and goes straight for Lilly.

"Son," my dad greets quickly before we both turn to watch Mum fawn over Lilly.

"Oh, darling, you look beautiful. Your gown is stunning."

"Thank you, Mrs. Dalton."

"Oh, please call me Elaine, dear. Mrs. Dalton makes me

feel old."

"Okay," Lilly says with a smile.

My mum briefly looks away from Lilly and glances at me. The look in her eyes hits me hard. She looks so happy. "Now, I want to know everything about you, Lilly. This is a first for me. I want to know why my son is so fascinated with you, other than your obvious beauty."

"I'm so sorry," my dad mutters to me. "I warned her not to do this but she's been waiting a long time to be introduced to a girlfriend."

"Lilly's not—" My dad raises one eyebrow at me and it stops me mid denial. "Fine, okay, I guess she is."

We both stand and watch as my mother grabs two glasses of champagne from a passing waiter and hands one to Lilly.

"Let's get a drink," Dad suggests, so we leave them too it and head to the bar.

"They're going to be requesting that we take our seats in a few minutes," my mum says as she and Lilly join us at the bar about thirty minutes later. I kept an eye on the two of them the whole time. They didn't stop chatting, and my mum didn't stop smiling. I think it's safe to say she approves of Lilly. "Don't let this one go, Luc, she's a keeper," Mum says with a wink.

This weird feeling settles in the pit of my stomach. I wasn't aware that I needed the approval of my parents. I'm big enough and ugly enough to do my own thing and make my own decisions, but it feels good knowing that my mum likes Lilly.

I look up to Lilly to see her reaction, but the face looking back at me isn't what I was expecting.

"Lilly, are you okay?" I ask. She looks pale. She's looking right at me but it's like she isn't seeing me. "Lilly?" I prompt when she doesn't respond.

It's only two seconds later that I see her fall. Both Dad and I jump forward and I thankfully manage to grab her before she hits the floor. I gently lower her down. "Lilly?" I ask again as I touch her face to see if it will bring her around. She doesn't respond, but she's really hot.

"Put her in the recovery position. I'm ringing an ambulance," Dad instructs, but I just panic. I stand up and back away, not knowing what to do or how to help.

Mum must see what I'm doing and immediately takes my place on the floor and rolls Lilly to her side.

The next hour is a total blur. The paramedics come. Thankfully Lilly is awake by the time they do, and tries to convince them she's fine, but they won't have it. They put her on to a trolley and push her out to the ambulance.

"Go on, Lucas," my mum says, pushing at my shoulder. "She needs you." I do as I'm told because that seems like the easiest thing, with my brain not functioning.

I sit in the back and hold Lilly's hand on the short journey to the hospital. I've only been in an ambulance once before and it's not really an experience I'd like to repeat or relive. My grip on Lilly's hand must be painful again as I try to keep my memories at bay. I need to be here for her right now, not lost in my own head.

Thirteen

Lilly

"I'm fine, I just haven't eaten anything all day, and then started drinking. Honestly," I plead with the doctor when he eventually appears in my bay.

All this is crazy. There's nothing wrong with me.

"Well I would like to do some bloods and take your blood pressure at the very minimum. People don't tend to pass out for no reason, Miss Morrison."

"Fine," I mutter.

I look over to Lucas, who is stood by my bed still looking

a little shell-shocked. As if the last few hours haven't already been bad enough, he had to catch me as I keeled over in the middle of the fancy event. When he told me he wanted to show me off, I don't think that was quite what he had in mind.

"Luc, I'm fine. Don't look so worried," I say softly, to try to reassure him.

"It's fine, I know," he says, but I have a suspicion he's just trying to look manly in front of the doctor. The look on Lucas' face tells a very different story.

"Your blood pressure is very low, Miss Morrison. I'll be back in a second to do a blood test. Hopefully that will tell us what's going on."

I look back to Lucas and he narrows his eyes at me. He doesn't need to say what he's thinking; I hear it loud and clear. Maybe something isn't right with me.

"Okay, we'll get these done and I'll be back with the results ASAP."

It's a long two hours later when the doctor reappears with some paperwork in his hand. His face is unreadable so I have no idea how bad the news could be that he's about to give us.

I look over at Lucas and see him swallow down a lump. He's obviously thinking the same thing.

"Okay, so I have your results…" the doctor says, and then pauses. I want to scream at him. We're not watching X-Factor—neither of us need the tension built by a long pause.

"You're pregnant, Miss Morrison. Congratulations."

I stare at him blankly for a solid minute.

"I'm sorry, you're going to need to say that again. I think I misheard you."

"You're pregnant," he repeats.

"No, I can't be. It's not possible. You're going to need to test again because something has gone wrong."

"That won't be necessary. We'll be sending you for a scan in a few minutes so you can see for yourself."

"But I can't get pregnant. I was told I can't. No, this can't be right."

"I need to go and fill out some paperwork, then I'll be back and we can get you upstairs for that scan."

I stare at him and watch the curtain fall back into place behind him. His words are on repeat inside my head. *You're pregnant. You're pregnant.*

"No, I can't be," I say out loud, even though he's gone.

"Lilly?"

I'd totally forgotten Lucas was in the room until I hear my name. I turn to look at him and I'm shocked by the look on his face. He looks like he's about to throw up.

"They're wrong, Lucas. I can't have kids," I say, in the hope of lessening his obvious panic.

"What do you mean?"

"It's a long story, but I've been told by doctors that I can't have kids. I never would have let this happen otherwise," I say, thinking about all the times we've had unprotected sex. I trusted Lucas when he said he was clean.

"But he just said."

"I know what he said, Lucas. But he's wrong. I can't have kids," I snap, getting angrier by the second. Why doesn't anyone understand what I'm saying? I can't have kids. Everything has been messed up down there for years, and then Jake happened and it all went totally down the pan.

If this is a joke, it's not a very funny one.

"Okay, the sonographer is waiting for you," a nurse says

when she appears around the curtain. She gives us directions and says I'm free to go, but that I must book a follow up appointment with my own GP and then a midwife.

I wanted to scream at her that I don't need a flipping midwife, but I know getting angry is not going to help.

Lucas continues to look ill as we make our way to the scanning department. We get lost twice before we manage to find the damn place. Neither of us are paying much attention to our surroundings.

I'm desperate to know what he's thinking, why he's freaking out so much about this. Doesn't he believe me either?

As soon as we walk into the reception area, we're ushered into a room by a young guy. I'm taken aback a little—I just presumed it would be a woman. Lucas gets told to sit on the chair while I get myself up on the bed after taking my gown off. It's only when the guy gives my outfit a funny look that I remember what I'm wearing.

It is the weirdest moment of my life. After being told I can't have kids, I never expected to ever be in the situation, or doing the things I'm being told to do.

After stripping out of the dress, I lay down on the bed feeling a little awkward seeing as I'm wearing the sexy set of lingerie Lucas bought to go with my dress. It's pretty clear the guy has no interest in me or any of the female population though; I think I'm more uncomfortable than he is. The sonographer covers my lower half with tissue, which I'm relieved about, and squirts gel on my belly. I expect it to be cold like it always is when you see it done on the TV, but it's surprisingly warm.

"Okay, let's see what's going on in here then, shall we?"

"You won't find anything. I can't have kids." He gives me a funny look, probably wondering why the hell I've been sent here if that's the case, but he continues nonetheless.

He pokes the wand thing into my belly a little too harshly, making me wince.

"I'm sorry, I'm just trying to get a good angle."

A couple of seconds later, a screen at the end of the bed flickers to life.

"If you both just look at the screen." I do as I'm told but what I see is not what I was expecting. There isn't a blank black screen. Instead, there is a fuzzy black screen with two obvious white shapes in the middle.

"Oh my God. Is that?"

"Yes, twins. Congratulations."

My entire body starts shaking and I try to bring my hand up to cover my gawping mouth but it doesn't make it.

I continue staring at the screen afraid that if I so much as blink then those two white blobs will disappear.

"Are you okay? Would you like some water?"

"No, I'm—" I stop when I look up at the guy, because he's not looking at me. He's looking past me to Lucas, who is sat with his head in his hands, slightly rocking back and forth.

"No, thank you," he mutters quietly.

The guy turns back to me. "Would you like some print outs while I'm here?"

I nod, unable make a sound as I continue to stare back at the screen.

"Okay, I'll try to get some good ones. I'd say you're a little over twelve weeks so that makes your due date November 5th."

I nod along to show that I am listening.

He finishes up, prints out the pictures and leaves me to get dressed again. We head to the little reception when we are done and get told to sit and wait for a nurse.

It's another hour before we get to leave the hospital. Neither of us have said anything. I think we're both too shocked.

Lucas rings for a taxi to go to my flat as it's closer than his house, and seeing as it's now almost 3am I don't argue with him. I'm too busy hugging the maternity pack that includes the photos from the scan to my chest to care much about anything else.

Five minutes before my flat, Lucas suddenly sits forward. "Can you pull in here?" he asks.

The driver pulls the car to a stop in the petrol station as Lucas reaches for the handle.

"Where are you going?"

He doesn't answer. He just gets out and I watch as he walks over to the twenty-four hour service window.

Two minutes later and he's sat back in the car like nothing happened. He doesn't say anything or give away where his thoughts might be.

I get out of the taxi while Lucas pays the driver. I head straight for the front door but Lucas hangs back. When I turn around, I see why. He's pulled a packet of cigarettes from his pocket and is in the middle of lighting one up.

"Since when do you smoke?" I ask. I didn't say anything when I saw him doing it last night. It was the first time I had seen or smelt any indication that it was a normal thing for him to do.

"Since I was about nine," he mutters around the cigarette

now hanging between his lips. "I'll meet you upstairs."

When I get in my flat, I'm relieved to see that Taylor's door is open and the room is empty. Lucas and I need to talk and it would be better if we were alone.

Reluctantly, I put the folder down on the coffee table before getting changed into something more comfortable. I go to the kitchen and make myself a hot chocolate, hoping the warm sugar will be exactly what I need, and then I make Lucas a coffee. I take them both into the living room and sit down on the sofa to wait for him.

After thirty minutes, I start to get concerned. Surely he's puffed himself through enough fags to start getting his head together? I know he's struggling with this. I could see it in every one of his features, but apparently this is happening, so we need to start discussing it.

I put on some shoes before making my way down to find him. On the way to the elevator, I can't help but look at the stairwell. It's a weird feeling. I thought everything that happened there that day had changed my life completely. But here I am with the one thing, or two, that I thought had been taken away from me forever.

Quickly pulling myself from my thoughts, I enter the lift when the doors open and head down. When I push the door open, a rush of cold night air hits me, reminding me that it's still early summer and here I am in only a vest top and a pair of thin pyjama bottoms. When I look around, it seems to be empty. Where is he?

I walk around the corner of the building in the hope he's sat himself on the one benches out here, but it's empty.

My heart starts to beat a little too fast as a feeling of dread starts to settle in my stomach.

He's gone.

Tears start pouring down my cheeks, but the events of the evening prevent me from crying properly. I think I'm in shock. This can't be happening.

I run around the building and through the car park looking for him, just in case I'm wrong, but I know I'm not. I know he's gone. I can feel it.

I clutch my stomach as I look up to the stars above me. What am I going to do now?

When the cold starts to get too much, I make my way back up to the flat. The sight of the two mugs sat on the coffee table next to the maternity folder I was given tip me over the edge and I collapse into the sofa. Whole body sobs engulf me as I replay the events of the night that led to this moment.

The confusion.

The disbelief.

The joy.

The devastation.

I can't focus on the joy. It's too early. I still don't believe it's actually true. It's the pain of being abandoned after everything that happened in the last twenty-four hours or so that overtakes every other feeling.

At some point, I must cry myself to sleep, because a loud banging on the front door wakes me. I jump off the sofa and run to the door, hoping that it's going to be Lucas, that he needed a few hours to get his head straight, but he's back and everything is going to be okay.

Before I pull the door open, I brush my hair back with my fingers and rub the sleep from my sore, cried out eyes.

The person standing before me when I do open the door

isn't the person I was expecting or hoping for, but it is a very welcome sight. I fall forward into his arms and the sobbing starts all over again.

"Thank God you're okay," he whispers in my ear as he holds me tight. "I've been going out of my mind all night. You weren't answering your phone, but I knew something was wrong. You scared the shit out of me again, Lilly."

Eventually, I compose myself enough to stand back and look at my brother.

"I'm so sorry, Dec. I didn't mean to scare you, I'm fine, I think."

"You think?"

"Come in, I'll explain."

"I'm going to fucking kill him when he reappears, Lilly. I swear to God. He doesn't get to treat you like that. For fuck's sake," Dec rants after I've told him everything.

I try to explain the little I know about Lucas' past, because I know that's the problem here, but Dec won't listen.

"I don't give a fuck about the dude's past. He needs to be here for you, stand by you."

I do agree, obviously, but also a part of me does understand what Lucas might be going through right now. We never talked about it but I can imagine him saying that he doesn't want kids. And here I am, walking around unknowingly with two of them growing inside me.

Dec looks over as another tear slips down my cheek.

"Oh, Lilly," he says as he wraps me in anther hug. "What are you going to do?"

I shrug and sniffle in response because I wish I had the answer to that question.

"It's time to tell Mum and Dad everything, Lilly." He's

right, I know he is but the prospect fills me with dread.

After booking a doctor's appointment for later that afternoon, Dec sends me to bed. I hate to think what a state I must look after a night with too little sleep and too much crying.

"Lilly, you need to wake up. Your appointment is in an hour," Dec says softly as he sits on my bed and places a cup of tea down on the side.

I try to drag my eyes open, but hours of tossing and turning mixed with the dried tears that are stuck to my eyelashes doesn't make the task very easy.

I'm hoping seeing my doctor will help. She can either convince me that this is all actually happening, or that I'm the butt of some really sick joke.

"Lilly Morrison," is called across the waiting room.

"Do you want me to come in with you?" Dec asks.

"Sure," I mutter, because it's not like I have anything to hide from my twin.

"How can I help you today, Lilly?" Dr. Bennett asks in her usual polite manner. She's been my doctor since I moved to Cheltenham. She's very soft and gentle, and I really appreciated that in the aftermath of Jake.

"Apparently, I'm pregnant," I state, and watch her brow furrow as she absorbs the information.

"Okay, have you done a test?"

"No. Last night I passed out and got taken to A&E. They did a blood test and then I had a scan."

"Oh, I see," she mutters, somewhat shocked.

"It's twins."

"Oh, Lilly. That's such wonderful news." My face clearly doesn't show the same excitement. "What's wrong? This is incredible news."

"I was told I couldn't get pregnant. And now here I am, apparently growing two babies, only a few weeks into a new relationship. He's freaked out and done a runner by the looks of it, and I'm here not knowing how the hell this happened because I was told I couldn't have children." I don't mean to sound angry but I can't help it. I'm emotional, tired and confused. I cannot be held responsible for my actions or words right now.

"Oh, you're not—" Dr. Bennett starts looking at Dec, who is sat in the chair next to me, holding my hand.

"No this is my twin brother. Apparently, it's genetic."

"Oh of course, we've talked about that before. I'm so sorry, Lilly. No one ever told you that not being able to have kids was final. The evidence showed that it would be very unlikely, but not totally impossible. I have to say I'm very shocked, but obviously, the time was right."

"Or he has super sperm," Dec helpfully chips in.

I turn and glare at him while Dr. Bennett bites her lip to contain her smile.

"Anyway, what happens next?" I ask, distracting both of them from their amusement.

"Well, you've already had the scan, so I presume you know your predicted due date."

I hand over everything I was given at the hospital last night and we sit in silence as she reads it then taps the information into the computer.

"Lilly, I know things aren't easy right now. But clearly, this was meant to happen. I know it's hard to believe after everything, but you need to embrace it and make the most of the next few months. No matter what happens with the father, life is going to get very…exciting for you." She doesn't need to tell me that; I've heard enough horror stories from my parents about how much work twins are.

Before leaving the surgery, I book a midwife appointment for later that week, then Dec drives me home in my car.

"You're going to need a new car. This rust bucket isn't any good for two babies," he says, referring to my almost clapped out old Volkswagen Polo.

I hear the words, but they don't resister. Instead, I sit there with my arms wrapped around my middle as I think about how my life is about to change.

Where am I going to live? Should I move home? How am I going to afford all the stuff I'm going to need? What about my career?

Dec's phone is ringing off the hook all the way home, so I convince him that I'm okay and that he can leave. He's not happy about leaving me alone, but I can see he's got a lot going on that he needs to deal with.

"Honestly, Dec. I'll be fine."

"And you'll talk to Mum and Dad?"

"Yes," I say, but I have no idea when or where to even start that conversation.

"Okay, I'll ring you when I get back."

"Okay, love you."

"Love you too, Lilly. You look after yourself," he says, gesturing to my belly before sliding his helmet on and swinging his leg over his bike.

I stand there long after the sounds of his bike have faded. I feel like if I go inside, I've got all this stuff to think about and deal with. I realise that I can't stand looking out over the car park forever though, and eventually head back up.

I find my phone between two of the sofa cushions with a flat battery. It must have fallen down there and died while I was trying to get through to Lucas last night.

I plug it in to the charger next to my bed and power it up. I'm hopeful that Lucas might have tried to get in touch, but I'm not surprised when the only voicemails and texts I see are from Dec, Imogen and Eve. I'd had loads of calls and texts from both Imogen and Eve after Lucas dragged me from the bar Friday night. I meant to get back to them; they must be going out of their minds wondering how I went from cleaning his room to dating him. But after his freak out that night and then everything else, I haven't managed it.

I go through them all and feel awful for not getting back them. I close down my messages and stare at the home screen. It's a picture of Taylor and me from last summer. Before my life went down the pan. It suddenly starts ringing in my hand.

"Oh my God," I mutter to myself as I look at the caller. I should have been at work this morning. I never even gave it a thought.

"Hello?" I don't need to put on a sick sounding voice. I can already tell that my lack of sleep is making me sound rough.

"Lilly, are you okay?" Hilary asks.

"Yes, I'm so sorry. I wasn't able to get to the phone," I lie with ease.

"Don't worry about that. We were all so worried. Neither Eve or Imogen have been able to get hold of you, and then you didn't show for work. We've been going crazy." I feel awful—I didn't even consider them in all of this.

"I'm so sorry. I'm fine. I'll be in tomorrow."

"As long as you're well enough."

We chat for a few more seconds before we both hang up. I lie back on my bed and think about having to be inside Lucas' suite at the hotel. The thought makes my stomach turn over and before I know what's happening, I'm running to the toilet to be sick.

I sit back against the cold tiles and let my head fall back with a light thud. "What am I going to do?"

I don't get a chance to ring Imogen and Eve back, because as soon as I leave the bathroom, the buzzer to the flat starts going crazy.

I buzz them up and open the door for them. I head to the kitchen to kick-start the coffee machine, knowing they'll want caffeine after their shift.

"Lilly, what the fuck is going on? You have a lot of explaining to do, young lady," Imogen announces as they enter the flat.

I turn towards them and they both stop in their tracks.

"Shit, what's wrong?" Eve asks, starting to move again with her arms open. She wraps me in a hug and I burst into tears. Imogen follows suit, and that's how Taylor finds us a few minutes later.

"Oh, gang bang in the kitchen. Just my style, ladies," he announces as he heads our way. That is, until the girls pull back and he gets a look at me.

"Shit, chica." He engulfs me in his arms and it's almost as comforting as a hug from Dec.

Taylor takes over coffee duty, seeing as he's had Morrison training on how to use the machine, and I get ushered to the sofa.

Imogen and Eve hold the questioning until Taylor joins

us with three coffees and a pot of tea for me.

"Go on then. And start from the beginning; we want to know how you ended up shagging the King."

I give them a basic run down of how that happened, while Taylor waits anxiously to find out the latest development.

"Is he as good as everyone says?" Imogen asks.

"I can't speak for Lilly, because I wasn't in the room. But it sounded fucking hot. He's a machine," Taylor answers for me.

When they both turn to look at me, I'm tomato red. It's clear I don't need to add anything to Taylor's statement.

"So what's happened to get you like this?" Taylor asks, skipping over the detail of sex with Lucas.

"I'm pregnant."

"You're what?" Taylor screeches in shock. He's the only one in the room who understands the significance of my statement, but he's loyal to the core and won't say anything until the girls have left.

"Oh my God! The King got you pregnant," both Imogen and Eve say at the same time.

"And it's twins."

"Of course it is," Taylor mutters as he takes a huge sip of his coffee, burning his mouth in the process. "I think I need something stronger than this."

"Lilly, how many cups of tea have you had?" Eve asks me when Taylor disappears.

"Uh…" I think about the answer, but I haven't really been keeping track. "Probably five or six today. Why?"

"You need to cut down. You can't have that much caffeine while you're pregnant."

"I haven't had any coffee," I say, trying to make it sound better because I feel awful that it hadn't occurred to me.

"You are going to need decaffeinated tea, Lilly." The look I give Eve in response must tell her exactly how I'm feeling. "It's okay, hon, you'll figure it out. You'll be better than me. I was clueless when I was pregnant with Elissa, but I managed and she's still alive and healthy," she says with a laugh as she squeezes my shoulders in support. "Any questions you have, just ask. I think I got every symptom in the book so I should have an answer for you."

Two hours later, Imogen and Eve leave. Taylor has been giving me the eye since my announcement earlier, so I know I'm in for another round of questions any minute. All I want to do though is collapse in my bed.

"Go on then, explain," he says, the second I've shut the door behind them.

"I can't really, Tay. I spoke to my doctor earlier and she said that no one ever said it was impossible, just unlikely. If I was aware there was any chance, we would have been using protection."

"I can't believe the prick's just disappeared on you. I knew he wasn't good enough for you. Didn't I say that?"

"No. I'm pretty sure you were too busy staring at him to say much," I say, trying to bring some humour into the conversation. It's only been a day and I'm already fed up of being in this strange mood.

"I'll see if I can put off my job for a bit," Taylor says when he comes back in with another drink each.

"Don't be stupid. You are not putting your life on hold because of my bad decisions."

"Are you sure? I don't want to leave you here alone."

"I'm not alone, I have those two nutters," I say, gesturing to the door where Imogen and Eve left a while ago. "Plus my family. I'll be fine."

Taylor nods, but I'm not sure he's convinced. I'm going to need to prove to him that I can cope with this.

Fourteen

Lilly

"Where did this come from?" Hilary asks when she finishes reading the letter I just handed over.

"It's been coming. Now I've finished uni, it's time to move on," I say in the hope she believes me.

I got up bright and early this morning so I could beat everyone else in. I didn't want to see anyone. I wanted to do this and get out—preferably without having to see or even have Lucas' name mentioned. The girls said yesterday that he wasn't there, so I was hopeful.

"We're really going to miss you, Lilly." Hilary says before giving me a hug. I feel myself tear up but I refuse to get emotional because that will lead to questions. I don't need questions.

I feel like I'm at a complete loose end when I walk out of the hotel I've worked at for the last two and a half years. I may not know what I'm going to do now, but I do know that it needs to not be working there, where I have constant reminders of Lucas and risk running into him. Handing my notice in with immediate effect wasn't a decision that took too long to make.

I walked out of that place with my head held high. I might not feel all that brave inside, but I wasn't going to let anyone see that Lucas Dalton had broken me. I'm stronger and prouder than that. I'm a Morrison.

I walk down the street from the hotel and order myself a decaf tea and a Danish pastry. The smell of coffee, like always, settles my nerves about what I just did. I find myself a seat in the back corner where I have little chance of anyone spotting me and pull my phone out. I send a group text to Imogen and Eve to meet me here after their shift. When I saw them yesterday I had no clue I was going to leave, so now I think I owe them an explanation. And I'm sure they'll have a load more questions to fire at me.

Deciding it's probably about time to learn about this pregnancy thing, I pull up the app store on my phone. I remember Connie and Molly showing me one they had that tracked the baby's progress, and it looked pretty helpful.

I find what I want and download it before putting all my details in.

I sit and look at the phone as it loads, and when an image appears of a baby, I have to fight the urge to puke. This is so surreal.

I look through everything I can find and by the time I'm finished, my tea is stone cold, but I have a bit more of a clue as to what's going on inside my body. I roughly know what size they should be and how developed they are, along with all the really exciting things I should be expecting from my body. Nausea, headaches, bleeding gums, a change in sexual desire—well, that happened from the moment I got up close and personal to Lucas. I can only hope that it will decrease again now he's gone, because I'm going to have an issue otherwise.

I feel the first waves of excitement about my pregnancy begin to bubble up as I sit and look at the app. So much so I decide to spend the rest of the morning while the girls are at work embracing it. I quickly eat my pastry and order another decaf tea to go before wandering down into town and looking around every shop that has either maternity or baby stuff in.

I buy myself some maternity leggings and a couple of tops but I don't go crazy. Reading the app, it looks like my little tadpoles are going to do some serious growing in the next few weeks so I think another shopping trip will be in order before long. I'm achingly aware of my financial situation though, so I'm hoping I may be able to borrow some stuff from Molly or Connie to make it a little easier. Just thinking about how much stuff the babies are going to need brings me out in a sweat, especially as I've just jacked in my only source of income. I ask myself for the millionth time what I'm doing, but just like all the other times, I don't have an answer.

I check the time on my phone and notice that Imogen and Eve should be finishing soon, so I grab my bags from the counter and begin walking back to the coffee shop. I stop at a cash point along the way to see how dire my situation is. I punch in my code and go to the balance area of the screen. I brace myself for how pathetic the amount is going to be, but when the figure appears my eyes nearly pop out of my head.

"What on earth?"

I cancel the transaction and pull my card out before marching inside the bank.

"Hi," I say in a rush when I get greeted by the assistant behind the glass screen. "I think there's been some error made on my account. I just checked my balance and it's got over twenty thousand pounds in it. I was expecting a couple of thousand at best."

"Okay, let's have a look. Pop your card into the machine." I do as I'm told and wait while she clicks around on her computer. "No, that seems to be correct, Miss Morrison. A payment was made into your account from an L Dalton about an hour ago, with a reference of *babies*." I lean forward with my elbow on the small counter and put my face in my hands. "Are you okay, Madam?" the assistant asks.

I lift my eyes and look at her though my fingers as I think about my answer. "Yes, I'm fine," is what I go for in the end as I pull my card out and walk away.

I don't know why I'm so shocked really. I almost feel stupid for not expecting something like this. Lucas isn't a horrible person. He wouldn't allow me to struggle. His presence would be much better than his money, mind you. She said the money only went in an hour ago, so I'm presuming he already knows about my resignation.

I find myself an empty bench outside the bank, pull my phone from my bag and dial his number. Just like all the other times, it goes straight to voicemail. Red smoke descends around me as his voice enters my brain.

"Lucas," I bark, sounding very unlike me, "you'd better ring me back when you get this. I'm outside the bank. What the hell do you think you're playing at? You don't get to just throw money at me in an attempt to clear your conscience. Money will not solve any of this. If you don't want anything to do with me and your babies, then that's fine, but at least have the decency to show your face and tell me in person. You don't get to buy me off, Lucas. You are just as much to blame for this situation as I am, so stop running away." I end the call with a sharp stab to my screen. I lower my hand and see that it's shaking. I'm so angry with him. How dare he treat me like this?

I've calmed down slightly when I get back to the coffee shop. I'm late though, so Imogen and Eve are already sat at a table with my tea. I plonk myself down in the seat and hold the mug in the palms of my hands, letting the heat soothe me.

"What's happened now, and why have you jacked your job in?"

I explain to Imogen and Eve the best I can, but it's hard when I really have no idea myself what I'm doing. They both look concerned, but don't question my decision.

I pull into my space outside our building just as an ambulance pulls in. My nosiness gets the better of me and I sit and wait to see what's going on. When I see paramedics wheel my elderly upstairs neighbour out of the back, I rush out of the car. Shelia has lived upstairs forever. I thought it had been quiet the last few days. I guess this explains it. As they turn the wheelchair around, I see that she has a cast on her leg.

"Lilly, my dear, how are you?" she asks with a smile as I rush over.

"I'm fine, what have you done?

"Oh, I slipped in the bathroom a few days ago and broke my damn ankle. On the plus side though, I've had a lovely young nurse looking after me," she says with a wink that makes me smile.

Shelia and her husband never had any kids. She's been alone since he died a few years ago. Taylor and I try to stop in and see her every now and then. I feel awful that I got swept away by Lucas and haven't managed to see her.

"If it's okay with you, I'd like to come up and help get you settled in. Perhaps I can bake something for you?"

"That would be lovely, dear."

I'm thrilled she says yes, because it means I'll have something to focus on for the next few hours.

The second I step into her flat, I realise that she might need a little more doing than just a pot of tea and a cake. The shock on my face must be evident as I look around, because Sheila cringes before saying, "Things have got a little on top of me recently."

I just about manage not to say, *you're telling me*. Instead I go with, "We can get it sorted in no time."

I spend the afternoon making some space in her living room so she can sit comfortably before blitzing the kitchen. It's a health hazard. By the time I've finished, every surface is gleaming and I'm brave enough to grab some ingredients from my flat and make Shelia her favourite lemon drizzle cake.

"You really didn't need to do all of this. I would have got to it."

"Shelia, you have a broken ankle," I point out in case she's forgotten already. "Plus, I'm more than happy to help. I actually needed the distraction."

"Oh," she says, prompting me to spill.

"It's a long story and you look like you need to have an early night," I say in the hope getting out of talking about it any more today. "I'll come back in the morning to finish the living room if that's okay with you."

"Don't you have your job at the hotel?"

"Uh…no, I actually handed my notice in. I'm free."

"Only if you're sure. I don't want to take up your time."

"I'm more than happy, Shelia."

After helping her to her bed, I leave her to it and head back downstairs. I see a parcel sitting in the middle of the sofa the second I walk in. It's wrapped perfectly and has Taylor's name written all over it with its pink and blue ribbons hanging from it. I carefully open it open and I almost cry with relief when I see an entire box of my favourite Teapigs tea bags staring back at me. The only difference to my usual order is that every single one in here is decaf. I make myself a quick pasta dish for dinner, seeing as Taylor is nowhere to be seen, before falling into my bed with a mug of rhubarb and ginger tea and a pregnancy magazine I picked up earlier.

I know I've been putting it off, but I convinced myself that talking to Mum and Dad could wait until this morning. I thought I'd go around a couple of hours before everyone usually appears for Sunday dinner and tell them everything. That way, they'll have all the details before I tell everyone else at dinner.

"Are you sure you don't want me to come?" Taylor asks from his slobbed out position on the sofa. It's obvious from here that he's still nursing last night's hangover.

"No, I'm fine. I think it's best I do this alone. They're going to be mad that I didn't tell them before now; I don't need to rub their noses in it that they were almost the last ones to find out."

"I guess. Well, if you change your mind, ring me and I'll be there," he offers.

"I will. Thank you." I walk over to him and place a kiss on his cheek. "Go and shower; you stink," I tell him before walking over to the front door and sliding my flip-flops on.

"Love you, too," he calls after me.

I pull the door open but I'm too busy rummaging inside my handbag for my car keys to pay much attention, so when I bump up against another person, I jump out of my skin.

"Ahh," I shout in panic.

"I'm so sorry," a soft female voice says in response as she puts her hands on my shoulders to steady me.

"What's wrong?" Taylor says, rushing to the door.

I look up to see a familiar sophisticated face looking back at me.

"Nothing, it's fine. Taylor, this is Elaine, Lucas' mum. Elaine, this is Taylor, my practically naked flat mate. Please ignore him; he's trying to sleep off his hangover." Taylor gives me a scowl and disappears back inside. Elaine doesn't look away quick enough and I catch her checking out his backside. I smile and raise an eyebrow at her.

"What?" she asks innocently. "Don't tell me you haven't," she adds with a laugh.

I make a non-committal noise in response, because she's not wrong, Taylor does have a good body. I think if he hadn't decided to be a photographer, he would have been just as good the other side of the camera.

Elaine shakes her head before looking serious. "I'm so sorry to just turn up like this, but I thought…well, I don't know what I thought, but…"

"It's okay, Elaine. Shall we go and get a coffee?" I ask.

Thankfully, when we get to the car park, she offers to drive. I slide into her brand new Mercedes, grateful that she isn't doing the same with my rust bucket.

Once we've got drinks and found a table, Elaine starts talking. I mean, it's pretty obvious why she's here, but I did presume she knew more than she obviously does.

"What's happened, Lilly? No one can get hold of Lucas. We have no idea where he is. We've called all our hotels but no one has seen him. He's not at his house. Sylvie hasn't seen sight nor sound of him. We've been so worried after what happened the other night, and then Christopher found out you'd handed your notice in with immediate effect, and I just didn't know what to think."

I let out a huge breath before I just go for it. "I'm pregnant, Elaine. That's why I passed out. I had no idea, I didn't even think I could have kids, but apparently, a miracle happened. I haven't seen Lucas since we got a taxi back from the hospital. I left him outside having a cigarette." I don't miss the way she curls her lip in disgust at that. "I've not seen or heard from him since. Apart from a large deposit of money into my bank account that I'm not too happy about."

"Oh my goodness, congratulations, Lilly," she says, her eyes shining with tears. "I'm going to be a grandmother?"

I nod at her question and grab her hand that's resting on the table. "It's twins," I admit. Her chin drops open in shock at the same time a tear drops from her eye.

"Oh, I never thought I'd ever be a grandmother," she says, sniffling as she rummages around in her bag for a tissue. "I'm sorry," she says, "I just didn't see this coming."

"It's okay. Trust me, I know it's a shock."

"I don't even know where to start," she says looking completely blindsided. "It would explain Lucas' disappearance, though. How much has he told you about his past?"

"Not a lot. I know you and Christopher adopted him and that his life before was awful. He told me he lived in London for a while, but that it wasn't a good time in his life. That's about it, really."

"That's more than I expected. He's been really trying to let you in, Lilly." I know she's right; I could see him trying and fighting the urge to keep everything hidden.

"I won't break his trust in me by telling you everything. I probably already said too much that day on the phone. Lucas is right—he had an awful childhood and because of that, he always swore he never wanted a family of his own. He's always had a fear that he would end up like his mum and he would never want to submit anyone to that kind of life. I can only imagine what's going on in his head right now."

I let that information sink in before saying anything.

None of it's a surprise; it's pretty much what I expected, but to hear it said aloud hits me deep. "So you haven't heard anything from him?"

"No, nothing. I've been ringing every day. I wanted to know you were alright."

We chat for a long time. She gives a little more information about Lucas, but nothing that I hadn't already guessed, before she tells me about how her and Christopher could never conceive which is why they jumped at the chance of adopting Lucas went they found him.

By the time there's a break in our conversation, I realise that I'm late for dinner at my parents'. Elaine drives me back to the flat so a can jump in my car and head over there. Before I leave, she gives me a huge hug and hands me a business card with her contact deals on, telling me she wants to be involved as much as I would like her to be. She also promises to be in touch if she hears anything from Lucas, and I promise to do the same. When we part, there are tears filling our eyes.

I sit in my car for a few minutes as I try to pull myself back together enough to face all my family. I realise I'm going to have to put off telling my parents until later, because I can't face doing in front of everyone.

"Lilly, there you are," my mum says as I walk into their packed dining room.

Everyone is here today, so Mum has had to add a fold away table to the end of our usual dining table and dragged in some of the garden chairs for everyone to sit on. All eyes turn to me at Mum's words, and I swallow down the sudden rush of emotion that being surrounded by my family brings on.

I walk towards my empty seat, pausing on the way to give Lois a kiss on the cheek. She gives me a smile and starts shouting, "Li Li," at the top of her voice.

"Are you okay? You look tired," Mum whispers to me when I take my seat next to her.

"Yes, I'm fine," I say, trying to sound as convincing as possible. "I'm starving," I add to try to distract her. I'm not lying though—the smell had my stomach rumbling the second I walked in the house.

"Lilly, do you want wine?" Dad asks when he gets to my glass.

"No thank you, I went out with Taylor last night and had plenty," I say, in the hope it will be enough to stop them questioning my refusal.

"Emma?" he asks.

"No thanks, Dad. Actually, before we start eating, Ruben and I have something we would like to tell you all."

All eyes snap to Emma. I glance at Mum to see a ginormous smile on her face; she knows as well as I do what's coming next. We all wait anxiously for her to spit it out.

"You're going to be grandparents," she says, looking between Mum and Dad. "To twins, obviously!"

Mum gets up with such force her chair goes flying back as she launches herself at my sister, while Dad sits there with a bemused look on his face. Okay, so when I said everyone knew what was coming, apparently that didn't include Dad, bless him.

"Everyone says their congratulations before questions start getting fired towards both Emma and Ruben.

"I'm nearly thirteen weeks so due beginning of November, but it's more likely to be October with it being twins."

I get lost in my own head as she continues to answer all the questions in the exact same way I could right now. I feel bad as she talks excitedly about her pregnancy, like I'm going to be taking something away from her when I announce mine. This is obviously something she and Ruben planned for and are so excited about, and here I am having an accident, an amazing one, but still an accident, and I'm going to take some of her limelight. I know she won't hold it against me in any way, but I already feel like I make her life that little bit harder by how much I look like Hannah. I don't need to do this to her as well.

"Sorry, I just need to pop to the loo," I say quietly in case anyone actually notices my disappearance. I give Emma a hug as I pass and Ruben a shoulder squeeze in congratulations.

I sit down on the closed toilet lid and put my head in my hands. I lose track of how long I sit there, totally lost in my thoughts. When I'm back with it, I realise I need to get a grip if I want to get through the next few hours without having a meltdown. *This would be so much easier if Dec was here*, I think as I splash cold water on my face.

"Are you sure you're okay?" Mum asks again when I sit back down.

"Hangover," I mutter in response and it appeases her for now because she turns back to Emma.

The next few hours are a blur of talking pregnancy, babies, childbirth and everything else that comes along with that stage of your life. I listen to some of it, especially Molly's giving birth story, because I have no clue about any of that. I've not even seen *One Born Every Minute*. I make a note to record it next time it's on.

Eventually, Emma starts yawning so Ruben takes her home, Lois starts grumbling so Molly and Ryan say their goodbyes to get her home to bed, and I'm left with my mum and dad. It's now or never.

"Hey, do you need help with that?" I ask them as walk into the kitchen.

"That would be great," Mum responds, "Dad's running a training course tomorrow in Birmingham. He's going to the hotel tonight so he can be prepared for the morning."

"Off you go and sort your stuff out then," I say to Dad as I take the tea towel from his hands and usher him out of the kitchen.

I don't want him to feel like I can't talk to him or don't want him here, but I am a little relieved I'm going to be able to tell Mum everything alone.

"Ring me when you get there," Mum says, giving Dad a kiss when he has his small case in his hand, ready to leave.

"I will. See you tomorrow. Bye love," he shouts over to me.

"Good luck."

"Right, angel. You're hovering; I'm guessing you have something you need to talk about." I look up at her from my seat on the sofa and I can't hold back my emotions any longer. My bottom lip starts to wobble and tears run down my cheeks. "Oh, it's okay," Mum says as she wraps me up in a hug.

"I don't know where to start," I admit when I pull back.

"The beginning, angel."

"You're going to be so mad because there's stuff I haven't told you."

"Stop stalling and just tell me. I'll make my mind up then."

"Okay. You remember I had a boyfriend last year?" Mum nods so I keep going. "Well…he was amazing at first. I thought he was too good to be true, and he was. He had been brought up by his grandparents and they both died a month or so apart. Jake didn't take it very well. He started drinking to begin with but it wasn't long before he started playing with drugs. I should have ended it, I know I should, but I felt guilty even thinking about it when he was hurting already. The more he drank and did drugs, the more unlike himself he became. He started getting angry at the smallest things, and jealous and paranoid that I was cheating on him.

"One night last summer, I'd been out with friends for some drinks. One of Taylor's friends walked me home. We said goodbye at the entrance but Jake obviously didn't see that. I hadn't been in the flat long before he started knocking at the front door. When I opened it, he was angrier than I'd ever seen him. He started accusing me of sleeping around. He threw me down the stairs and knocked me out," my mum's hand comes up to cover her mouth as she sucks in a huge gasp of air at my words. "And then he stabbed me."

"Oh my goodness," she says in a rush and pulls me to her. She squeezes me within an inch of my life. I'm just about to complain that I can't breathe when she lets go.

"Dec knew something was going on, and thankfully when he phoned I was able to answer. Anyway, he got an ambulance and…"

"And he never told us about this?"

"Don't be mad at him. I told him not to tell you. I begged him."

"Why?"

"Because you've already been through so much with Hannah, I couldn't do it to you."

"Oh, Lilly, angel. Please don't ever think that. Please don't hide something this serious from us because of that. You're my baby, I want to be there to help you." I can see her getting more upset so I apologise and continue with my story.

"We told you that I had the flu while I recovered. I had to have surgery because of the blood loss but the stab wound was so low that the surgery caused adhesions that they said would make my chances of having kids even lower than before. Basically impossible.

"I got a promotion at work." I can see Mum's confusion at my sudden change of direction but I don't give her time to question me because now I'm this far in I need to keep going. "I got given the King's suite to clean." I don't need to explain farther than that because I've told Mum about it in the past. "I started the day Connie had Noah, and Lucas, the King, found me a bit of an emotional wreck on his sofa. Well, one thing led to another, and we sort of started dating—"

"You started dating your boss? The one that no one likes?"

"Yeah, that's the one. He's actually not that bad outside work."

"Well, I should hope not."

"Anyway, he took me to a charity action last weekend, but we didn't even make it to dinner because I passed out—"

"Oh my God, you're pregnant!"

My chin drops. "How do you know that?"

"Because that's exactly how I found out I was expecting you and Declan. I was in a supermarket buying bread and the next thing I knew I was on the floor with shop assistants staring down at me."

I smile at her, a little relieved I wasn't in a supermarket when it happened. "Yeah, I'm pregnant."

"With twins, by any chance?"

"Yes."

"Oh my goodness, what a day. How far along? When can we meet…Lucas, was it?" she fires all these questions at me to the extent that I don't know what to answer first.

"I'm pretty much the same as Emma. Thirteen weeks and due beginning of November. And as for Lucas, well, there's my next problem. He's done a runner. Basically, he found out about me being pregnant and I haven't seen or heard from him since, other than a deposit of money into my account."

"What a…" Mum pauses for the appropriate name, "idiot." I almost laugh. Yes, idiot is one way to describe him.

"I've quit my job because I can't work there anymore. I can't just run into him. I don't really know what I'm going to do though. Taylor has landed himself a job in London and I'm never going to get one now. Oh, and the reason I was late is because Lucas' mum was at my front door when I went to leave. She hasn't heard from him either and is worried."

"Wow, Lilly. That is a lot of information to take on all of a sudden. I don't know where to start."

Fifteen

Lucas

"Lucas? Oh my gosh, are you okay? Where are you? What are you doing? Do you know it's Lilly's twenty week scan tomorrow?" Mum practically shouts down the phone at me

"Mum, calm down. I'm fine. I've just been working and trying to get my head straight. And yes, I'm aware of the scan tomorrow."

"You've been getting your head straight?" she fumes. My mum hardly ever gets angry, but I can feel her practically vibrating with fury down the phone. "Well, I hope you've had some great epiphany because while you've been off doing that, Lilly has been here wondering what the hell she did wrong and having to deal with everything alone. Do you have any idea how scared and confused she is?"

"Yes, actually, I do."

"You left her, Lucas. She came looking for you and you had just gone. Disappeared into thin air. Did you not think to warn her? To tell her you needed some time? She'd have understood, Lucas."

"I—" I go to say more, but clearly, she hasn't finished.

"She's been a mess, Lucas. She's needed you and none of us could find you. You could have been dead in a ditch somewhere for all we knew. You've got two babies on the way, you cannot be that selfish any more, Lucas Dalton."

Whoa, my full name...she means business.

"I know, Mum. I'm sorry."

"Don't apologise to me. There's only one person you should be apologising to."

"Yes, I know. I will."

"You had better have something big up your sleeve, my boy, because nothing short of one seriously grand gesture to show her what she means to you is going to get her back. You might be my son but I won't defend you after the way you've behaved."

Ouch, that hurt. I thought my mum of all people would understand my need to escape. Obviously not.

"I've been working on something for her," I admit.

"Good."

I barely get a chance to put the phone down before it's ringing again. My heart jumps into my throat but I reason with myself that Mum couldn't have told Lilly I was in contact that quickly. I breathe a sigh of relief when I see Joe's name on my screen.

"What the fuck is going on, Dalton? You fall of the face of the earth for weeks on end and then when I look at your accounts they're all but empty." That's the greeting I get from my friend and accountant. I shouldn't be surprised really, after the amount of money I've spent in the last few weeks. I probably should have warned him.

"I made an investment."

"You don't fucking say. I hope it was a wise one."

"Yeah, me too," I say, picturing what I've been working on. I hope it's worth it too. "Lilly's pregnant," I admit. Joe is the first person I've said it aloud to, and it feels fucking weird.

"No shit, man. That's awesome."

"Is it?"

"Yeah, I think a sprog is just what you need."

"Two."

"What?"

"She's having twins."

"Fuck me."

"Nah, you're alright."

Once Joe's shock wears off and I manage to convince him I haven't totally lost my mind, I turn the light out and attempt to get some sleep. That's wishful thinking though, with the prospect of seeing Lilly and our babies at tomorrow's scan. *If* she allows me to attend.

I know running away wasn't the most mature thing to do but images of my childhood were on repeat in my brain from the second the doctor announced Lilly was pregnant. I always feel like I'm one mistake away from turning into my mother. I'm further from it since I moved away from London but I know I have the same addictive personality as her, and my fear of becoming like her made me run.

Lilly and the babies would be much better off without me if there was even a chance of me being a parent like that.

As the weeks without her have gone on though, I soon realised that being with them wasn't the scariest part—being without them was worse. So much fucking worse.

I realised I couldn't just turn up on her doorstep with a bunch of flowers and say I'm sorry. That wasn't going to cut it. So I got on the internet and found something I hope she is going to love. I've worked my arse off to make it a reality for her, but now it's pretty much ready I'm petrified I've made a mistake, that she's going to want nothing to do with me after the way I've treated her, let alone what I've done.

"I'm here for Lilly Morrison's appointment," I say to the lady at the reception desk. She looks at me and then behind me—I guess for Lilly—but when she doesn't see anyone she looks back, waiting for me to explain. "We're arriving separately; she'll be here shortly." I don't add that she might cause me physical harm for turning up like this. It took some serious convincing to even get someone to tell me what time this appointment was, but I soon realised after leaving her building that day that I wasn't missing it for anything. All I have is the memory of those white shapes on that original scan. I need to see more to help convince me that this is really happening and to tell myself that everything I've done isn't for nothing.

I sit myself in the back corner. I want to see Lilly before

she sees me. I sit there for ages, but that's my own fault for being so early.

Eventually, I hear familiar soft footsteps behind me. I brace myself for her to round the corner and when she does, my breath catches in my throat. She looks beautiful. Her long blonde hair is hanging down her back and she has on a light summer dress. Everything in me craves her. I wrap my fingers around the edges of the chair to keep me in place.

I watch as she goes to the desk to check herself in before turning around. She takes two steps towards the seating area before she sees me. Her whole body stills and her mouth drops open. I make the most of her shocked state to run my eyes down the front of her body, over the bump of her belly. I get this weird feeling come over me as I think about my babies growing in there.

Lilly is pulled from her shock when a woman, who I can only presume is her mother because she is just an older version of Lilly, crashes into the back of her. The woman follows Lilly's gaze and turns to look at me as well. Her features harden as she stares at me. I think her anger may rival my mother's, by the look of it.

Lilly's mother just goes to step forward when the door opens next to me and a young woman steps out. "Lilly Morrison?" she asks.

Lilly pulls her eyes away from me and heads towards the woman at the same time I stand from my chair. The sonographer can obviously tell something is going on, because she looks between the three of us before asking Lilly if everything is okay.

Lilly doesn't say anything; she just nods her head.

"Can he attend?" she asks, looking back at me.

"Well, they are his," Lilly snaps as she walks through the door, turning her back on me. I can't lie; her harshness stings a little.

I stand by the door awkwardly as Lilly goes through the same process as last time. She slips her leggings down her hips a little and lifts her loose dress to reveal her swollen belly. My eyes are locked on to her rounded skin. She looks perfect and the fact my babies are growing under there has me frozen to the spot.

"Do you need to sit?" someone says, and it takes a few minutes to realise that it's Lilly's mother with her hand on my arm, gesturing towards the chair.

I nod and do as she suggests because I'm not feeling very stable right now.

I watch from the sidelines as Lilly lies on the bed, holding her mother's hand. The sonographer soon has an image up on screen, and I'm even more enthralled by that image than I am with Lilly's swollen belly.

My babies.

She seems to be there ages, moving the wand thing around and getting different angles. Eventually though, she looks up to Lilly and asks, "Would you like to know their sex?"

I look back at Lilly and watch as she bites down on her bottom lip in thought. After a few seconds, her eyes find mine. Her excitement and happiness is infectious and for the first time, it's not just dread I feel about this situation.

"I'm happy either way, as long as they're both healthy," I say, my voice full of emotion and barely recognisable to my own ears.

Lilly looks to her mum who smiles at her and says, "It's

your call, angel."

"I want to know."

"Okay, well it looks to me like you've got one of each. This one on the left of the screen is a girl, and the one on the right is a boy."

I stare at the screen for the longest time, looking at my almost ready-made family of four, trying to allow it to sink in. In a matter of weeks, really, I'm going to be a dad to not just one kid, but two. I'm going to have a son and a daughter.

Sniffling to my right eventually makes me rip my eyes away from the screen. Lilly has tears streaming down her face but she also has the biggest smile I think I've ever seen.

Without thinking, I get up and walk over to her. In seconds, I have my hand on her belly and my lips against hers.

I expect her to push me away but to my surprise she relaxes under my touch and her lips soften against mine— until someone else in the room clears their throat to distract us.

"I'm sorry," I whisper as I pull back. I know that isn't enough to cover what I've done, but it's all I've got right now.

I continue looking down at Lilly as I stand to full height once again, and I see the tension and anger descend like I was expecting when I went to kiss her.

"One kiss changes nothing, Lucas." I nod because there is nothing I can say right now to try to make any of this better.

I sit back down and allow the sonographer to finish what she's got to do. I listen to everything Lilly says in the hope it will give me some insight into what I've missed so far with this pregnancy.

"Well…thanks for coming. It's nice to know you care about these two," Lilly says sadly when we're back in the waiting room.

"Of course I care, Lilly. That has never been in question. It's—"

"Stop," she interrupts. "I'm not interested. If it was that important, you would have found a way to tell me before now. Here," she snaps as she hands me one of the scan photos she just had printed. "I'll see you around—maybe at the birth, if you can be bothered."

"Lilly, please," I start to beg as she and her mother turn to walk away.

"No, Lucas. You made your bed when you walked away. Now you've got to lie in it. It's been eight weeks. I've moved on and have more important things to worry about," she says, placing a protective hand on her belly.

I keep my mouth shut this time and watch her walk out. The pain in my chest is well deserved after doing the same to her. I freaked out. I know I should have manned up and followed her into her flat, explained properly about my childhood, about my birth mother and how scared I am to turn into that kind of parent. But I didn't. I took the easy route and I ran. It wasn't very long before I regretted that decision, but I didn't know how to rectify it.

There is only one place to go after the hospital appointment, and that is to my parents' house to face my mother's wrath.

Her anger at me lessens somewhat when I flash the scan picture in front of her but it only lasts so long.

"What the hell are you going to do, Lucas? Your babies

need you. Lilly needs you. I can't imagine bringing up twins singlehandedly."

"I have a plan."

"You have a plan that will make her forget what a selfish bastard you've been? That must be one hell of a plan, Luc."

I pull up the photo on my phone and hand it over to her.

"What have you done?"

"It's for her?"

"Why?"

"Because it's important to her."

"But it's miles away, Lucas. Why on earth?" Mum doesn't finish her sentence as she starts swiping through the photos. "I hope you're right and this works," is all she says before handing my phone back.

I'm not sure what I was expecting her reaction to be, but what she said didn't fill me with hope. Maybe I'd gone about this all wrong and I've made a massive mistake.

I jump out of the car and jog across the car park outside Lilly's building. I'm like a drowned rat by the time I get there, which just about matches my attitude.

I hold my finger down on the button for the longest time. I can only presume Taylor has already left for London, and I have no idea if Lilly would have had to find another flat mate. I fucking well hope not. The thought of Lilly living with someone else gets my temper flaring. I slam my palm down on the wall next to the buzzers.

"FUCK," I shout out into the grey and wet day.

"So you decided to show your face at last," a soft female voice says from behind me.

When I turn, I see an elderly lady with a crutch and a bag of shopping. "Uh…"

"Well, I have to say I didn't think I'd ever see the day. I thought Lilly was stupid, holding on to hope that you would reappear when you saw fit. She'd be a fool to take you back though."

"Okay. Who are you?" I ask. Lilly never mentioned a grandmother, but there's a lot we didn't get a chance to talk about.

"It doesn't matter. What matters is that I know who you are and what you've done to my lovely Lilly." The lady goes to pass me and opens the door. "And don't even try to sneak in after me. She's not here. She's at yoga with her sister at the sports centre," she calls over her shoulder before the door closes behind her. *She obviously isn't that against me if she's telling me where Lilly is*, I think as I make the dash back towards my car.

I press my foot down and take off for the sports centre, hoping I'll get a better reception from Lilly than I did this morning. I know it's wishful thinking. After the way I've behaved, I couldn't blame her if she never wants to talk to me again.

Lilly

"He was just sat there waiting for you?" Emma whispers over from her mat a foot or so over from mine.

"Yeah."

"I can't believe you let him into the scan with you."

"He's their dad, Em. No matter how he behaves, he is and always will be their dad."

"I guess."

"Ladies at the back, either take this seriously or take your gossiping elsewhere," the instructor says, looking less than amused.

We both mutter our apologies and go back to what where meant to be doing.

"I still can't believe the cheek of him. No contact for two months and then there he is? How did he even find out about the appointment anyway?" Emma continues ranting when we leave the hall.

"I presume his mum. Lucas tends to get whatever it is he wants, so I shouldn't have been sur—" my sentence is halted when I catch sight of the suit-clad figure waiting in reception who is turning every woman's head as they walk past. "No way."

"What?" Emma asks, looking over at me. I nod my head in his direction. "Holy shit, is that him?"

"Yes. Why the hell is he here?"

"Looks like he's back with vengeance, Lills. And he wants you." I don't miss the way Lucas' eyes run over my Lycra-clad body either. "Christ, he looks like he could melt those clothes off your body right here with that look. Good luck," Emma says with a laugh. I think she's right, but I'm going to need more than luck to keep some much distance from him.

"Lucas, what are you doing here?"

I watch as he looks between Emma and me, then at our matching bellies. I don't miss how his eyes darken when he looks at me though.

"Is it safe for you to be doing that?" he asks, gesturing to the direction we've just come from.

I stick my hands on my hips and stare at him, hoping that I look as irritated by him as I feel. Emma doesn't seem to notice, as she answers for me. "Yes, it's pregnancy yoga. It's designed for pregnant women."

I watch as Lucas takes on that bit of information before nodding and stating that we need to talk.

"I agree, but now's not a good time."

"Well, when is?"

"I don't know, Lucas. When I don't feel like trying to kill you with whatever weapon I can find. It's been two months. Two. I've just about got my life somewhat sorted and now here you are. Well, you don't get to call all the shots. I'll talk to you when I'm ready, but that's not now. Let's go," I add, looking at Emma.

"Don't you think you should—"

"Emma, don't," I warn, knowing exactly where she's going. She holds her hands up in defeat and begins walking towards the car park.

"Lilly, please. I'm not above begging," Lucas says quietly.

"Good to know," I say, before striding off after Emma.

"I can't believe I just did that," I admit, before bursting into tears in Emma's car.

"I'm proud of you, Lills."

"I told myself over and over again I wouldn't cave to him when—if—I ever saw him again, but I didn't think I would be strong enough."

Emma reaches over and takes my hand in hers for support as I continue to splutter and sob very unattractively.

"He doesn't look like the kind of man who takes being told no easily," Emma says eventually.

"He's not. I'm not stupid enough to think that's the last I'm going to see of him."

After Emma drops me off, I head up to my flat to have a quick shower. It's weird being here alone now. Although towards the end Taylor wasn't around much, it's still strange knowing he isn't going to appear at some point.

I pull on some comfortable clothes and don't bother doing anything with my hair before heading upstairs to sort Shelia out. Since the day I helped her settle back in, I've been helping her out with her chores. She's so grateful for the help, she's insisted on paying me. I refused to accept it for a long time, but I had to cave in the end, and if I'm honest the money is a great help now I'm pregnant and unemployed. I've picked up some shifts in Mum's coffee shop, so that, along with the little bit that Shelia gives me, is keeping me going at the moment.

I've only made one purchase with the money Lucas stashed in my account, and I'm determined not to spend any more, but I couldn't resist buying myself a more comfortable bed. I put up with aching hips for a week before I headed to the bed shop for an upgrade. So far, it's the best purchase I've ever made.

I'm not in Shelia's flat five minutes before I discover how Lucas found me at my yoga class. Shelia is angry with him after everything I've told her, but I still feel like she might have a sweet spot for him, even though she's only met him briefly. She spends the rest of my visit telling me I need to hear him out, that holding off will only make everything harder.

I know she's right. I'd like to have everything sorted out between us before these two appear. I'm just not sure I want to hear it. There have been weeks where it was all I wanted—to open the front door and find him stood there. But I've grown since then. I've realised that I don't need him, that I can do this alone. I don't want to, but I know I can.

It seems being able to ignore Lucas now he has reappeared is going to be impossible. I look around my living room at all the deliveries I've received throughout this week and sigh. It's covered with bunches of all colours of lilies, boxes of chocolates, and some mummy-to-be sets.

I decide I've put it off long enough and unlock my phone. I find his name and stare at it for a few seconds as I try to decide if this is the right thing to do or not.

"Lilly," he says, sounding relieved.

"You can't buy me back, Lucas," I snap, a little harsher than I intended. I didn't ring for a fight.

"I know that. I just wanted you to know that I'm thinking of you. That I never stopped, Lilly."

"It would have saved you a lot of brain power if you'd just stuck around." I hear his sharp intake of breath at my words. It makes me want to apologise for being short with him, but I stand my ground. He's in the wrong here.

"Please can we talk? I could come over," he asks, hope in his voice. This was what I was afraid of—that I would reach out and suddenly he would think everything was okay.

"NO," I shout in panic

"No?"

"Don't come here." *I don't trust myself.* I'm already struggling with my pregnancy-heightened sex drive; I really don't need to be alone in the same room as him. I'll end up climbing him or something embarrassing. "I'll meet you in the coffee shop around the corner."

"What I need to tell you isn't something I want to discuss in public, Lilly."

"Well, that's all I'm offering. Take it or leave it."

"Okay. I'll meet you there in thirty minutes."

I was hoping for a little more time to prepare but I mutter my agreement and head back to my bedroom to get ready.

I'm just walking through the main door to my building when my phone starts ringing. Hope flares that it might me Lucas cancelling and I won't have to do this, but the second I pull my phone out and see Nicole's name, I hate to say I'm a little disappointed, although I'm kind of relieved I now have a reason to be late.

I sit down on the bench overlooking the grounds and put my phone to my ear.

"Lilly, I'm so sorry I didn't get back to you last night. I had a bit of a crazy day with mum."

"It's okay, don't worry."

"Everything's okay with the babies then, I'm guessing, looking at the scan picture."

"Yes ,they're perfect. Lucas showed up."

"NO!"

"Yep, just sat there in the waiting room. I couldn't believe it."

"Fucking dick," Nic mutters under her breath. "What did you do?"

"What *could* I do? We were in a hospital, and he is the dad, after all."

"You let him in?"

"Of course. I can put aside how he's treated me for the benefit of our babies."

"Well, that's big of you, Lills. I'm not sure I could have done the same thing. Do you think you'll see him again?"

"I'm actually on my way to meet him now. You're

currently making me suitably late. I'm quite happy for him to sit there, sweating about whether I'm going to turn up or not."

"I can't believe you haven't told him where to stick it." I think if any one of my friends were in my current situation, I would be saying exactly the same things, but it's different when it's actually happening to you. They don't know Lucas like I do. I know he's not a horrible person. I'm pretty sure that whatever made him run off was to do with the skeletons in his closet about his own childhood. It will be different if I discover I'm wrong, and it's because he thinks I got myself pregnant on purpose to trap him or something. I try not to let thoughts like that enter my head, because I'm pretty sure he knows me better than that as well, and that he believed me when I told him I didn't think falling pregnant was a possibility.

"I think there's more to it. He has a reason."

"No reason is good enough to do what he did, Lilly. He abandoned you."

"I know," I whisper as the hurt I've been dealing with the last few weeks creeps its way back in. "How're things with you?" I ask, changing the subject. I'm already in for an afternoon discussing the situation with Lucas; I could do without it now.

"Same. She's still declining, just slowly. It feels like it's never-ending." I hate hearing her sound so defeated, and I hate even more that me wishing for it to get better means I'm wishing for her mum to pass away.

We chat for a while longer before I decide I've probably made him wait long enough. We say our goodbyes and I hang up. She won't tell me what she plans to do when her mum's gone. I have no idea if she's planning on staying up there or even moving to the other side of the world. She won't commit to anything. I totally understand why, but I'd love to know she's possibly considering a move back down here. We may not be family by blood, but she's my sister in every other way, and I know my parents love her. Dec not so much, but he's not here anyway.

Thinking about my brother makes my heart a little heavy. I really miss him at the moment. I mean, I always miss him, but since finding out I'm pregnant it's even worse. We've gone through everything in life together, and I hate not having him here for this. It's made me think more seriously about whether to make the move down there with him, but the thought of leaving the support of my parents when I'm going to have two babies puts me off somewhat.

I let out a sigh and try to put thoughts of my future aside as I slide my phone back into my bag. Mum and Dad have offered for me to go back home so they can help, and they've also said I can stay in the flat rent-free, but I have no idea what I want. Ideally, I want to be with Lucas, but I have no idea if that's going to be an option.

"I thought you'd changed your mind," Lucas says when I step up to the table he's sat at. I stood at the window of the coffee shop watching him for a few minutes before entering. He looked totally lost, sat there staring into space. It's not a look I'm used to seeing on him. He usually looks so in control of everything.

The second he registered me walking through the door, his expression completely changed. Gone was the sad and lost look, and in its place was relief. A lot of relief.

"I wouldn't do that to you," I say, but don't really think

about the words.

"I'm so sorry, Lilly," Lucas says, and it makes me realise that he thought I was going to abandon him like he did me. "I got you a tea, but it's probably cold now." I look to the table where there's a pot of tea, a teacup and saucer, along with a blueberry muffin.

"That's okay. I need decaf anyway. I'll get another one," I say, going to move towards the counter.

"It *is* decaf, Lilly," he says sadly, making me stop in my tracks and turn around. He must see the question in my eyes because he quietly says, "I've looked everything up. I know what you should and shouldn't have."

My heart melts. He may have been God knows where these last few weeks, but he's read up on pregnancy.

"Sit down, I'll get you a fresh pot."

I do as I'm told and plonk my arse in the chair he pulls out for me, and watch as he walks off to get me a new tea. My heart flutters as I think about Lucas sat reading pregnancy magazines just like I have. I wonder if he's looked at baby stuff as well. The thoughts get my hopes up that maybe he does want this and that he's willing to deal with whatever it was that caused him to bolt.

"Here you go," he says as he places the new pot in front of me and sits down.

We stare at each other across the table, both taking each other in. Remembering each other's features.

He looks the same as I remember, only more stressed and tired than I've ever seen him before.

I open my mouth to say something to break the awkward silence that's descended over us, but he beats me to it.

"You look beautiful, Lilly. I always thought it was bullshit when I heard people describe pregnant women as glowing, but you really are. Pregnancy suits you."

"Thank you," I mutter.

"I mean it."

"I know."

Another silence falls upon us. It was never this awkward between us before. It was one of the things I loved about spending time with him. I was always comfortable in his company—even at the beginning, when I thought he was a pretentious prick.

"I'm so sorry, Lilly. I never meant to hurt you. I just…I panicked and freaked out. There is no good enough excuse for what I did. It's just…my mother was…" he looks around to see if anyone is paying us any attention. They're not, of course, but he still pauses, which makes me think he really is uncomfortable discussing this in public.

"It's okay, you can tell me the details another time," I say.

"That's why I suggested your place."

"I can't have you there yet. I don't trust—" I stop myself before he gets the wrong, or right, idea. It's too late though, because I see his eyes light up.

"I read about that too," he admits with a sudden sparkle in his eye.

"You left, Lucas. I was waiting for you to come up and you just disappeared. How do you think that felt? I'd just received the most shocking news of my life and the one person I needed upped and left," I say, reminding him of why we're here. My libido might be raging with hormones, but I will not allow him to think everything is okay. "I had no idea if you were mad because of me, whether you thought I'd done it on purpose or if you just didn't want anything to do with them and were too weak to tell me to my face. I was a mess, Luc, and you just left me." I don't mean to lay it all out there like that, and the look on his face makes me feel awful for bringing it all up in one go, but I was annoyed by his earlier hope that I'd allow him to pick up where we left off. "You left me, and everyone else had to pick up the pieces."

He scoots his chair closer to me when he sees me start to get upset, but he doesn't reach out to touch me. "Lilly, I'm so sorry. Trust me, it wasn't anything to do with you or these," he admits as he tentatively reaches out a hand and places it on my belly. He looks up to my eyes and he relaxes when he realises I'm okay with his hand there. "It was me, my fears for what kind of father I might be. I'm so scared I'll turn into *her*. I freaked out. I should have talked to you, I know, but the thought of telling you all that ugliness when you should have been happy…I just couldn't do it."

"And you thought leaving would hurt me less than you telling me all that?"

"I don't know. I wasn't thinking straight. I was just thinking of the damage I could do to them," he says, rubbing my belly gently. "To you."

"You can't hurt me more by being here, Lucas. We need you."

Hope flares in his eyes and his lips quirk up at the corners in the beginnings of a smile. I feel the same hope begin to bubble up in my belly. Maybe this is all going to be okay and I'm not going to have to choose between living as a single mum in my flat or with my parents. Maybe my babies will have two parents who are together. That's still a few too many maybes for my liking, but it's better than an hour ago.

Sixteen

Lucas

I thought she was going to back away from me when I reached out to her belly. I've been gone for weeks, and I've already missed so much. It's such a weird feeling, being so far away from someone but feeling so connected to them at the same time. She's the one carrying them, and I've only seen scan pictures, but I already know these two in here are going to rule my life—along with their mother, of course.

I never wanted kids. I never wanted to get the chance to find out if I would be like *her* or not. I'm still petrified that old habits will resurface when things get tough, but I'm getting more and more convinced that with Lilly by my side, those things won't happen. She seems, rightly or wrongly, to have faith in me, so I need to have some in myself. I can be a good man for her and I can be a good father to my children, I tell myself.

"Whoa, what was that?" I ask when I feel something weird beneath my palm. It's kind of like a flutter of a butterfly wing against my skin.

"They're kicking. Give me your other hand." I lift my arm and she directs my hand to the right spot and presses down.

"Oh my God, that's incredible. How long have they been doing that?"

"It's only this week I've been able to feel it with my hand. Before that, it kind of felt like I kept getting a sudden belt of nerves. It's quite early to feel them but it's more common with twins and the consultant said they are already a good size, so getting a little squished up in there."

I can't help the wide smile that stretches across my face as I think about my babies already fighting with each other in there like Marcus and I used to do.

"Have you bought anything yet?"

"No. Everyone has tried to get me out shopping but I've been holding off. I think I was holding out hope that their father might reappear and we could do it together."

"Let's go then," I say, before finishing my coffee and standing up.

"Could I eat this first?" Lilly asks, looking longingly at the muffin. It's a nice change to see her wanting to eat.

"Sorry, of course."

"I have to eat every two hours, otherwise it's like I'm starving."

"Tell me what symptoms you've had. Any morning sickness? Any cravings?"

I sit and listen like it's the most important information in the world as Lilly explains about the weeks I've missed. When she's finished her muffin, we walk out together. Just like I hoped we would.

We spend the afternoon visiting every baby shop I can find in the area. I've spent hours online looking at everything they're going to need, much to Lilly's surprise. I don't think she's done the same; she's been putting it all off. To be fair though, she had enough other stuff to deal with, along with growing them.

"I've got a shortlist of three double buggies I thought might be good," I admit when we stop in another coffee shop to feed Lilly again. I never thought I'd see her eat like this.

"What?" she asks around a mouthful of cheese sandwich.

"I have a shortlist—"

"That's what I thought you said. You really do want to be involved with this, don't you?" The fact she still doubts me stings a little, but it's only what I deserve.

"Yes. The first few minutes after finding out were a little weird, but I've known all along that I wanted this—them—with you. It was my shit I couldn't cope with. It wasn't because I didn't want them.

By the time we get back to Lilly's flat, we are loaded down with stuff, most of which I never in a million years thought I'd buy. We ordered a pushchair after discussing each one's pros and cons over a coffee and decaf tea together, and then again with the sales assistant. Because we know the sex of the babies, we were able to have the fabric parts the correct colour, so one half is baby pink and cream and the other baby blue. For something I never thought I'd buy, let alone research, it's safe to say I'm pretty excited about it, much to Lilly's amusement.

I don't know about her, but spending time together this afternoon has been like the last few weeks never happened. It's safe to say I'm brought back to earth with a bump when we unload the shopping at Lilly's building and she hesitates when I go to help her up.

"Let me just carry it all up. I can leave it in your living room if you don't want me there."

I hate myself again for the pain I've caused her. The sight of her confusion as to whether she should allow me in or not guts me.

"Okay, thank you," she says quietly.

Once everything is up, we stand looking at each other awkwardly for a few minutes. I desperately want to pull her into my arms but I know I need to take my cues from her, and her body language is currently telling me to stay away.

"Thank you for allowing me today. I really appreciate it. When can I see you again?"

"I don't know, Luc. It's going to take time."

"I understand," I say sadly, because I do. It doesn't mean it's what I want, though.

"I'll call you. We still need to choose furniture."

This is true. We looked today, but Lilly, being an interior designer, wanted to do more research to get the room perfect. I was glad of this because if my plans for her work the way I'm hoping, Taylor's old room will never be a nursery.

I give Lilly a gentle kiss on the cheek before walking away. Just like the last time I walked away from this building, my heart stays with her.

I hear nothing from Lilly for days. Well that's not entirely true. I text her every day, at least once, and she does reply when I ask if she and the babies are okay. She's yet to arrange a time for us to get together again though. To say I'm getting impatient would be an understatement. I've already missed so much and I desperately want to experience the rest of her pregnancy with her.

By Friday afternoon, I've had enough of her elusive messages and decide that as soon as my final meeting with my boring interior designer is over, I'm heading to her flat. I need to talk to her, and the longer we are apart, the easier I fear it is for her to ignore me. I need to show I'm here to stay this time and that I want her.

Everything looks normal when I arrive and I'm thrilled to find Lilly's elderly neighbour by the entrance to the building again. She's slightly more pleasant to me this time and tells me how Lilly allowed her to come and look at all the stuff we bought. It thrills me that Lilly must have said some good things about me, because she allows me to enter the building with her.

I wish her a good evening before stepping out of the lift onto Lilly's floor.

The door is wide open.

That really isn't like her. I may have only been here a few times, but I've noticed she's obsessive with making sure it's shut and locked.

I pick up my pace and head towards the doorway. When

I step in and see what's going on in front of me, I swear my life flashes before my eyes.

Lilly

I know I should have arranged to see Lucas again, but I keep putting it off. I tried to tell myself that I hated him when he left and that I'd never forgive him, but in one afternoon, all my previous feelings I thought I'd banished came flooding back. It was clear I was still in love with him, and now I'm carrying his babies I swear it's only stronger.

Shopping with him for baby stuff wasn't like I imagined it would be because I thought he'd be walking around completely clueless. I was not expecting him to already know which breast pump was rated the best by other mums, or that you could get a machine that made perfect bottles ready to drink every time. It seemed he used the time he was away very effectively when it came to baby stuff. It warmed my heart that he didn't go because he didn't want us, but at the same time I hate that we couldn't have found all that stuff out together.

Getting him to leave when he brought up all the stuff was the hardest thing I think I've ever done. Every fibre of my being was screaming at me to let him stay, but I knew it wouldn't be helpful in the long run. Before I let him back in properly, I need to be 100% convinced he's not going to freak out and leave again. And that includes having him open up about his past, no matter how painful that will be for him. I also need to tell him about Jake and how I got to this point in my life as well.

I spend Friday morning with Emma, Connie and Noah at

my flat, and by the time they leave, I'd decide I've put off calling him long enough.

I've psyched myself up so much with what I want to say to him that when it goes to voicemail, a huge ball of disappointment hangs heavy in my stomach. I've been in a weird mood all day. I guess it's just pregnancy stuff.

I've just put my phone down when someone starts knocking. It's very unusual that anyone knocks before buzzing up from the main door, but the first thing that pops into my head is that Taylor has come back for the weekend. He's been promising he'd visit, and knowing he still has his keys so he could get in if I wasn't here has me convinced it's him.

I rush over to the door and pull it open as I announce, "I've missed you," and hold my arms open. But instead of large strong arms wrapping around me, I feel a pair of hands push harshly at my shoulders, making me fall to the floor with a thud.

My eyes blur with tears as a bolt of pain goes up my back. It's not until he's in my face that I realise who it is.

Jake.

"Good afternoon, Lilly Lou," he snarls.

I start to scrabble away from him but he stalks forward. He looks menacing, glaring down at me from his full height. I'm aware of how vulnerable I am, so I fight to get back on my feet. When I manage it, I'm aware that he's backed me into a corner.

I look around frantically for a weapon but there is nothing close enough to grab. His eyes look exactly like the last time I saw them: glazed, absent and dangerous.

"Wha…what do you want, Jake?"

"You, Lilly. Always you. I've given you time. Enough to realise you still love me."

I'm totally lost for words. If I argue and say I don't love him, it's going to hurt, I know it. But I also don't want to pretend. I never want to back down to him.

"Fuck you," I whisper.

His head snaps back at my rare use of the word.

"Excuse me?"

"You heard. Just leave me alone. You've already caused me enough damage."

"See, I would have left you alone but it seems you've found yourself a replacement and I can't have that. Either I have you, or no one does."

"Ow," I complain when he reaches behind, grabs a handful of my hair and pulls so my head snaps back.

"You're mine, Lilly, and it's time we showed your new man who you belong to." He pulls harder. It feels like thousands of needles being pressed into my scalp. "Phone him now. End it," he demands as he shoves my phone into my chest.

"No."

"It wasn't a choice, Lilly. Do it now."

"No," I repeat, although it doesn't have the same strength behind it this time. His eyes are getting angrier and it makes me more and more aware of how serious this is. He left me for dead last time, but it was only me then. Now, I've got more to worry about. I've got my babies. The thought makes me wrap my arms around my middle. Jake sees the move though, and his eyes almost pop out of his head as he takes in my protruding stomach. He obviously hasn't been watching me that closely.

"YOU WHORE," he bellows as his hand connects with my cheek. The force of the hit sends me crashing down to the ground. I cry out in pain as my head connects with the oak flooring.

His hands grasp my upper arms harshly and he drags me back on to my feet.

"You're mine. You're mine. You're mine," he chants at me. His eyes have no focus and his hands shake as they hold me.

"Let me go, Jake. We'll talk," I say softly, in the hope he'll be able to see some sense in his drugged-up state.

"Never," he growls before he releases me. It's only for a second though, because one hand grabs me around the neck and squeezes.

He stares at me with an evil smirk on his face as everything around me starts to get a little hazy. The last thing I remember thinking again is that I don't want to die with him being the last thing I see.

I'm aware of a noise. It sounds like a wild animal. Wait, where am I?

Suddenly, the pressure around my neck is gone. My legs are unable to hold me up and I crumble to the ground. One hand goes to my neck while the other holds my belly.

I hear something metal clatter against the floor, and when I look up, I see a knife skidding across the living room.

My eyes snap up in the direction it came from, and my breath catches in my throat at the sight.

Jake's broken body is cowering in the corner of the kitchen with a very pumped up and angry looking Lucas staring down at him.

Lucas says something to Jake but his voice is so

menacingly low that I only catch the end. "The next time I see you, it will be your last." A shiver runs through me.

I watch in a daze as Lucas drags Jake's passed out body from the flat and, I presume, the building because he's gone for a few minutes.

I sag back against the wall and the sudden silence allows me to relive what just happened. My entire body begins to shake with my sobs. I wrap my arms around my belly and rock back and forth.

I thought he'd gone. I thought Dec and Taylor sorted it.

The sound of heavy footsteps heading my way has my body on alert again. When I look up and see a familiar suited figure running towards me, my sobs reignite again.

"Fuck, Lilly," Lucas whispers as he pulls me up from the floor and cradles me in his arms. He walks us over to the sofa and sits with me across his lap. He holds me a little too tightly but I don't complain, I'm just glad it's over.

Eventually, I need to move, because not only is my head pounding but my throat is throbbing, along with every muscle in my body.

"No," Lucas whispers. "I'm not ready. Fuck, Lilly. I've seen some crazy shit but that was by far the worst. When I saw him with that knife pulled back, I thought I was going to lose all of you."

When I look up at him, a huge lump forms in my throat. My dominant and ruthless businessman is on the verge of tears.

"I'm okay," I whisper, because it's all I can manage.

His arms wrap back around me and he holds me for a long time. Eventually though, the pain gets too much and I have to do something. "Lucas, please could you get me some painkillers and a drink?"

"What's wrong?" I turn to look at him face on and the blood drains from his face. "MOTHERFUCKER," he shouts as his hand comes up to my temple. It's throbbing where it collided with the floor, so I can only imagine what it looks like.

"It's fine," I say, trying to ease his worry.

"No, it's fucking not, Lilly. He put his hands on you. He hurt you. He was going to…" It's then that I see the realisation hit him. "Son of a bitch," he says quietly as he shakes his head from side to side. "Please tell me this is the first time this has happened." When I don't speak up, I feel his body shake beneath me as the anger washes through him.

Lucas gently puts me down on the sofa before standing. He begins pacing the length of the living room. His hands go through his hair, and he rubs them over his face before running them through his hair again. When they come back to his sides, they clench and unclench. His chest is heaving and his eyes are dark with anger. If I didn't know him so well, I think I'd be scared, but I know he won't hurt me. His anger is reserved for Jake. What I am scared of though, I realise as I sit and watch him, is what he's going to do about it. Right now, he doesn't look like a man who's going to let this go easy.

"We should ring the police," I say, realising that if I dealt with it properly the first time, this wouldn't have happened.

"That won't be necessary. He's never going to get the chance to get his hands on you ever again."

"Lucas," I say, standing and walking over to him. "Promise me you're not going to put yourself in any danger."

"You just worry about yourself and these two," he says,

putting both his large hands on my belly. I want to argue but the look in his eyes stop me. They are still a little wet, but the dark anger has transformed into a soft concerned and protective look. It's not a look I can argue with.

Lucas must see my legs start to get weak as we stand and stare at each other, because he lifts me and moves me back to the sofa. No words were exchanged out loud as we stood there but many were spoken silently. Promises were made and apologies were accepted.

"Let me look after you," he says when he has me settled. "Where are your painkillers?"

"Bathroom cabinet. I can't have ibro—"

"Ibroprofen," he finishes for me. "I know. Paracetamol only."

It's like my entire body smiles at his words as I'm reminded of what he spent his time doing when he was away.

After a few minutes, he returns with a box of tablets. He grabs a glass from the kitchen and fills it with water before handing me both.

"I'm running you a bath. Not too hot," he adds when he sees my mouth open to say something, although commenting on the temperature of a pregnant woman's bath was the last thing on my mind.

"Thank you, that sounds perfect."

"I should warn you, I'm not leaving you though. You could have concussion."

Even if I wanted to, I don't have the energy in me to disagree. "Okay," I mutter, much to Lucas' surprise.

Once the glass is empty, Lucas holds onto my waist and together we walk to the bathroom. He helps me pull my maxi dress off, but thankfully allows me to take control of my underwear. I keep my back to him, painfully aware that my body has changed so much since the last time he saw it.

"Lilly. Please let me see you." I might have refused if his voice wasn't so sad.

Slowly, I turn towards him, anxious as to what he'll think about my new lumps and bumps. Not only is my belly growing at a rapid rate, but my hips are wider and my boobs bigger.

I stand, squirming a little as he runs his eyes from the top of my head to my toes and back again. They finally come to rest on my belly.

"You're growing our babies, Lilly," he says, like it's only just occurred to him. "There are literally two whole people inside you right now. Two heads, two hearts, four arms and four legs." He stops in thought for a second. "Twenty fingers and twenty toes." The look on his face is one I'll never forget. The admiration of what I'm doing is written all over his face and it causes warmth to spread through my entire body. You'd think I was the only woman to ever be pregnant with the way he's looking at me.

Once Lucas has had his fill, he helps me into the bath. There is a heat in his eyes that I recognise and I'm unbelievably grateful it's still there. I had no idea what he would think of me now, but he actually looks even more excited by my body—evidenced by his need to rearrange himself after he's helped lower me into the water.

"Everything okay?" I ask with a smile as I watch him. He may have his back to me, but it's pretty obvious what he's doing.

"Yeah. I'm better than I have been in a long time," he

admits, looking over his shoulder at me. When he sees my smirk, he laughs in understanding. "Was it that obvious?"

I relax back with a laugh surrounded by bubbles as Lucas pulls his tie off and undoes the top few buttons of his shirt before sitting himself down on the closed toilet seat. I know he's itching to ask for more information about Jake, and I will give it to him, just not right this minute. I need the peace and tranquillity he's offering me right now.

"Do you want a drink?" I ask Lucas once I'm dressed.

"Sure."

Presuming he doesn't mean a soft one after the evening of this evening, I pull out a bottle of whiskey I bought for him before he disappeared. I pour him a generous amount before taking it through with a glass of water for myself.

"Thank you. I-" he begins to say something but I cut him off. It's now or never.

Lucas sits and listens as I pretty much relay the story I told to my mum a few weeks ago about Jake. Fair play to him because he sits and listens even as his anger increases.

"Declan and Taylor didn't do a very good job," is all he says when I've finished, and I can't help but agree with him. "He won't bother you again."

"Lucas, I'm serious, do not put yourself in any danger."

"Don't worry, Lilly. Everything will be fine."

"Okay," I mutter, feeling like it will be anything but. "Your turn," I say. He must know what I mean, because he necks his remaining whiskey before squaring his shoulders and looking straight ahead at the black TV screen.

"My mother was a druggie. She wasn't fussy—if she could get her hands on it, she would use it. I don't know if she was always like that or if something started it when I was young. All I know is that she was like it from my earliest memory. She used to promise us she'd get clean and when I was young I believed her like the naïve kid I was. It was never going to happen though. She was just about as addicted as anyone could get.

"Her priority was drugs. It wasn't me or Marcus. It wasn't putting food on the table or making sure we had clothes to wear.

"She would go out on a bender and leave us alone in the shithole of a flat we lived in with no heating, no food and nothing to do. We had no TV, no radio, no toys. Nothing.

"She would bring random men back. We had no idea what they were doing; we were too young to understand in the beginning but as I got older it became obvious.

"She would give us the odd bit of money to keep us going but nowhere near enough. She would always give us plenty though when we were sent to meet one of her *friends* to pick up supplies for her. I was always more than happy to go because more often than not there were a few pennies left over that I could save to put towards stuff Marcus and I needed."

"Jesus, Lucas." I don't know what else to say. I had kind of presumed some of this, but not to that extent. I guess growing up with a loving family shields you from the reality of others' lives.

"This one guy that used to come around was horrible. He was huge with greasy long hair and practically black eyes. His hands were always disgusting. I remember the stains on them and the blackness under his nails. Unfortunately, the reason I know that is because they were often flying towards me." I suck in a breath at his words. As if life wasn't bad enough.

"If he wasn't wasted, he was going at either my mother or me. I managed to keep him off Marcus. He was only ten at the time. I used to lock Marcus in our bedroom when I knew it was coming. I could read his moods well.

"Anyway, one day he really went to town. I don't know what upset him that day or what my mother or I had done wrong but I swear he was going to kill me. He was getting on a bit and wasn't exactly in good shape. I knew from past experiences he used to wear himself out pretty quickly, so I bided my time and eventually my chance came. He bent over at the waist and put his hands on his knees while he wheezed out some breaths. I broke my eye contact with him and grabbed the ashtray on the coffee table. I pulled my arm back and with as much force as my tiny thirteen-year-old body could muster, I hit him in the head. Then, I ran.

"I ran as fast and as long as I could. When I felt I was going to pass out from the exertion—bear in mind I probably hadn't eaten in days—I turned into a building. I had no idea what it was; I just hoped I could hide until I got my breath back. What I didn't expect was that I'd run straight into a man in a suit."

"Christopher?" I guess, and it must be correct because Lucas nods.

"He took me to his office and attempted to clean me up. I must have looked a fucking mess. Then, he did the most amazing thing. He called the kitchen and ordered me a three-course meal. That was the best fucking food I've ever tasted.

"A long story and a few foster homes later, and

Christopher and Elaine finally got approved to adopt me. Elaine told me that she knew I'd run into their lives that day for a reason, and she wasn't taking no for an answer. Fair play to them, because I'm not sure I would have wanted to adopt me. They must have known they were in for a world of pain."

"Why would you say that?"

"No kid who has grown up in squalor like that suddenly accepts a nice life. It never happens."

"Oh," I say, because I've never really thought about it.

"Once I was looking and feeling better, they enrolled me into the local secondary school. I hated it. I was the outcast from the bad side of town. I isolated myself and eventually found myself befriending another outcast called Nathan. I'd see him trying to hide the same bruises I used to. We never talked about it, but I knew what he was going through.

"We both already smoked but it wasn't long before the standard cigarettes were accompanied by weed. I'd always told myself I would never touch the stuff as a kid, but being a teenager was different. By the time we were fifteen, we were looking for the next thing and cocaine somehow fell into our laps. By the time we'd finished school and failed everything, we were addicted. We'd talked for years about going to London once we were free and at the first opportunity we had, we went. My parents were horrified and tried to get me back. They even came and got me a few times, but it always failed.

"Nathan and I had fallen further and further into the pits of hell. He had already started shooting up heroin, and if I'm honest I was only days away from starting as well. We made money dealing, and we lived in squats, whether they were empty flats or abandoned warehouses.

"I had no idea until it was too late that Nathan had been dealing for different people. A gang. A well known gang that was notorious for giving young lads a load of gear with promises of thousands of pounds, but the whole thing was always a set up. If I'd have known…"

I reach over and take Lucas' hand in mine, though I'm pretty sure he's so lost in his memories he doesn't even feel it.

"He convinced me to go with him but it got ugly. Really ugly. One minute we were being jumped by a load of guys, and the next I was waking up in hospital with my parents looking down on me, grief stricken.

"Nathan was dead and I had been very close."

I suck in another breath at his words, but remain silent.

"They brought me home, helped me get clean, and my dad stupidly handed me the company to keep me busy. It was a huge fucking risk, but one that worked. I think he knew me better than I knew myself back then.

"If Nathan hadn't have died, I don't think it would have worked. We would have ended up back there, but the next time something like that happened, we probably would have both ended up dead."

After his admission about his past, Lucas takes my hand and gently pulls me to my bedroom. He pulls the covers down and encourages me to get in. He strips down to his boxers and sits on the edge.

"Is that what the scars are from?" I whisper.

"Yes."

"And the tattoo? A phoenix is a bird of freedom, right?"

"Yes. I got it after I got clean. It's freedom from all the shit of my past. A reminder of why I can't lose myself again. I have her addictive personality, Lilly. I have to fight not to drown and I know I'm going to be fighting until the day I die. When I found out you were pregnant, all I could see was her and the pain she caused me and Marcus. I'm so scared to become that."

"You are not her, Luc," I say as I curl into his side once he's laying down. "You are so much more than that."

"I pray you're right, Lilly. I would never want you or our babies to experience what I did."

His disappearance makes even more sense to me. I'm still angry that he did it, that by trying to get himself together he hurt me anyway, but I don't bring that up. I ask another question that's been bothering me. "What happened to Marcus?"

"I don't know. It haunts me every day that I left him in that shithole with them. I've been too ashamed to find him," he admits.

"Would you like to? Find him, that is."

"Maybe one day."

That is the last either of us speak. We just lie there in each other's arms until we drift off to sleep.

Seventeen

Lucas

I lie listening to Lilly's breathing as she sleeps in my arms. I probably shouldn't have let her sleep; it sounded like she hit her head pretty hard and she might have mild concussion. She was exhausted though, so I figured that as long as I keep an eye on her, she'll be fine.

I run through all the events of the last few weeks over and over in my head. Even if Lilly forgives me for what I did, I don't think I'm ever going to be able to forgive myself. It may have only been eight weeks, but I feel like I've missed so much. When I get to what happened tonight, I feel the anger I felt when I see Lilly pinned up against the wall wash through me. After everything I've been through in my life, I think that image is going to be the one that haunts me. I was too close to losing everything in that moment.

When I hear Lilly's phone vibrating on the sideboard, I slide out from under her before grabbing it. When I see it's exactly who I suspected it would be, I silently sneak out into the living room so I can answer it.

"Lilly, what's wrong?"

"She's fine," I reply to his panicked tone. "I thought you'd put an end to Lilly's ex last year?"

"Who's this?" Dec asks, but I'm fairly sure he knows.

"Lucas. The guy who just stopped that psycho from ploughing another knife into your sister."

"FUCK," he bellows down the phone. "I thought we had."

"Well, you didn't do a good enough job. I need a favour from you."

"Why would I do anything for you? After what you've done to Lilly, I owe you nothing," he asks, clearly pissed off.

"Well, aside from the fact I just saved her life, I'm the father to her babies and I think I…love her," I admit quietly. Those are three words I never thought I'd hear myself say, and I'm surprised by how at ease I feel doing so.

"Well, shit me," Dec says with a laugh. "It's about time you did the right thing by her." From what Lilly has told me about Dec and his way with women, this comment makes him sound like a total hypocrite, but I don't mention it.

"So…the favour."

"Go on."

I explain everything to Dec about what I've been up to and what I want him to do. He's pretty shocked, but I can tell he's on board with my plan for Lilly.

Once he hangs up, I grab my phone and make the call that's going to put things in motion to end that motherfucker Jake.

I feel a little calmer when I slide back into bed beside Lilly, knowing I have things in place.

"Lucas," Lilly mutters in her sleep as she puts her arm around me. I kiss the top of her head before wrapping myself around her. What I said to Dec is true. Over the last few weeks away from Lilly, my feelings have become very obvious. All I need to do now is to get her to forgive me and show her how serious I am.

"Are you awake?" Lilly asks when the sun is starting to stream through the curtains.

"Yes, I've been keeping an eye on you."

"I told you, I'm fine."

"Are you sure? No pain or anything? Are the babies moving okay?"

"Yes, we're all fine."

"Good. You need to pack some stuff."

"Why?"

"We're going to my house."

"Lucas," she warns. "Just because I've had a knock to the head, it doesn't mean I've forgotten what happened."

"I know that, but I'm not having you here just in case he comes back for you. I need the three of you safe."

"Oh," she says, a small smile twitching the corners of her lips.

"I will not have you in any danger, Lilly. You're too important to me."

"Is that right?"

I have no idea if I'm allowed, but I lean forward and place my lips on to hers. I don't push for any more, and thankfully she doesn't push me away.

When we break apart, she looks up through her lashes at me. "It's like we're starting again, Lucas. It's going to take time. You can't just pick up where you left off."

"I know. I'm going to show you how much I want this."

"You already are."

As soon as Lilly has got up, I demand to know where her suitcase is so she can start packing. I won't have her here a minute longer, and I certainly don't want her here alone while I know that piece of shit is still walking the streets.

We spend the weekend hibernating inside my house. The only time we leave is to go to a supermarket because Lilly wants a certain brand of tea. I haven't been here since I left, and I'm glad I didn't come back, because it would be nothing without her here. It's bad enough now that she's demanding to sleep in the spare bedroom. How am I meant to sleep at night, knowing her sexy body is down the hall alone?

Dec did exactly as I asked and not long after we got to my place, her phone rang. I watched her arse sway as she walked off towards the living room so she could have some privacy.

Lilly

"Are you okay? I can't believe that dick had the balls to show his face again."

"I'm fine. Wait, how do you know about that?"

"Did you think I wouldn't know?"

"I guess," I admit, because he always knows when something is wrong with me. Just like I do him. Thankfully for me though, his life isn't quite as dramatic, and I don't get the feeling very often.

"Lucas answered when I rang you last night. He told me what happened. Why the fuck did you answer the door, Lilly?"

"I presumed it was Taylor coming back to visit, because no one buzzed, so I thought he's used his key."

"I can't believe you'd be so stupid."

"Yeah, thanks. I don't really need to hear that, Dec."

"Sorry," he mutters.

"Lucas demanded I came to his house, so I should be safe. You don't have to worry."

"Actually, that's kind of why I'm ringing. Do you fancy a few days by the sea next weekend? You can chill out on the beach and get some sun. I'll cook for you. You can totally relax." Dec is a great cook, although it's not common knowledge. I'm pretty sure he keeps it that way so that the women he hooks up with don't find out and try to dig their claws in any deeper. He'll be the perfect husband for someone one day.

"That sounds perfect. Shame my cocktails will have to be virgin."

"Awesome. How about I come and pick you up Thursday night?"

"Don't be silly. I can drive myself."

"You are not driving yourself and my niece and nephew in that rust bucket you call a car. No way. And I know for a fact Lucas will say the same thing."

"Okay, but I can't get on the back of your bike. You haven't seen me for a few weeks now, Dec. I've grown."

"I wouldn't even try to fit you on, Lills. I'll come in the van. Plenty of space for your fat belly then."

"Thanks," I mutter, trying to sound annoyed, but Dec knows it's hard for him to really irritate me.

"I'll see you Thursday. Send me the postcode for Lucas' house and I'll pick you up there."

"Okay. Love you."

"You too, bye." His response makes me smile. It's the only clue I get that he isn't currently alone. Dec is more than happy to tell me he loves me behind closed doors; as soon as he has company though, he locks it down. It's probably one of the reasons no woman has managed to get close to him. He's like a concrete wall until you really get to know him.

I find Lucas in the kitchen once I'm off the phone, as I expected. What I don't expect is to find him cooking. After his last failed attempt, I didn't think he'd try again.

I stand in the doorway and look around at the cluttered counter tops and steaming saucepans.

"What happened?"

"I know I made a mess," he says, looking around him.

"I didn't mean the mess; I meant you're cooking and nothing is burning."

"I'm learning to cook."

"You're learning to cook?" I repeat, because I can't quite believe it.

"Yes. I'm going to be a father soon, and I want to be able to help out." His words make me swoon.

"Lucas," I say softly as I walk over to him.

"I just thought that you're going to get so big you're probably not going to be able to move, so someone needs to keep you fed!"

"And to think I thought it was sweet," I say with a laugh as I playfully slap him on the shoulder.

I am pleasantly surprised by Lucas' first attempt at spaghetti bolognese. I think he may have a talent he didn't realise, and I'm more than happy for him to explore it.

The week is almost over before I know it. I was worried that spending too much time with him would mean we'd fall back into our old routine. I really want to still be annoyed at him for leaving me, but he's put so much effort into everything these last few days that I'm already starting to forget about it. I never thought it would happen so fast, but he's showing me every chance he gets that this is what he wants.

I still refuse to sleep in his bed, though. I'm standing by my decision to keep things slow. He may have found his way back in to my heart, although I'm not sure he ever really left. But he's going to have to wait a little until I let him have my body again. Although he isn't pleased with my decision, he is respecting it.

At 6pm Thursday night. I'm sat in the kitchen with my bags packed, ready to head to Devon for a long weekend. I may have been there plenty of times before, but I'm so excited to go and chill out with Dec and have a walk on the beach. I also think it will do Lucas and I some good to have a few days apart again. Other than him going to the hotel, we've been in each other's pockets since he rescued me on Friday night.

"Here's some food to keep you going on the journey,"

Lucas says, walking over to me with a bag in his hands.

"I thought you were making yourself dinner?"

"I was, but I did this for you, too." Lucas is really taking this cooking thing seriously. I love it!

"Thank you. Oh, he's here," I say, as a black van with 'Dec's Surf' in multicolour pulls into the driveway. "Are you ready to meet my brother?" It's very rare that Lucas looks unsure of himself, but this is definitely one of those times. He knows how close Dec and I are, and he's aware how important it is for them to get along. "You'll be fine." Dec was unsure about Lucas before, but since finding out he saved my life on Friday, he's warmed to him a little.

I swing the front door open and run as much as I can towards Dec as he steps out of his van.

"Oh my God, Lilly. Look at you," he says with his eyes fixed on my belly. I ignore his comment and wrap my arms around his neck. I breathe in his scent and I suddenly feel calm. I hadn't realised it, but I think Friday night may have been playing on my mind. Being with Dec releases it. I feel a little bad that Lucas wasn't the one to do that for me, but the connection Dec and I have is irreplaceable. Lucas is going to need to accept that he's a part of me.

When I step back, I see Dec's eyes lock onto something—or some*one*—behind me.

"Declan," Lucas states formally.

"It's Dec. Nice to meet you at least," Dec says, sticking his hand out for Lucas to shake.

"You too."

"Are you ready to get going, Lills?"

"Do you want a drink or anything before heading back?" I ask, because I'm aware of how many hours he's going to be driving today.

"I'm good. Could do with a leak, though."

"First door on the right as you go in," Lucas instructs and we watch as Dec walks off.

"He doesn't like me," Lucas whispers when Dec is out of earshot.

"Are you surprised, Luc? You left me without so much as a warning. He was the one to pick up the pieces."

I look up at Lucas as he swallows and thinks about what I've just said. "Lilly, I'm—"

"It's okay. We're moving on," I say, interrupting another apology.

He nods before lowering his lips to mine.

"Break it up, kids," Dec shouts over when he reappears. He goes about putting my mountain of stuff into the back of the van while he mutters about the fact I'm only staying a few days, not a month, while Lucas and I say goodbye.

It's stupid, I know, but as Dec pulls out of Lucas' driveway, I burst into tears.

"Shit, Lills. What's wrong?"

"N…nothing," I stutter out between sobs. "Just pregnancy stuff."

"Hmmm, maybe I should have thought twice about inviting a hormonal pregnant woman to stay for the weekend."

"Shut up. I'll be fine. Have you warned the others?"

"Of course. They said they'd keep themselves scarce for the weekend."

Dec lives in a huge house he bought a few months ago. It was a bargain, and also a complete dump. He allows his mates to stay rent-free as long as they help out with the renovation. It's worked pretty well for him, because the photos he's sent me of the place look stunning.

"Lilly, we're here." My eyes pop open and it takes a couple of seconds to realise who the house belongs to that I'm staring at, and that it's Dec shaking me awake.

"How long have I been asleep?"

"You lasted about twenty minutes."

"Whoops. Sorry."

"S'alright."

"I'm starving," I admit. Dec better get used to hearing that, because I seem to say it every few hours these days.

"We'll order something. Let's get you settled."

Dec helps me from the van and grabs my stuff before leading the way. I get a whistle stop tour of the ground floor on the way up to the spare bedroom.

"This place is amazing." The last time I was here, Dec was still living in a student flat and this place wasn't much more than a pile of bricks.

"It's not bad for a few novices, is it?" Dec asks, referring to himself, Liam and Ben—or BJ, as they call him—who've done almost all the work. I'm yet to use Ben's nickname. I really hope they call him it because of his initials, but I'm not convinced and I'm too scared to ask.

"Can I have the WiFi password please?" I ask Dec when I reappear after a long shower. God knows how my numb arse and stiff back didn't wake me on the journey but the power shower in the guest bathroom helped ease it.

"Sure," he says, walking over to the router and handing me a piece of plastic with the password on. I punch it in before opening Facebook Messenger.

I'm waiting for a message, although I'm scared it may never come. When Lucas left for work on Monday I started searching for his brother. He'd been much more open about talking about his past since his initial confession on Friday, so when I asked for his old surname he offered it up immediately.

There were quite a few profiles for Marcus Knightly, but I eventually narrowed it down to a couple and sent them a private message in the hope the right one would get in touch.

I wait for the app to load and a buzz of excitement goes through me when I see a new message. I'd turned the notifications off in fear of Lucas getting to my phone first. I stare down at Marcus' name on my screen and take a breath before opening it.

Lilly,

You've found the correct Marcus. What can I do for you?

My breath catches in my throat. Not only have I found him but he hasn't told me where to go.

"Are you okay?" Dec asks when he hears my reaction.

"Yeah, fine." I'm not ready to tell anyone about this yet. I want to see if Marcus is willing to get in contact with Lucas, and the rest of their stories aren't mine to tell.

I quickly type a message back, giving him a little information about me in the hope it will help him to open up to me.

Dec orders us a curry and we spend the night catching up with each other. Liam and Ben don't appear so I can only presume he's banished them for the night. It's great to spend some quality time together. It doesn't happen often these days. It's usually a phone call or a Sunday at our parents' when I have to share him with everyone else.

"Good morning, did you sleep well?" Dec asks when I appear the next morning.

"Yes, that bed is incredible and huge!"

"Good. I've got a surprise for you today."

"Oh yeah?"

"Yep. Here, have breakfast; then, we're going out."

"Don't you have to work?"

"No, Liam's got it covered, so we're good."

"Where are we going?" I ask when Dec gets me in the van.

"Can't tell you. Actually, it's probably best you wear these."

"Are you serious?" I ask, looking at the blindfold he's holding out for me.

"Deadly."

I reluctantly do as I'm told. I'm not very good with secrets, which Dec knows, so I figure the quicker I do, the sooner I'll find out what's going on.

The journey seems to take forever when I can't see where I'm going. Both babies are asleep so I can't even distract myself with their movements.

Eventually, the van starts to slow down as we drive onto what feels like gravel.

"Okay, we're here. I'm coming around to get you."

"Can't I take them off now we're here?"

"No," he states before jumping out and slamming the door.

I'm directed to God knows where by Dec, who is stood behind me with his hands on my hips.

"Okay, stop here."

"Where the hell are we?" I'm totally lost. We walked across the gravel we drove on before walking up some stairs, and now I'm stood on what I think is tiles.

"Here," Dec announces before pulling my blindfold off.

"What the…?" I ask as I spin around and take in my surroundings. "But this is…Oh my God. He has, hasn't he?" I ask, but Dec doesn't say anything. Instead, he grabs my hand and pulls me towards a bank of elevators.

I walk alongside him as my mind spins. While we wait for the doors to open, I look back at a hotel entrance hall I'm very familiar with. It's perfect and exactly as I designed.

Dec hits the button for the top floor and butterflies erupt in my stomach because when I'm usually heading to the top floor of a hotel, there is one person up there—or at least his room.

"Shit," I whisper as I wipe my sweating palms on the fabric of my skirt.

"Are you okay?" Dec asks. It's not very often he hears me swear.

"I don't know," I admit. "It depends on what I'm about to find." He winks at me but says nothing.

When we are stood outside of what I presume is the penthouse, I let out a huge breath to try to steady myself. I could be wrong about what's inside, but I'm pretty sure I'm not.

"Lilly, you're shaking. Are you sure you're okay?"

"Just open the door, Dec."

He does as I say and the door flies open to reveal plush cream carpet, a gorgeous oak unit and a huge mirror inside the entryway to the suite. Dec once again grabs my hands to get me to move. He slowly pulls me through the entrance to a living area. Just like downstairs, it is exactly as I designed it. Every piece of furniture, every colour and fabric… it's perfect.

My heart drops a little when I realise the living room is empty. That is, until Dec coughs loudly as if announcing our arrival and starts moving towards a closed door.

My eyes automatically shut as he reaches out for the handle. When I open them, I find exactly what I was expecting. Lucas is stood in the most stunning bedroom I think I've ever seen. My hands come up to cover my mouth as tears begin to stream down my cheeks.

In no time at all, Dec has left my side and I'm being wrapped in Lucas' arms.

"It wasn't meant to make you cry," he whispers in my ear soothingly.

"Lucas, it's…it's incredible. How did you—?

"I took copies of your designs one night when you were asleep."

"The hotel?"

"It's what I was doing while I was away," he admits. "Once I realised I'd made a catastrophic mistake I thought maybe I should do something to show you how serious I am about us." He places a hand on my belly. "So I found this place for sale and worked my arse off to get it ready for you. I want everything perfect for our family, and that includes you being near your brother."

"You want us to move here?"

"That's what I was thinking. How amazing will it be for these two to grow up by the sea? We can have birthday parties on the beach, Dec can teach them to surf…" he continues to paint this amazing picture of our future and I can't help but get carried away.

"That all sounds amazing-"

"But?" he adds for me.

"I'm sorry, but I'm not bringing two kids up in a hotel." I look over his shoulder at the two cots that sit at one side of the bed.

"There's more. Come on." He takes my hand and once again I'm being pulled along behind him with no idea where we're going. I'm almost disappointed that I don't get a chance to check out the rest of my designs, but the anticipation of what's next distracts me.

"This is for you," Lucas announces as he pulls into a driveway. I look up to my left at the dilapidated house sat into the cliffside, with incredible sea views.

"What?"

"This house, it's for you. Do whatever you wish to it to make it our home. We'll move in here once it's done."

"You're kidding."

"Nope," he says, holding the keys out for me.

"Oh my God," I squeal as I take the keys from him.

I let myself in and run around the downstairs. I come to a grinding halt when I come across a bottle of champagne, a small carton of orange juice and a little black box sitting on the kitchen worktop.

"There's one more thing," Lucas says when he comes over and sees where my focus is.

"I don't think I can cope with any more," I admit, but it doesn't stop him.

He walks over to the box and picks it up and turns to look at me.

"I want us to be a proper family, and that means we all

have the same name. I love you, Lilly. Will you marry me?"

"Lucas, this is crazy. We've only just got back together. You've been gone for weeks. This—"

"I know all that, Lilly. But no amount of time will make me surer of what I want. I want you. I want these two," he says, caressing my belly. "I want us forever."

"I do, too," I admit.

"Is that a yes?"

"Yes, it's a yes." Before I've finished talking I'm up in Lucas' arms and spinning around the room. His lips descend on mind and I lose myself in him. I forgot how all-consuming one kiss from him is.

When he pulls back, I'm shamelessly panting, my pregnancy libido well and truly stoked.

"You're going to be Mrs. Lilly Dalton," Lucas says with a smile.

"Take me back to the hotel, Luc," I say.

"I didn't think you were ever going to ask."

Lucas sweeps me up in his arms and carries me back out to the car, along with the bottle of champagne and carton of orange he swiped off the side on our way out.

Eighteen

Lucas

The hotel and the house were well planned. The proposal was a little more of a spur of the moment thing. I realised Friday night that I never want to be without her again. So the first thing I did Monday morning when she thought I was going to the hotel was head into town to a few jewellery shops. That was an experience. I must have looked so lost after all the questions that had been thrown at me in the first shop that the shop assistant took pity on me and explained everything I might ever need to know about rings and diamonds. She didn't need to tell me all that though, because I knew the one the second I laid eyes on it. It was a simple 1.5 carat, brilliant cut diamond on a platinum band. Okay, so maybe I did listen to her diamond master class. She seemed pretty happy about my choice, although I'm pretty sure that had something to do with the hefty commission I'm sure she'll get from the sale.

Waiting for Dec to arrive with Lilly was the most painful wait of my life. I was fairly confident she would love the hotel—after all, she designed almost every inch of the place—but waiting to see the look on her face when she walked into the bedroom was hell. The same can't be said for letting her walk ahead into what is going to be our new home. I knew that ring was sat on the worktop and I was so nervous I could have thrown up. I never get nervous, ever. But there I was, feeling like a right pussy in case my girl turned me down. Let's face it, she had every right to after what I've put her through.

We fall silent as I pull the car to a stop back outside the hotel again. Lilly has only said a handful of words of the drive back. I'm hoping she's just overwhelmed by everything and not having second thoughts.

Before I get to say anything, she's out of the car and heading towards the main doors. I jog up behind her and grab her hand. My thumb rubs over the new piece of jewellery wrapped about her finger and my stomach flips over. She's going to be my wife.

"Are you okay?"

"I'm a little overwhelmed, Luc. This was all a bit of a shock but I'm good. I'm more than good, actually." The smile she gives me when she looks up at me warms my entire body.

The second we step into the lift, she presses her front to me—as best she can with the bump—and places her lips to mine. When I feel her tongue run along my bottom lip, a bolt of electricity shoots down my spine. It's been so long since I've kissed her properly, held her, loved her.

"I need you," I mutter against her lips.

She doesn't respond. Instead, she kisses me deeper as her hands run down my back and cup my arse. I completely lose myself to the kiss and to images of what I want to do to her that are running through my head. It's not until I feel her pull back and grab my hand that I realise the lift doors are open. She pulls me out and down towards the room. She doesn't stop in the living area like I expect her to; she just keeps going until we're in the bedroom.

I stop by the door as I shut it behind me and watch her continue over to the bed. Lilly doesn't waste any time. She slips her flip-flops off before pulling her dress up and over her head. It gets thrown of the floor before she turns back towards me.

My hands clench at my side as I take her in. She was always beautiful, but now, with my babies growing inside her…Fuck. She looks unbelievable. Her tits are fuller and her belly rounded.

"Are you sure about this?" I ask, trying to do the right thing. She said she wanted to take it slow and I'm more than happy to do that. I think.

"I'm sure, Luc. I need this, you, please."

She hasn't finished talking and I already have my suit jacket and tie off. I'm halfway through undoing the buttons when I step up in front of her and she bats my hands away to continue herself. Once it's undone, she runs her hands up the length of my exposed skin before pushing the fabric from my shoulders. The feel of her hands against my skin has me containing a groan. I can't even put into words how much I've missed her and her touch.

She immediately goes for the waistband of my trousers. Her slim hands fumble with the button and I take over for her.

"You're in a hurry," I comment as she sits back on the bed in her lace underwear.

"You've no idea what these two have done to me."

"Oh yeah?" I ask with a smirk. I read all about raging hormones and their side effects.

"Yeah. I've needed you for weeks," she says, and the little reminder is like a knife to my heart. Although I know she doesn't mean it, it hurts.

"Well then, let's see what we can do to help you out. Hands and knees," I demand.

She immediately does as she's told and I reach out to pull the fabric of her knickers down over her arse and off her ankles. I drop my trousers and boxers before adding them and my socks to our pile of clothing.

I look at Lilly lying there, squirming as she waits for me, and I can't help but think of the difference from the first time we were together. She was a little unsure of herself then. Right now though, she is anything but. She knows exactly what she wants, what she needs.

I lower down and blow a gentle stream of air across her sensitive skin. I see her whole body shutter at the sensation.

"Are you ready for this, Lilly?" I ask. My nose is so close to her centre that the smell of her makes my mouth water for a taste.

"Yes." Her voice is already a little husky, like I've had her screaming for me.

I blow out again just to see her reaction, but I can't hold off any longer and I latch my mouth on to her clit. She says she needs this so I'm going to have her crying out in a matter of minutes.

"Lucas, oh my god. Luc," she whimpers as I continue lick and suck at her clit. When I slide a finger insider her, she starts chanting, "Yes, yes, yes."

"I fucking love how much you want this," I admit when I pull back for a second.

"Keep going," she pants and I can't deny her. I put my mouth back and increase the tempo inside her until she screams out my name. Her muscles squeeze down on my fingers, making me wish I had my dick inside her. I grab on to myself as Lilly comes down from her high. I pump myself a few times before she looks back at me. Her eyes drop down to my cock and she smiles. She goes to turn but as good as her mouth will feel right now, what I need is her pussy.

"That can come later. I need to be inside you right now." She doesn't argue; she just turns back and sticks her arse higher up in the air, giving me a great view. "Fuck, Lilly. Your body is so fucking sexy right now."

"Really?' she asks, showing her first sign of insecurity about her pregnant body.

"Fuck me, yeah. Your curves are fucking perfect." The second I finish talking, I line myself up against her. "This isn't going to be gentle," I warn. We both let out moans as I seat myself inside her.

I hold still for a moment, mainly because it's been a while

for her and I want to make sure she's ready, but also so I can steady myself a bit. This has been a long time coming and I don't want it over before it's really started. I can only hold off so long though, and when I feel her wiggle her arse, the only thing I can do is start to move.

"I'm going to own this arse on day soon, Lilly," I warn. She groans in response so I take that as an approval.

I reach around and palm Lilly's lace covered tits, pinching her nipples when I find them peaked. The action makes make her groan again and push back farther on to me. I skim my hands down her sides before grabbing on to her hips to help her out.

"I need to feel you, Lilly," I warn as my own orgasm approaches at a rapid rate, but I refuse to let go until she has.

"Uh huh," she grunts

One of my hands slides around to find her clit and it's only a minute or two more until I feel the first signs of her orgasm.

"Ohhhhhh," she cries as her entire body starts to spasm with her release. She squeezes me so fucking tight that I fall over the edge with her only a few seconds later.

I fold myself over her back as we both pant out breaths.

"Luc?"

"Yeah, baby?"

"I'm stuck."

"What?" I ask, standing back up and pulling out of her.

"I can't move. Will you give me a little nudge so I fall onto my side?" I can't help but smile at her. "You'd better not be laughing at me."

"Never, baby, never." I do as she asked and I watch as she falls down onto the mattress before stretching her legs out.

"Wow, that isn't as easy as it used to be. It feels different, too," she adds.

"Good different?"

"I don't know. I mean it was good, but I don't know it if was better. Just different."

I sit down next to her and sweep back a piece of sweaty blonde hair from her forehead. "It was incredible," I whisper before kissing her.

When I pull back, she looks up at me with sleepy but happy eyes.

"I love you, Lucas. I don't think I said it earlier."

"You didn't. But I know." She wouldn't be here and wearing my ring if she didn't. I've given her enough reason not to.

I cover Lilly up with the duvet and give her a kiss on the nose before leaving her to have a sleep.

Lilly

I'm totally confused when I wake up. I have no idea where I am. It's takes a good few seconds for everything that's happened to filter into my brain. I quickly uncover my left hand to check that I've not dreamt the whole thing. But no, because there on my hand is a huge rock.

Good lord, I'm engaged!

I did not see that coming in a million years. Well, any of this, actually. I can't believe Lucas has bought a hotel and a house here in Devon so I can be close to Dec. It's completely crazy.

Speaking of Dec, I reach down to grab my handbag from

where I dropped it on the floor when we got here earlier and pull my phone out. I find his name and hit call. He answers on the second ring.

"How'd it go?"

"You knew about all this and didn't tell me?" I'm amazed Dec could keep his mouth shut; he isn't very good with secrets. Plus, I don't think he likes Lucas, although he's never said it out loud, so I'm surprised he did any favours for him.

"Yeah. Did you not notice I hadn't spoken to you that much this week?" he asks and I think back. Yeah, we had a long chat after Jake appeared Friday night, but other than a few texts, that had been about it. So, that was Dec keeping a secret then!

"I didn't think you liked Lucas. Why'd you help him?"

"I don't not like him, Lilly. He seems okay. I just don't like the way he treated you when he left. He does seem to want to make up for it though. I mean, how much money do you think he dropped on all that?"

"I know, it's crazy. And the ring," I say, once again looking down at my hand.

"What ring?"

"The engagement ring," I hear Dec's sharp intake of breath. "Didn't you know about that bit?"

"No. He asked you to marry him?" Dec asks, and I'm not sure if he's just shocked or angry from his voice. A little of both, I think. "You said yes, didn't you?"

"Of course I did, Dec. I love him and we're having twins together."

"Are you sure—"

"I know what I'm doing, Dec," I say, cutting him off.

"Are you sure? What happens if he gets freaked out and

disappears again?"

"He won't," I say, with complete confidence in Lucas. He's opened up to me now, and I'm confident he'll be able to talk to me before running.

"Hmmm... I'm sorry, Lills, but I've got to go. It's crazy busy down here today. Enjoy the rest of your day celebrating," he says before hanging up, but I'm still not sure he's entirely happy about this.

"Hey, baby. Who was that?"

"Dec. You didn't tell him about this?" I ask, sticking my hand out towards him.

"No. I didn't think he should know first. Shit, I was meant to ask your dad, wasn't I?" Lucas asks suddenly.

"It's tradition, but I'm sure my dad will get over it. You may just have to buy him an expensive bottle of whiskey!"

"That I can do. So, when do you want to become Mrs. Dalton?"

"Ugh, when I can fit into my dream dress," I say, running a hand over my belly.

"Oh," is Lucas' response, along with a sad looking face.

"What?"

"I was hoping for sooner than that. I was us all to be a family."

"We will be. We are, Luc."

"But you'll still be Lilly Morrison."

"Luc, as much as I want to marry you—and I do, I promise—I also want to have time to plan it properly exactly as I, I mean we, want it. I don't want it to be a shotgun wedding just because I'm pregnant. I want to be able to go dress shopping and try on every dress in the store, not just the ones that will fit me."

"What if I organised it?" he asks hopefully.

"What, the wedding?"

"Yeah. I could do it, take the stress away from you."

"But my dress," I pout.

"Okay, let's compromise. I hear that's what relationships are all about anyway. We have a small wedding now and then a proper big celebration when the babies are here. They could be bridesmaid and pageboy."

I stare into his excited and happy blue eyes, and although I really want to hold out for my perfect day, I know this is really important to him. Having a proper family. "Okay, fine. But it's going to be small and you're planning it. I have enough on my plate as it is," I say once again, rubbing my belly. "I'd like to just turn up and have it happen." I know that sounds harsh, but he knows what I mean, I hope. "Then I'll plan the proper wedding for a couple of years' time. How's that?"

"Perfect, thank you," he says, before pushing me down on the mattress and kissing the life out of me.

The rest of the weekend is mostly spent in the hotel suite bedroom. And trust me when I say I'm not complaining. After weeks of being a horny mess, I more than got what I needed. It's just a shame I have to have nap after almost every orgasm these days!

"I think we should get married here in Cheltenham before we move down south. What do you think?"

"You know what I think, Luc. I think *you* sort it out. As long as I know when we're leaving so I've said goodbye to everyone, I'm good."

We've been back almost three weeks. The weather is

sweltingly hot and I'm massive. How I still have fifteen weeks to go is beyond me; I swear I'm going to explode. Although, every time I see the midwife or consultant they tell me I'm not going to make full term. They think I'll be lucky to get to thirty-six weeks. And as much as I'm enjoying being pregnant, I think I'll be more than ready for it to be over by then.

"Okay. What are you doing today?" he asks as my phone pings again with another incoming message.

I don't pick it up just in case he decides to be nosey and look at it. "Oh, I'm...uh...just meeting the girls for coffee after their shift. Then I'm not sure." Lucas looks at me and raises an eyebrow. I'm a useless liar so he can obviously tell something's up.

"Right."

I get myself ready once Lucas has left for the hotel. He's already pretty much handed the reins over to Catherine so he could stay home and work, but he says he feels more productive working away from home. Even if it means he is working in the penthouse.

It feels amazing to be able to go out now without worrying about someone watching me, that he could be around the corner. Knowing I'm totally free from him is an amazing feeling. I don't want to feel happy and relieved that he's gone. That's not the kind of person I am. But it is great.

Lucas was noticeably much more relaxed when we got back from Devon. I just put it down to the fact he wasn't keeping secrets from me anymore. But a couple of days later I went over to my flat to check the post and I found a blank envelope with all my other letters. I took them all up to the flat so I could grab some more bits before sitting on the sofa to go through it all. I opened the envelope, not having a clue what I was going to find. A small and thin square of paper slid out on to my lap. When I turned it over and read the headline, I had no idea what to think. A weird mix of happiness, relief and sadness washed through me. I had some great memories from the beginning of our relationship.

Body found Sunday morning has been named as Jake Ashworth.

I read through the short article about how his body was found in a derelict warehouse that was well known for its drug dealing and unsavoury goings on. A post-mortem showed a very high level of heroin in his system.

I let the article drop to my lap as I think about my time with Jake. Unfortunately, all the happy memories I have of us have been muted by the horrific ones towards the end.

Once I've pulled myself together a little, I look back at the envelope and check inside to see if there's any clue as to who it's come from. There isn't anything, but I'm fairly sure this isn't a coincidence or an accident. I'm not stupid enough to ask questions about it though. It's best left alone.

I take the envelope and article to the bathroom. I pull out my box of matches in the cabinet usually used for candle lighting and I light the corner. I let the charred remains drip into the toilet. I feel a weird sense of closure from the whole thing as I push the flush and watch it all disappear. I have a new life now. New priorities. Jake is well and truly in the past.

I grab a bottle of water and throw it in my bag before rushing out to my car. I don't know what it is about being pregnant, but it's like suddenly I can't get anywhere on time. I don't think I realised how long everything would take, being the size of a small rhino!

I'm only ten minutes late as I walk through the entrance of the coffee shop. I only partly lied to Lucas this morning. I am going for coffee, just not with the girls. I'm meeting Marcus.

I sent him a selfie of me a few days ago so he would recognise me—not that it's really necessary. I'm not sure many blonde women will turn up in the few minutes he'll have been waiting for me with a belly this size. I look around the room after I let the door close behind me and I find him immediately. My breath catches at how much he looks like Lucas. His hair is the same colour, although shaved close to his head. His eyes, from a distance, look a little darker, and he's a slimmer build than his older counterpart.

He begins to look more and more unsure of himself the closer I get to him.

"Marcus?"

I watch him swallow nervously before he cautiously sticks his hand out towards me. "Lilly?"

"It's so good to meet you at last. What can I get you to drink?"

"You sit down. I'll go."

I give Marcus my order and watch as he heads over to the bar. Their similarities are mind-blowing. You could easily mistake them as twins.

"Thank you for agreeing to meet me," I say when he sits back down. I know it wasn't easy for him. He told me many time over message about how he doesn't want to bring up the past and I understand why that might be the case from the little bit I do know about his and Lucas' childhood.

"You're welcome. Tell me about him. Lucas. What's he like now? What does he do?"

I'd only given basic snippets about Lucas when we were messaging and although I'm a little more open with the details now, I'm still aware that Lucas might not want him to know too much.

"I always knew he would do well for himself," Marcus says with a look of pure awe on his face when I talk about the hotels. "I idolised him growing up. Even after he left, because it wasn't until then I realised how much he did for me," he says with a sadness suddenly washing over him.

I sit quietly as Marcus gets lost in his memories for a few seconds. It's clear that the pain is still very raw, even now he's twenty-six.

When he comes back to me he starts to tell me about his life now. It doesn't escape my notice that he ignores anything before his twenties. I can only imagine what life must have been like for him once Lucas got out. I was expecting him to be angry with him, but it doesn't seem that way. Not to me, anyway. It may be different when—if—they meet. Marcus is a mechanic. He tells me how he's always loved cars and how it's his dream job. He has a small garage with a studio flat above not that far from here.

I'm shocked when I learn how close to each other Lucas and Marcus have been and didn't even realise it. I know Lucas ran to London for a while but I'm surprised they are both now so close to where they grew up. If I was in their place, I'm not sure I'd want to be living locally to where all that went on. But then, what do I know about it all, really?

Marcus is busy chatting about his life when suddenly he stops mid-sentence. His mouth drops open as he stares intently over my shoulder.

Nineteen

Lucas

Lilly just lied to me.

I don't do lies. I grew up around enough bullshit. I don't need it now. Especially from the woman who is wearing my ring, carrying my babies and claiming that she loves me.

I go to work like normal so I don't raise her suspicions, but I keep an eye on my phone to track where she is. I'm relieved when she arrives at the coffee shop like she said she would. I almost close the app and put the whole weird encounter down to her pregnancy this morning. Lilly has been pretty easy to live with so far. She hasn't complained as much as some of the people I've read about online. She seems to be taking all the symptoms in her stride.

Something in me stops me from forgetting about it though, so I finish up what I'm doing and head out. I walk the short trip to where I know Lilly currently is and stand what I hope is out of sight, and look through the window.

The second I see her sat opposite another man I feel a wave of anger wash through me, just like when I found Jake with his hands on her. I knew my paranoia this morning was for a reason. I continue to stand and watch them as they talk and laugh together.

After a couple of minutes, I can't stand unnoticed any longer, and I walk around to the doors and start to head towards them. I'm barely inside the coffee shop when I'm able to get a better look at the guy Lilly is sat with. Suddenly, it feels like someone's taken a baseball bat to my chest because my breath catches and my hands shake a little.

Marcus.

I stand just inside the doorway in everyone's way, staring at him, taking in all his features that are still so similar to my own. Just like when we were kids. He always was a miniature version of me.

Marcus must feel my stare because after a minute or two he looks my way. It takes a few seconds for him to focus on me and I see the same shock that must be on my face reflected back at me.

A flash of blonde catches my eye as Lilly's hair whips around to see where Marcus' attention is. Her eyes widen when she sees me. I'm not sure if it's horror or just shock.

She looks back and forth between us a few times before her mouth opens to say something, but nothing happens.

Deciding we've stared at each other across the room for long enough, I move forward until I'm stood at their table.

"Lilly?" I ask.

"I…uh…I was going to tell you, Luc. But Marcus wanted to meet me first, find out a little more about you. I swear I was going to tell you," Lilly rambles on, thinking I'm mad. I guess I am mad that she lied to me, but I can sort of see why. What I'm currently feeling is a long way from anger, though. Lilly has gone out of her way to hunt down my brother. I've looked a couple of times but was never successful, and I always convinced myself he wouldn't want to hear from me anyway after I left him in that hell hole.

"It's okay," I say, giving her shoulder a squeeze before turning to my brother. "Marcus, you look good," I say awkwardly. I have no idea what the right thing to say right now is, but I have a huge desire to apologise. "I'm so sorr—"

"Don't, Lucas. None of that was your fault. You got lucky after a fuck load of bad luck. You don't need to apologise," he says, surprising the shit out of me.

"But I abandoned you," I say in shock.

"Yeah, and I was utterly devastated, but I got over it. Being devastated made me weak, and I don't need to explain to you what that meant." No, he doesn't need to explain. I know all too well.

"Grab a chair, Luc," Lilly says, still looking between the two of us as if we're aliens. I'm not sure if it's the similarity between us or the fact Marcus hasn't tried to kill me yet for what I did to him.

Reluctantly, I ask the question that I'm not sure I want

the answer to. "What happened to her?"

"Dead," Marcus says coldly. "Overdose a few years back. She lasted longer than I ever thought she would." I can't help but agree with him. If she kept up the life she had while I was there, I'd have put money on her dying much younger. "And him?"

"Left for a new bottle of vodka one morning and never reappeared. No idea if he's alive or dead, but at least he's gone." I hate the feelings that talking about those two wastes of space drag up in me, so I quickly change the subject.

"So, what are you up to now?"

I forget all about work and spend the next few hours sat chatting to someone I never thought I'd get the chance to see ever again. It's the oddest feeling, because we chat like fifteen years haven't passed by. Marcus tells me all about his business and I feel so much pride for what he's achieved despite everything that I'm worried my chest is going to explode.

"I can't believe you did that, Lilly," I say the second we both walk through the front door later that day. "I never thought I'd see him again," I admit.

"I looked for him after you told me about your past. I didn't honestly think I would find him or that he's still be local, but after a couple of wrong hits I found him. I can't imagine not being close to Dec, so I thought it was worth a shot. I could tell how much he meant to you as a child and how much leaving him must have hurt you."

"You're incredible," I say as I grab her wrist and pull her to me for a kiss.

I slide my tongue against hers as I try to show her what

she means to me. I kiss her until we are both panting for breath. Eventually, I pull back and run kisses along her jaw and down her neck.

"Luc," she moans when I suck on the sensitive skin behind her ear.

"Bedroom," I whisper back. Once upon a time I would have had her right here up against the wall, but she needs a little more comfort these days. I'm seriously looking forward to when I'm able to do that again though.

"I need to eat first," she admits and I can't help but smile at her.

I grab her hand and lead her in a different direction than I was picturing a few seconds ago.

"Okay, we're good to go now," Lilly announces an hour later once she's eaten a sandwich.

"Ah, you're so romantic," I comment with a laugh. She just shrugs at me.

I grab both of her hands and pull her up from the chair. "Have I told you how beautiful you look?" She shakes her head with a shy smile on her lips. "So beautiful. I love this look on you," I say as I run my hands over her belly. There's a sudden bump against the palm of my hand and I don't think I could smile any wider if I tried, knowing that was one of my babies.

"They love hearing your voice. It always sends them crazy."

For the second time in one day, I pull Lilly along behind me, but not towards the bedroom. Instead, I get her to sit on the sofa. I lower myself to my knees next to her, place my hands back on her belly and talk to my babies.

Lilly looks down at me with tears in her eyes and a soppy look on her face.

"What?" I ask.

"Nothing. Just you."

"What have I done?"

"You're just you. You're going to be an incredible dad, you know that?"

I pray that's true. Although I feel a little better about the whole parenting thing since opening up to Lilly, I still worry. I only want the best for my babies and I really hope that I will be that. Lilly seems to think I am, so I have to trust her judgement.

I look back up at her as I feel my babies move beneath my hands and I can't believe how lucky I am. Not only have I got Lilly and soon to be two babies, but she's brought my brother back to me after all these years. And he doesn't hate me—that's a massive fucking bonus.

"I can't wait to make you mine," I admit, thinking about all the planning I've been doing. Lilly doesn't know it because I got her to sign the change of date paperwork when she was half asleep, but we're going to be saying our vows very soon.

Lilly

"LILLY?"

I roll over in bed as I try to find another comfortable position to lie in.

"LILLY," I hear shouted and my eyes fly open. Maybe it wasn't my back and hips that woke me then.

"Lilly, why are you still in bed? Get the hell up, woman,"

Molly demands as she comes marching into my room with Lois propped on her hip.

Molly is followed by my mum, Connie, and then a waddling Emma. Mum goes straight to the window and pulls the curtains back to allow the sun in while Molly pulls the covers back off me. Thankfully, I'm wearing pyjamas.

"What are you guys doing?" I ask, still half asleep and completely confused.

"Guess what today is?"

"I've no ide… Oh my God, it's today, isn't it? I'm getting married?"

"Yes, Lilly. It's today. Three o'clock to be precise, so you need to shift your arse."

I glance over at the clock. "Em, it's only ten. What's the rush?"

"Um…it's your wedding day. Firstly, you need to be awake to enjoy it, and secondly, we need to make you perfect, ready to say 'I do' to your man," Molly says with her hands on her hips.

Her words run through my brain and a huge ball of nerves and excitement explodes in my belly. I'm marrying Lucas today.

As much as I want to launch myself out of bed, I have to settle for slowly swinging my legs over the side before trying to haul myself up with one arm. I never pictured me being thirty-two weeks pregnant and huge when I wore my wedding dress.

I get taken downstairs where I discover the kitchen-diner looking like wedding fair has exploded in it. There are balloons, banners and confetti everywhere. Sylvie is going to hate us for this.

I look over to the table and my stomach grumbles on cue as I take in the amazing breakfast spread over the table. It's the prefect continental breakfast with everything I could want. I continue towards it with Emma, who also seems to be eyeing up the food greedily.

"Em, you only ate in the car on the way over," Connie says with a laugh.

"And, I'm growing two kids over here. It's hungry work."

"Agreed," I mutter before showing a croissant in my mouth. "You only grew one, you have no idea," I add with a wink, because I know it will wind her up. In reality, it doesn't matter Connie only had one, because she had a hell of a time being pregnant with Noah.

"Where is the munchkin, anyway?" I ask when I've swallowed a gorgeous buttery mouthful.

"With the guys. You should see his little suit, it's too cute for words."

Emma and I are still making our way through the buffet when the doorbell goes.

"Oh, that must be hair and make-up," Mum says excitedly, clapping her hands in front of her before hightailing it from the room.

We all stop our conversations and look up towards the doorway when we hear an excited squeal from Mum. We only have to wait a few seconds because she comes bouncing back into the kitchen with a very suave suited and booted Taylor behind her.

"Tay," I shout as I slowly get up. He takes pity on my pathetic state and in seconds is in front of me and pulling me to my feet for a hug. "I've missed you," I say as the first tears hit.

"Hey, don't cry," he says as he holds me.

"Sorry, it's the hormones and the fact I'm getting married today. Can you believe it?"

"No, not really," he says, half serious and half joking. I know Taylor's opinion of Lucas is similar to Dec's. I'm hopeful Lucas will win them around though.

"Why aren't you with the boys?" Molly asks.

"You really need to ask that?"

"I guess not."

"Hair and make-up is way more my thing than whatever boring shit they're doing. Plus, I'm the official photographer and Lilly is a much prettier subject. Although saying that, Lucas is a fine specimen of a man," Taylor admits, reminding me of the first time he saw Lucas.

Much to my horror, I see my mum nodding her head in agreement. Thankfully, the doorbell rings again, presumably with the hair and make-up team this time.

"I can't believe you're here," I say, turning back to Taylor.

"I wouldn't miss it for the world, Lilly," he says, kissing my cheek. "You look really…well."

"You mean huge, right?"

"Yeah, pretty much. Everything still going okay?"

"Yes, perfect."

"Who wants tea or coffee?" Connie calls out as she heads towards the coffee machine I moved here from my flat.

"I'll help," Taylor offers. "It's all I seem to do these days anyway," he mutters to himself as he walks off. I feel bad for him because he went off to London thinking he had his dream job, but his fears were confirmed on his first day. He's basically the gofer who gets the coffee for the real photographers. His time will come; he just needs to suck it up for now.

When Mum reappears this time, it's still not with who we're expecting. This time she's hiding behind a huge bunch of flowers. She puts them down in front of me after Molly clears some space.

I briefly appreciate their beauty before grabbing the card.
Lilly,
Congratulations on your wedding day.
I'm so sorry I can't be there with you but you are in my thoughts.
All my love
Nicole
Xxx

More tears fill my eyes as I think about her up there dealing with everything still. When I spoke to her the other day, things were still the same, and she sounded more defeated than ever.

Thankfully, I'm distracted from my thoughts when the hair and make-up team do show their faces. They set up camp in the formal dining room where the light is the best and set to work.

"Do I get to see my dress?" I ask Mum when the others have disappeared.

"When you're ready you can see it."

"Have you seen it?"

"Of course. I helped pick it."

"Really? You went shopping with Lucas for it?"

"Yes. Did you really think I'd let him do something that important alone?"

I never thought Lucas would have asked for any help with all this, so I'm a little surprised.

A couple of hours later, I'm stood in front of a full-length mirror that has a sheet over it. I haven't seen myself at all yet.

"Ready?" Mum asks.

I take a deep breath and nod. She pulls the fabric away and I stare at myself. My hair is down with the ends curled and a diamante slide, holding one side away from my face. My make-up is so soft it's almost like I'm not wearing any. The only way I can really tell is that the bags under my eyes from lack of sleep are magically gone. I run my eyes down my dress. It's simple and stunning, a satin sleeveless gown with a cowl neck that skims over my belly and pools on the floor. It has a diamante sash around the middle that catches the light as I turn to the side to look at the back.

It may not have been what I would have chosen if I wasn't pregnant, but it's utterly perfect. I look up at Mum, who has a huge smile on her face and tears in her eyes.

"You look stunning, Lilly."

"Thank you. Can we leave now?" I ask, getting impatient.

"The cars will be here any minute."

In no time at all, I'm stood outside the small function room at the hotel with my dad by my side. I was kind of expecting to be going to the registry office. I don't know why I didn't think he'd use the hotel.

Every surface of reception is covered is flowers that match my bouquet—simple cream flowers with just a few sparkles thrown in to catch the light.

I caught a fleeting glimpse of Catherine as I walked into reception, but one look at me had her marching out with a scowl on her face.

"Are you ready, baby?" Dad asks when the music starts.

"As ready as I'll ever be."

Two members of staff open the double doors for us. I keep my eyes down for a few seconds, trying to prepare myself for what will be ahead of me.

I take a deep breath and raise my eyes. The first and only thing I see is Lucas. He's stood at the opposite end of the room to me in a grey suit with a cream tie. He isn't rocking his usual slick look though, because his hair isn't pulled back. It's falling over his face, exactly as I like it. It's a little hint of the bad boy beneath the expensive suit.

I feel a tug on my arm as Dad starts to move and my legs must start to work without any instruction from my brain, because in no time at all I'm stood in front of Lucas.

"Hey, beautiful."

"Hey, handsome."

"Happy wedding day. Do you like it?"

"I love it, Luc. Thank you."

We get distracted when the registrar welcomes everyone and gets the ceremony started.

The whole thing is a total blur. I try to focus and remember every second, but it's so hard when I'm standing there looking at Lucas. It's not until an applause sounds out from behind me that I realise it's over.

We've done it.

We're married.

In little over only six months, I have everything I have ever wanted but a year ago never thought I'd get.

Twenty

Lilly

A phone ringing wakes me up. I open my eyes but it's pointless because the blackout curtains mean I can't even see my hand in front of my face.

"Is that yours?" Lucas asks in a husky voice.

"Yeah it is. Please could you get it for me?" Usually I would go myself, but it will take me about a week and I have a dreadful feeling in the pit of my stomach that I know who it is and what it's about. Usually I would ignore it—not that my phone ever rings in the middle of the night.

It's stopped ringing by the time Lucas hands it to me, but seeing as my suspicion is correct, I call straight back.

"She's gone, Lilly," Nic says in floods of tears.

"I'm so sorry, hun." My heart breaks for her. I desperately want to be there with her right now. "She's been getting worse and worse the last few weeks, not even opening her eyes. I could tell something wasn't right yesterday so I sat up with her. She just stopped breathing. It was so peaceful, Lills. Exactly as she wanted—well, apart from the long wait to get here. Lilly?"

"Yeah?"

"Is it awful that I have this huge feeling of relief?"

"Of course not. Don't you dare feel guilty about feeling like that. It's only natural; this has gone on for so long. You putting your life on hold isn't what she would have wanted. She's probably feeling relieved for you."

"I hope you're right."

"No one can tell you what's right or wrong right now, Nic. Only you know what you've been through. You're allowed to feel anything. If people don't understand how you're feeling they clearly don't understand what you've been through."

"Thank you," she whispers.

"I wish I could be there."

"Don't be silly; you're thirty-four weeks pregnant. You could pop at any time."

"When do you think the funeral will be?"

"I hope it's not a long wait. Now this has happened I want to get it all done and try to figure out what the hell I'm going to do with my life."

"Tell me as soon as you know. I want to be there."

"Lilly, don't be stupid. You can't."

"Yes I can, and as long as I'm not in labour, I'll be there." I can feel Lucas' stare burning into me as I say this, because I know he isn't going to agree.

"We'll worry about it closer to the time. It could happen any day," she says, like I need the reminder.

"You are not going," Lucas warns when I hang up the phone.

"She's my best friend and she's just lost her mum. If I can be there, I will be. You can come, or I'll go on my own. There's no discussion about it."

I can see he's desperate to argue but we both know we're not backing down, so instead he pulls me back down to the bed and wraps his arm around me as much as he can with the size of me.

"I can't believe I'm allowing this to happen," Lucas says two weeks later as he watches Dec get behind the wheel of my wedding present, a white Audi Q7. It's a ridiculous size and I look utterly stupid driving it, but Lucas is right, and it will fit everything in that we need for two babies.

"It will be fine. We will only be gone two days. I don't feel like anything's going to happen."

"That doesn't make me feel any better," Lucas complains. Typically, the day of the funeral is also the day Lucas has interviews for management jobs at the hotel, so he can't come. Thankfully, Dec agreed to be my chauffeur, much to his delight.

"It'll be fine. Just make sure you keep your phone on loud, just in case," I say but when I see the look on his face, I realise it was the wrong thing to say. "I love you, Lucas.

Everything will be fine."

"You'd better be right. And I love you, too," he says before lowering his lips to mine.

"Are we going or what?" Dec shouts from the car.

"Yes, let's go."

"I can't believe you talked me into this, Lills."

"Oh, why's that? Because you don't like Nic, or because you may have to deliver two babies at any moment?" I ask with a laugh.

"All of the above."

"But you love me, so you're going to suck it up and get on with it, even if you have to play midwife on the hard shoulder of the motorway." He glances over at me in the passenger seat and doesn't look amused by my comment. "It'll be fine," I say again, just like I did to Lucas an hour or so ago.

"Oh my God, you made it," Nic shouts over when she spots me waddling towards her after Dec drops me off right outside the crematorium where the funeral is being held.

"I told you I would. Come here," I say, trying to give her a hug.

"Lilly, you are fucking massive," she says, putting her hands on my colossal belly.

"I know. I feel ridiculous."

"Oh, I didn't know Dec was bringing you," Nic comments when he appears from the car park.

"Didn't I mention it?" I ask innocently, because I know full well I didn't tell her.

"No, you didn't."

"Whoops."

"Nicole, I'm sorry for your loss," Dec says politely as he

steps up to us.

"Thank you," she mutters, before excusing herself.

I glance over at Dec.

"What? I was perfectly polite. What did you want me to do? Pull her in for a hug?" He has a point, but I don't really know what I expected. They haven't seen each other for years; they aren't suddenly going to start getting along now.

The service is short and sweet, with only a handful of people in attendance, making me glad I made the effort. When Nic and her mum moved up here, Natalie was either looking after her parents or working, so she never really made many friends before she got ill.

Nicole ushers me to a chair right next to the buffet table when we get to the pub the wake is being held in, and I couldn't be more grateful because I'm starving, as usual.

We're probably there for an hour before it happens.

"Oh shit."

"What?" Dec asks in a slight panic because of my language.

"I think…um…I think my waters have just broken."

"Please tell me you're fucking joking, Lilly."

I stand up to head to the toilet to check it out, but the second my arse leaves the chair I feel fluid run down my legs.

"Uh…nope, pretty sure it's really happened." I'd been having weird twinges for a few hours, but I put it down to the long car journey to get up here. Apparently, I should have taken them more seriously.

"Fuck. What do we do?" Dec asks, totally flustered. It's quite amusing for me because he hardly ever gets worked up.

"Firstly, calm down." I'm not entirely sure why I'm so calm about all of this. Some kind of natural instinct, I guess.

"There's a blue and white striped bag in the boot of the car. Please go and get it for me."

"Are there instructions in there?"

"Just go and get it." I watch Dec stop and say something to Nic before he rushes out of the pub.

Nic runs over to me, her eyes wide and a huge smile on her face. "The babies are coming?"

"It looks that way. When Dec reappears, will you help me to the toilet? You might have to apologise to the owner about the state of his chair," I say.

When Dec comes back, I hand him the paperwork I printed out for the local hospital. He gives me a questioning look when I hand it over. "What? I was just being prepared. As you all said, it could happen at moment, so I wanted to have everything in place. Now ring them, tell them my waters have broken but I haven't had any…argh," I say as a pain goes across my lower belly. "No, tell them my contractions have just started."

Dec immediately goes to pull his phone out of his pocket as Nic grabs the bag he brought in and helps me towards the toilets. "Oh," I shout over my shoulder towards Dec, "and maybe call Lucas."

After an hour, my contractions start coming hard and fast so the midwife tells Dec to bring me in.

"I'm so sorry for ruining your mum's day," I say to Nic.

"Are you crazy? She would have loved it. She always wanted to be a midwife. Come one, let's go."

"Aren't you staying here?"

"Seriously?" she asks, looking around.

She has a point; the only people left here for the wake are a couple of elderly neighbours who are propping up the bar and watching the horse racing on the TV. "Okay, come on then."

Nic helps me get in the car after laying out a waterproof cover on the seat. They're maternity pads but I'm fairly sure I could have picked up the exact same thing in the puppy training department in our local pet shop.

"Hurry up," Dec says anxiously from the driver's seat.

"Seriously, Dec. You need to chill out a little."

"You are about to push out two kids. Two, Lilly. Not one, like most normal people. Two. How are you so calm?"

"What's the point in panicking? There's nothing I can do to slow this down. It will happen as it will happen. Have you managed to get hold of Lucas yet?"

"No, still no answer." So much for me telling him to keep his phone on loud just in case.

"Lucas is on his way," Dec announces as he walks back in the room after answering his phone.

"About bloody time," I grate out as I feel another oncoming contraction. "He'd better not miss this."

Five hours later, I'm on my back with Dec holding one leg up and Nic the other while the midwife looks intently at my nether regions. If I cared about anything right now, I would feel sorry for my poor brother, but I don't. My only focus is the pain I'm currently experiencing.

I was planning on having an epidural. The midwife agreed, but there was an issue with another woman and by the time the anaesthetist actually made it to my room, it was too late. So here I am, enduring the joys of labour with only gas and air to dull the pain. And let me tell you right now, that stuff does shit all.

"Argh," I groan as one contraction rolls straight into another. It wasn't so bad earlier when I got a break in between, but this is torture.

"That's it, Lilly. I saw the head. A few more like that and baby number one will be here."

"Lucas," I mutter. "Need Lucas."

"He'll be here, honey," Nic says softly. I'm so glad she's here. I'm not sure how I would have done this without her. Dec's great and all, but he's like a fish out of water. Nic seems to know what I need and when.

"Okay, one more like that and we'll have a baby, Lilly. Come on, you can do it."

I clamp down on Dec and Nic's hands as I give it everything I've got. I'm vaguely aware of a bang, but that's about it as I focus on the task in hand.

Lucas

Fuck knows how I got here in one piece or without being pulled over. The second I saw Declan's name on my screen, I was running for the car. I just knew it was happening. I told her not to fucking go.

I pull the car into an empty disabled space outside the maternity ward and run as fast as I can while taking in the signs for the right way.

A midwife or nurse or someone points me in the right direction for Lilly when I briefly stop at reception. She can obviously tell I'm in a rush from the look of me.

I just swing the door to the room open as I hear the midwife say, "That's it, Lilly. One big push." I'm frozen to the spot as I take in the sight in front of me.

"Lucas," Dec shouts. When I look up, I see that he's in almost as much of a panic as I am. "For fuck's sake, come here."

My legs do as he says, although my brain is elsewhere. *I'm about to become a father.*

I take over Dec's position as Lilly grunts and groans. I look up at her and I think I fall in love with her all over again. Her hair is matted all around her head with strands stuck to her sweaty skin. Her face is red and covered in sweat. Her eyes are closed as she focuses on pushing. I don't think she's even aware I'm here.

Seconds later, I hear the words I never thought I'd hear.

"Congratulations, you've got a daughter."

There's a few seconds of silence before a tiny cry fills the room. I look over to the midwife, who's holding this tiny person in her arms before she passes her to Lilly, whose eyes are now wide and filled with tears.

"Dad, would you like to cut the cord?"

"Uh—" I start as I pull my eyes away from my wife and daughter. I've read all about this, but right now, everything I've ever learnt has gone as I stand and stare at this little person.

"Lucas?" Nicole prompts.

"Yes, sorry."

The midwife tells me what to do and I follow her instructions exactly. Once the cord is cut, I turn my eyes back to the most precious people in my life.

It's not until I put my hand over Lilly's on our daughter's back that she looks up and registers that I'm there.

"You made it," she says as her first tear drops.

"I wouldn't miss it for the world, Lilly. You did amazing."

"You weren't here; how can you say that?"

"Because she's perfect, just like her mummy."

After a few minutes, the midwife takes my daughter from Lilly to get her cleaned up, checked over and weighed.

"Are you ready for number two?" the other midwife in the room asks just Lilly lets out groan. "I'll take that as a yes."

I briefly look around and see that both Declan and Nicole have disappeared.

"Come on, baby, you can do this. I want to meet my son."

Lilly was incredible. I want to say that I helped, but I think I pretty much stood there gawping as my son was born. It was the most amazing and surreal experience.

Although both babies are a good size for twins at just over 5lbs each, they get whisked off to special care to be checked over properly. I diligently follow them so they're not alone while the midwives attend to Lilly. She's so exhausted that I don't think she even hears me tell her where I'm going, let alone realises that I leave the room.

I stand in the corner of the room and watch as the nurses check every inch of both babies. I guess they do the technical things I read about, like checking their oxygen levels and that kind of thing, but I'm too busy staring at the perfection that is my children. My daughter has a light dusting of blonde hair and a cute little button nose like her mummy, and my son has dark hair like me.

I thought I loved Lilly before, but having just watched her deliver my babies into the world has blown away what I felt for her before. Lilly and the two little people in front of me are my life. Fuck all the bad stuff that happened in the past. I have my own family now, and I'm going to show them every day how amazing and important they are.

The nurses nod me over when they are finished. They explain everything they've done and that they're happy with both of them; they just need to monitor them for a while to make sure they progress and eat as they should.

I sit down between my two little people and look between them. I feel like I could look at them for days and it would never be enough.

Eventually, I get distracted by voices in front of me. When I look up I see Lilly in a wheelchair with one of the midwives behind her.

"Are they okay?" Lilly asks in a panic.

"They're perfect. This is just a precaution because they're early."

"Oh thank God. I was so worried when I realised they were here," she says, starting to tear up.

Lilly thanks the midwife before standing on unsteady legs so she can see them properly.

"Sit here," I say, giving her my seat. After all, she did all the hard work; she should be the one making use of it.

"Look what we made," she says softly, looking between the two cots.

"Look what you did. You were incredible. I'm sorry I almost missed it."

"You didn't though. You got here."

"So, names then," I suggest. "Are we going with what we agreed?"

"Yes, I think they're perfect. Especially hers," she says, nodding towards my daughter.

"Okay, so Natalie Elaine and Nathan Christopher.

Welcome to the world," I say, giving them both a kiss on the nose." When I look up, Lilly has tears streaming down her cheeks and a huge smile on her face.

I lean down and put my lips to hers for a sweet but innocent kiss. "I love you, Lilly Dalton," I say when I pull back. "Thank you."

"What for?"

"For trusting me. For believing in me. For becoming my wife. For giving me the most perfect children in the world." Her tears continue to fall as she listens to me.

"You make it easy, Luc." Now I'm not sure how true that is, but I accept the words from her anyway.

"Okay, lovely, are you ready to have a go at feeding these gorgeous little ones?"

Lilly excitedly agrees. I know she's dying to hold them properly.

The midwife pulls the curtain around and I watch as Lilly has her first attempt at feeding. I find the whole thing incredible. Not only has she grown both of those perfect little humans, she's now keeping them feed and watered. I'm in complete awe.

"You have some visitors at reception. It's technically not visiting hours, but I'll let them in for a few minutes. You'll need to be quiet though," a nurse says when she pops her head in.

"Shit, I forgot all about them," I admit.

"They look a little exhausted," the nurse says with a laugh.

"Let them in."

"When I was wheeled down here they were both fast asleep in the corridor," Lilly says. "The midwife wanted to wake them up but I said no. Nicole had her head on Dec's shoulder; they looked so sweet. I've never seen them like that before."

"Hey, how's it going you two—or should I say four?" Dec asks when he gets to us.

"They're prefect."

"Of course they are. You made them, Lills."

"Congratulations, hun. You were amazing," Nicole says, coming over to give Lilly a hug.

"So, who've we got here then?" Dec asks, looking down into the cots.

I let Lilly tell them their names and the reasons behind them. Nicole bursts into tears when she hears what we've called our little lady.

"I hate to distract you from these two, but I'm kind of stranded here now and it occurred to me that you two have two cars. Any chance of me taking one back?" Dec asks to my horror. Lilly's car has all the baby paraphernalia in it, so we need that one. That means I'm going to have to give him the keys to my Jag. The huge smile on Declan's face tells me he knows that, as well.

"Stay in the slow lane and do not go over seventy. Actually, on second thoughts, don't go on the motorway at all."

"Yeah right, whatever," he says, still smiling. I swear he looks way more excited about the prospect of driving my car than meeting his niece and nephew.

"I'm serious. If you damage her, I'll damage you." My threat is laughed at by everyone in the room but me. "Just be careful," I say, reluctantly handing Declan the keys.

"Can I come and see you again tomorrow?" Nicole asks

Lilly.

"Of course you can. I'm sorry for ruining today."

"Are you kidding? It's been amazing. Being able to be there for you and these two has been incredible. Thank you for allowing me to help."

"I wouldn't have had it any other way—well, unless he was here on time," she says, nodding to me. I just shrug. What's done is done. She rolls her eyes at me before turning towards Declan. "Thank you," she says, giving him a hug. "You were amazing. A little frantic, but amazing. I hope you're calmer when it's your kids being born." I can't help but laugh at the look on his face when she says that.

"I used to think that too, Declan, but look at me now. Your time will come whether you want it or not. You mark my words," I warn as I look at Lilly. No, she wasn't what I wanted, but now I couldn't imagine my life without her. The same will happen to Declan one day. I really hope I get to watch it happen; it should be entertaining, watching him get whipped.

We all say our goodbyes before Lilly and I take up our previous positions of staring at our babies.

"What time is it?"

"Just gone 3am. You should get some sleep."

Twenty-one

Lilly

We end up staying in hospital for seven days as Nathan has some trouble eating. The week passes by in a total blur though. I try to memorise every moment with Natalie and Nathan, knowing I'm never going to get these first hours back, but still, it's gone before I really realise it's happened.

Putting them both in the car to come home I think is the scariest thing about the whole giving birth and being new parents thing. In the baby unit, there was always someone on hand to help if we weren't sure, but we're about to be let loose to go it alone, and that scares the pants off me.

It's the longest journey ever, seeing as we have to stop every two hours to feed them. Giving birth to twins six hours away from home wasn't the best plan, but it is what it is, and we'll get home at some point today—or maybe tomorrow. If we were more prepared, we could've got a hotel for the night, or even stopped at my parents', but we don't have anything for them to sleep in, along with all the other stuff we're going to need.

"Lilly, we're home," I hear Lucas say quietly as the car engine shuts off. I drag my eyes open and immediately look behind me into the mirrors that allow me to see my babies. "They're fine. Slept as soundly as you. Come on, let's get them out of those seats."

Lucas insists on carrying them both and refuses to let me help with anything. The first few seconds of being left alone with both of them is daunting, even though Lucas has only gone back down to the car. I'm responsible for both of their lives, for everything they're going to need. The thought freaks me out somewhat.

"I've got a surprise for you," Lucas announces when he reappears.

"Okay."

"I've already given them a talking to about backing off if needed, because I don't want you to be overwhelmed or smothered, but I thought you might want them here."

Excitement bubbles inside, because if he's talking about who I think he is, then yes, I desperately want to see them and for them to meet Natalie and Nathan. I smile and nod at him to get a move on.

When Lucas reopens the hotel room door, as expected, my mum and dad are stood there smiling with arms full of pink and blue gift bags.

"Let me see my babies," Mum demands after she's given me a huge hug.

"Thank you," I mouth to Lucas.

I look at my mum and dad cooing over our babies and my world feels complete. I have everything I've ever wanted, and it's more than I could possibly imagine.

Epilogue

Lilly

In just a few days, my babies are going to be six months old. I have no idea where the time has gone.

Mum and Dad stayed for a week after we got back to Devon with the twins. They loved spending time with us all, but they were soon on their way back to Oxford when they got the phone call from Ruben to tell them their next set of grandkids were on their way. Emma gave birth a long thirty-six hours later to a healthy baby girl and boy. They called them Alice and Harry, and they are almost as cute as our two.

I finish up cleaning a mountain of bottles and put them in the steriliser before going to find out what's going on. It's suspiciously quiet upstairs, where Lucas should be getting

Natalie and Nathan ready for bed.

I walk through our house and it makes me smile, like always. We moved in a few weeks ago, and I love it. I also love not being in a hotel. I insisted that we had to be in for the six-month mark, because I was not starting weaning in a hotel penthouse with no kitchen. It just wasn't happening.

I make my way upstairs and I stop in the doorway of the nursery. Lucas has his back to me. He's got a baby in each arm as he sways from side to side singing Twinkle Twinkle Little Star. My heart melts. This man, who was so freaked out about the idea of becoming a parent that he ran away, is the most incredible dad. He puts them both first in everything he does.

As I stand and watch, I continue to fall deeper in love with him, just like I do every day.

When I got that promotion to clean his suite back in Cheltenham just over a year ago, I never could have imagined that he would become not only the love of my life, but the father of my kids. It just shows that you really have no idea what life holds for you.

I continue to stand there silently as Lucas puts each of them into their cots. Although he showed no sign of knowing he was being watched, he must have known because when he turns around, he has a smile on his face. The closer he gets to me, the darker his eyes get.

"They're out for the count. Let's make the most of it."

I try to keep the surprised squeal in when he picks me up and throws me over his shoulder. We just get to the doorway to our bedroom when a loud knocking sounds from downstairs.

"Leave it," Lucas growls. "If it's important, they can ring

or come back."

"Okay," I agree. But only seconds later, there's more banging, along with my name being called.

Lucas lets out a huge breath before turning us around and heading downstairs. I'm still over his shoulder and staring at his fine arse when he pulls the front door open.

"Shit, what happened?" he asks in shock, making me fight to get down and see what's going on.

When I do, my heart drops. There are two guys stood in our porch. One I vaguely recognise from somewhere, although I have no idea where, and the other, who is leaning against the first for support and is covered in dried blood and the beginnings of some serious bruising, is Taylor.

"Shit, Taylor. What happened to him?" I ask as Lucas takes his other side and helps to get him in. "I know you," I say to the other guy once we have Taylor on the sofa, "But I can't place you."

"I'm Caleb, Beth's brother. Taylor lives with me."

Tracy Lorraine

Taylor and Caleb's story is next and out now…

Acknowledgments

I hope you all enjoyed Lilly and Lucas' story. I'm a little bit in love with Lucas and I'm sad to say goodbye to them. It's only for now though, because just like all the others, they will make appearances in future books in the series.

Where do I start with everyone who has helped bring Lilly's story to life?

Michelle, thank you so much for beta reading Lilly when none of my sentences made sense and you had to guess every other word. I really appreciate your honest feedback, even when you think you're being little harsh.

Evelyn at Pinpoint Editing, thank you for working your magic on Lilly and making her as perfect as possible. And thank you for the time you have put in to not only Lilly, but all the other books in the series these last couple of months.

Thank you to Colleen at Itsy Bitsy Book Bits for always going out of your way to help me. I really appreciate everything you do to help get my books out there. Your reviewers, as always, are incredible and write the most amazing reviews.

Nicole, I don't know how to thank you enough for everything you've done the last few months. Your support, encouragement and advice are priceless. I almost feel like I know what I'm doing now. Well, I have some sort of a plan of action at least!

As always, a huge thank you to my husband and little girl who allow me time to do what I need to do. I love you both so much.

Deanna, my biggest stalker! What would I do without you? You fill up my notifications every day with your pimping of my books. I can't thank you enough for all the time you put in to help me. It's only been a couple of weeks but our new blog—Laid-back Book Bitches for those of you who don't know already— is doing amazingly well and it's all because of you. I knew you could do it. We have exciting things ahead of us and I can't wait to see where it takes us.

And last but not least, Lindsay. This one is for you, and not just because of the random medical questions I threw at you to ensure Lilly's story was realistic. From the day I told you about my secret writing career, you have been behind me 100%. I can't thank you enough for supporting me and loving my stories and characters almost as much as me. I promise to keep them coming for as long as I can. It's been fourteen years since we met, but it only feels like yesterday we were trying to sell curtains to people who didn't think we knew what we were talking about. We've both been through so much since then and I'm so glad to have had you by my side all the way. Whatever life throws at us next—the good, the bed and the ugly—we'll get through it together.

Taylor's is next in the series so you can find out what he's been up—or not as the case may be—to with Caleb.

About the Author

Tracy Lorraine is a M/F and M/M contemporary romance author. Tracy has just turned thirty and lives in a cute Cotswold village in England with her husband, baby girl and lovable but slightly crazy dog. Having always been a bookaholic with her head stuck in her Kindle, Tracy decided to try her hand at a story idea she dreamt up and hasn't looked back since.

Find out more at:

www.tracylorraine.com

More books by Tracy Lorraine

Falling Series

Falling For Ryan: Part One
Falling For Ryan: Part Two
Falling Fr Jax
Falling For Daniel
Falling For Ruben
Falling For Fin
Falling For Lucas
Falling For Caleb
Falling For Declan
Falling For Liam

Chasing Series

Chasing Logan

Ruined Series

Ruined Plans
Ruined by Lies
Ruined Promises

Tracy Lorraine

Never Forget Series

Never Forget Him
Never Forget Us
Everywhere & Nowhere

The Cocktail Girls

His Manhattan
Her Kensington

The Halloween Honeys

His Sorority Sweetheart

Printed in Poland
by Amazon Fulfillment
Poland Sp. z o.o., Wrocław